A Wolf Before the Storm
Wolves of Stormfall Book 1

by

J.W. Golan

© 2022 by J.W. Golan

All rights reserved.

This is a work of fiction. Names, characters, places and incidents are the products of the author's imagination or are used fictitiously. Any resemblance to actual events, places, or persons, whether living or dead, is entirely coincidental.
Cover designed by L.N. Golan.

J.W. GOLAN

Collected Maps

Western Lands

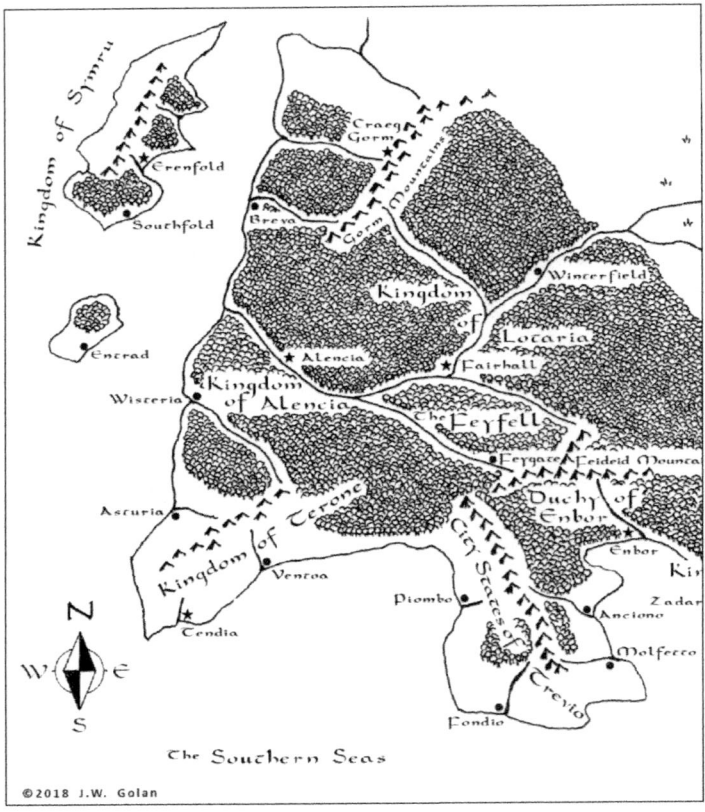

Eastern Lands

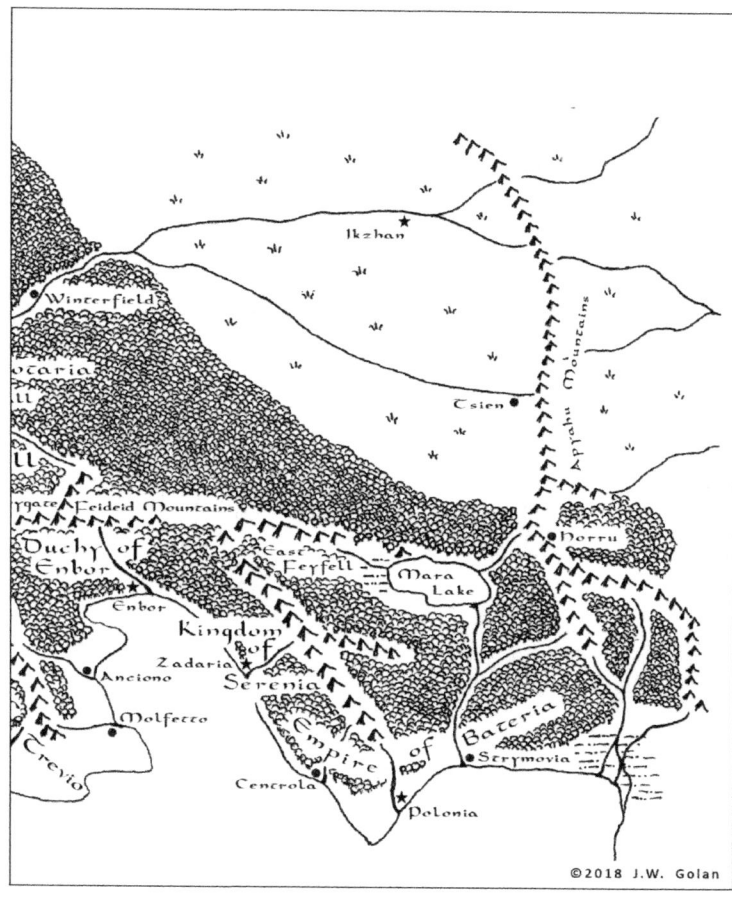

J.W. GOLAN

Chapter 1

Dear grandma,
They have a job set up for tomorrow. I'll be doing the burglary. Some wealthy travelers or such. At the inn. Pontus has arranged to clear the upper floor, first thing in the morning.
I'm excited. I'm the best lockpick in the gang. I wish you could be there to see me, yah-yah. I know it's not the life you imagined for me. But I live for moments like these.

* * *

Callisto lowered herself to the balcony, dropping down onto all fours in a practiced crouch. A lanky girl. All knees and elbow, her instructor would say.

The doorway had been left open, as planned and paid for. The hallway within, however, was unlit – too dark to peer into from outside.

There was a certain thrill, she had to admit, in these kinds of jobs. The only time she was ever really free. Completely on her own, left to her own wits and abilities to survive.

The hallway ahead was quiet, but it was always a risk, plunging into the unknown. She calmed her nerves, drinking in the sensations, testing for movement. The floorboards, cool against her fingertips, betrayed no hint of footsteps.

Birds chirped and leaves rustled in the breeze. Pots and pans were banging in the kitchen below. Drudges stoked ovens. A familiar, breakfast routine. From the hallway ahead, however, all remained silent.

She inhaled deeply. Salty sea air intermingled with the savory scents drifting from the kitchen below. Fresh bread, cheese, and eggs. Slivered, sauteed mushrooms – a rare delicacy this time of year. Her stomach growled. It was no wonder the upper floor had been cleared for the morning meal. The merchants, officials and other wealthy travelers were eating well today. From the hallway ahead, however, only the scents of leather and linens floated through the air.

Satisfied she had taken every precaution, Callisto arose from her crouch, stepping lightly into the hallway. If she was caught, she'd have to pose as a cleaning servant.

The plain white blouse and dark trousers she wore matched the unadorned clothing of the inn's staff. With her short, dark hair, she could readily pass for a boy – a fact which often worked to her advantage. But her chest was beginning to show the first promise of womanhood. It was an illusion she wouldn't be able to maintain for much longer.

The hallway was dim, with only the light from the window at the other end to guide her. She knew these halls, however. Without waiting for her eyes to adjust, she headed towards the door she had been told was her destination this day. The third one on her left. It was unremarkable, with a dark metal knob and keyhole below it. She lowered herself to examine the keyway.

From her satchel, she withdrew a pair of metal picks. Their smooth surfaces fit snugly into her hand. It was a simple, guarded lock. The kind she had opened dozens of times before. A couple of seconds, a turn, and the door swung open.

The room within was quiet. A pair of stitched leather travel bags with metal clasps rested on the beds. A silver charm with some symbol dangled from one of them: an outstretched hand, palm facing forward.

She entered, closing the door behind. A silver comb and hand mirror sat on a small table, next to a washbasin. There was a coin purse secured to the outside of one of the travel bags. She ignored them both for the moment. She knew what she had been sent for.

Moving across the room, towards the open window, she spotted it: a metal box resting on the floor, on the far side of the bed. It had a dark, almost black finish with a handle and lock on its front face. Raised patterns in a brightly polished brass decorated its edges and corners.

Callisto bent over it, running her fingers across. The patterns depicted trees and animals, carved in exquisite detail. Even the shiny metal handle with the lock in its corner had been sculpted to resemble a tree limb, complete with vines and leaves. She knew fine craftsmanship when she saw it. No artisan in Centrola could have produced anything like this. No artisan in Bateria, for that matter. It was undoubtedly gnome-made.

She'd only seen a gnome once or twice before. The little, waist-high people seldom ventured this far east. Their metalworking and mechanical skills, however, were renowned. A gnome lock box would not be so easily opened.

She drew a folded cloth from her satchel, opening it on the floor alongside the box. Rows of pockets held shiny metal tools of different sizes, arranged from largest to smallest.

She selected two of the finer picks from her collection and slid the pair into the lock. A flat metal plate for turning the mechanism, and a curved pick with a wavy pattern for raking the locking pins. She listened, her fingertips sensing as each pin was pressed into place. One . . . two . . . three . . . there was a click as they released the latch.

Callisto stopped, her body tense. She had felt the pins sliding into place, but the sound of the latch had been wrong. The tone was off, as if the lock was inside its own, smaller metal cavity. It sounded . . . hollow.

She delicately removed her lock picks, relaxing her tension and allowing the pins to spring back into their locked position. She was careful not to turn or touch the handle.

Her tools freed, she examined the face of the box more closely, testing the raised portion decorating the face. There was a hare, carved into one corner. The darker metal around it had score marks, as if something had scratched it repeatedly. She pressed on it, and the hare moved – rotating out of the way, revealing another lock.

The lock in the handle had been a trap! It either engaged a second lock, jamming the mechanism closed, or else released a defensive measure – a poison tipped needle or something similar. She had heard of traps like this but had never seen one herself.

Callisto slid her picks into the second lock, feeling the pins sliding into place as she raked the pick across. One, two, three . . . there was a satisfying click as all the pins aligned and the cylinder released. She pulled gently on the handle – pulling, but not turning. It opened to reveal a dark, padded interior.

There was a folded leather pouch, a necklace, and a couple of bracelets. She drew them out. They glittered in the dim, shuttered room. She didn't have time to inspect them more closely. She hurriedly shoved them into her satchel.

She opened the leather pouch. There were papers inside. They were folded, with tiny holes along their crease, as if they had once been bound into a larger volume. Handwritten, with a signature on each page. Herrick, it read. It looked like a personal journal. The name sounded vaguely familiar, like something she had heard of, long ago.

She stuffed the papers back into the leather pouch. She was tempted to leave them. They didn't appear to be anything important, but she had been instructed to retrieve the contents of the lockbox. She stuffed the leather pouch into her satchel and closed the box. The lock latched shut.

Callisto replaced her picks, sliding her tools back into her satchel. She had what she had been sent for. She needed to get out before anyone returned from breakfast. She smiled mischievously. Wherever had Pontus found such a rare delicacy this time of year? It was something she would have to learn for herself, if she ever wanted to strike out on her own.

Heading towards the door, she paused at the stitched leather bag, the one with the coin purse. A missing coin purse would be noticed immediately, but a couple of silver coins . . .

There was another of those metal charms, shaped into a hand, palm facing forward, dangling from its drawstring. It wasn't from a guild or religious order she was familiar with. She loosened the drawstring just enough to draw out two silver coins, then drew it shut again. She slid the coins into a hidden pocket on her belt.

Satisfied with another job well-done, she waited at the door, listening. Not a sound from the hallway. She turned the handle, tentatively, peering out. The hallway was still deserted. She exited, closing the door behind her. A quick turn from her larger lock picks, and the door had been locked shut again.

She headed towards the far end of the hall, her padded boots muffling her steps as she made for the open door and balcony. She was almost disappointed it was over. Other than the trick latch in the lockbox, it had been an easy job – for one with her skills. She smiled at the thought. She'd love to see one of those other clods try to open a box like that. Without her sense of hearing . . .

Wait! Footsteps. On the stairs behind her. She was almost to the exit. Yes! Two sets of heavy boots, climbing!

A surge of apprehension shot through her, sending shivers down her spine. She needed to make herself scarce – and fast.

Callisto sprinted towards the balcony. She raced through the open door, lifting her knees higher. The footsteps were growing louder, their sounds amplified by the narrow stairwell. They pounded in her ears like a warning drum. Her foot touched-off against the edge of the handrail. It was a two story fall below. Her heart hammering, the thrill of the chase coursing through her. It would all come down this. Success or failure, in those last few seconds.

Chapter 2

The alley separating the inn from the neighboring structure was broad enough for a fully loaded wagon to pass comfortably between. Too broad for most thieves to jump. Certainly not if they were aiming for a narrow window on the other side. But Callisto had a running start – and she had been preparing for moments like this for years.

She pushed off from the railing, every muscle alive, every sinew in motion. It coursed through her; eyes fixed on the open window ahead as if closing on her prey. She leapt up, stretching out. A moment of shear exhilaration, suspended in mid-air, the wind streaming past. She tucked her body into a roll as she sailed through the open window and crashed onto the wooden floor.

She rolled to her feet, crouching low – watching, listening. The wooden floorboards still vibrated from her landing. She could feel the motion beneath her boots and fingertips. The dry dusty scent of the attic filled her nostrils. Her heart was pounding. Her muscles poised to flee or pounce.

From the balcony across the way, a tall, burly man stepped out. His expression was curious, perhaps perplexed, but not alarmed. He had a grey mustache and wore a saber at his hip. Probably a hired sword serving as a guard for one of the travelers.

Callisto remained in her crouch, letting the darkness of the shuttered attic shield her. He peered out, then down onto the street below. He had probably heard something, coming up the stairs. She remained still. He glanced each way, scratching the stubble of his beard. Callisto schooled her breathing, waiting. At length, apparently satisfied, he withdrew, shutting the balcony door behind him.

No cries of alarm. No rushing footsteps of pursuit. In the alleyway below, kitchen drudges shouted at dogs. Porters unloaded wagons. Callisto grinned. Despite her sore and bruised legs and back, she had made it with seconds to spare. Her reputation within the gang would remain untarnished.

She rose to her feet, checking herself for bruises or cuts. The muffled sound of voices and boot steps filtered from the storeroom below. There was no sign of anyone responding to her rough landing. Everything was exactly as it should have been, the product of endless preparation.

The attic was a cluttered array of cast-offs: winter supplies, storm shutters, leftover paints and stained brushes. There were worn tools which needed to be either repaired or discarded, but which had instead been piled onto broken tables, all dimly visible in the light which leaked in through the worn shutters.

Callisto had cleared a path through the debris when she had arrived the night before. She had ensured there would be ample room for the rolling landing which she had just accomplished. The upscale inn had proved a fruitful target over the years, one worth cultivating contacts in, and escape routes from. She didn't know whom Pontus paid to leave the balcony door open, nor did she know whether the proprietor of the shop below was aware of her presence. The system worked, however, and that was good enough for her.

She drew her change of clothes from a corner, from behind an empty wooden crate. A long pale skirt which matched her blouse, followed by a darker vest. She wrapped a white scarf around her head, hiding her short hair, and slipped her satchel across her shoulder. She adjusted the vest. There! She'd look like a typical shop owner's daughter, going about her morning errands.

There was a stairway leading down to the storeroom and storefront below. Instead, however, she made her way to a window on the opposite side of the attic, navigating through narrow aisles between tables, crates and assorted detritus. She stuck her head out of the window, observing the alleyway below. No sign of anyone watching.

A copper drainpipe extended from the roof, collecting rainwater into a cistern. Callisto swung herself out, gripping the drainpipe as she lowered herself to the alleyway. It was a well-practiced exercise. She touched lightly onto the worn, cobbled stones below. Still no sign anyone had noticed. From there, she made her way out, onto the street – on the side opposite from the inn.

The city of Centrola was still waking up. Cart herds prodded mules or donkeys forward. Shop keepers were unshuttering their stores. Callisto walked towards the opposite side of town, blending in with the people and bustle of the morning. There were no sounds of pursuit. With any luck, the travelers she had fleeced would be in the next town before they opened the box and realized they had been robbed.

The exhilaration of the chase was wearing off. It was a long trek back, and Callisto had time to think. How had she fallen into this life? The constant threats. Perpetually trapped or on the rung. Even after the thrill, after she succeeded wildly, it still felt like the victory was never hers. Probably because it wasn't.

She passed through the central market. Farmers and fishermen were still setting up stalls, laying out their wares. A few industrious women were waiting in line to get first pick at the season's vegetables or the latest catch. Callisto watched them, young women like herself, smiling and joking with sisters or friends. Going about their ordinary lives. It was hard not to feel resentful. The pretty girls who could turn every boy's head. Sisters laughing loudly as they exchanged gossip. Drawing glances from passersby as they bantered. Callisto, in contrast, had practiced how to disappear. How to make herself invisible.

A breeze carried the scent of fresh bread, and her stomach turned again. The constant hunger, even when she had enough silver in her pocket for bread. Sometimes she imagined herself running away. Escaping to somewhere new, where she could be the master of her own destiny. Then her reality would come crashing back down on her.

There was no place in Bateria she could go where Pontus wouldn't find her. He had too many connections. Too many friends who owed him favors. Lethe had run. Callisto shuddered. Lethe. The doleful pleas still haunted Callisto's dreams.

Glancing around to make sure no one was watching, she doubled back, retracing her steps. She was close to the eastern dockyards now. No signs anyone was following her. She turned into an alleyway, slipping into the shadowed gloom.

She followed the alley to a green door with peeling paint. She glanced up and down for whomever might be watching.

She could spot Atreus at the other end of the building, leaning against the wall – on lookout. He was one of the younger members of the gang. He had one of those cherubim faces which usually kept him out of trouble. He gave her a smile and a silent nod as she rapped on the door: two quick knocks, a pause, and then a third. The door unlocked and cracked opened.

One of the older boys was at the door.

"You can send her in," came a voice from another room.

The door swung wide, and Callisto entered. The room was dimly lit by a single lamp. An older man with dark hair and a long, trimmed beard sat behind a table. Grey hairs bristled from his intent eyebrows and from his temples.

Pontus sat at the table with a magnifying glass and scales in front of him. He wore a long coat, too long and warm for this time of year. It draped around his shoulders and reached nearly to the ground from the tall chair where he sat. Candlesticks, platters, broaches, rings and bracelets – all alike were laid out in front of him. They were sorted by silver or gold content, or by the color and quality of their stones.

"You're back early," Pontus said, looking her up and down. "Were you able to open the lockbox?"

"Of course," Callisto said, laying the satchel on the table and opening the flap. She gave it a little shake and the necklace and bracelets spilled out. Pontus eagerly snatched them up, bringing them under the magnifying glass and leaning closer to look.

"The stones are cloudy. I would have expected something better." Pontus set the necklace aside and peered at the first bracelet. "This is all there was? I thought these travelers were rich."

"Those and this pouch," Callisto replied, shaking the folded leather pouch from her bag. She slid it across the table towards him.

Pontus gripped her wrist, staring at her. "You wouldn't be holding out on me, would you? You know I'll find out."

"I'm not holding out. This is all there was."

"You know what happens if I catch you stealing from me." Pontus pulled aside his cloak to reveal the silver handle of a knife. Her arms itched painfully with the memory. She could almost feel its cold edge.

He released her, still watching her suspiciously. She rubbed at her wrist, at the phantom scars of her memory. "That's all there was. I swear."

Pontus went back to examining the bracelet.

"The lockbox was gnome made," Callisto said. "The lock in the handle was fake – probably tripped a trap."

Pontus grunted. "They flashed a lot of coins around the inn. I would have expected more."

"They had small silver amulets on their bags. A palm-faced hand."

"Some religious cult from Trevio," Pontus muttered. "The order of Marcus Maximus." He cast the bracelets into a pile and reached for the folded leather packet. "I expected more than this."

Callisto waited, as Pontus opened the leather packet and drew out the handwritten pages. He thumbed through them, his scowl slowly relaxing, a perplexed look furrowing his brow. "You said the bags all shared this religious symbol?"

"Yes. Nothing from around here."

Pontus replaced the papers into the pouch. His mood had improved. "I have to go see someone, find out what these are. You can be done for the day."

Callisto remained standing, all but blocking his path. He turned, glaring at her.

"You wanted something?"

"You said I could have another lesson with Erebus."

Pontus regarded her coldly. "Tomorrow. I have to go now."

Pontus gathered the leather packet with its letters, stuffing them into a bag. He whispered instructions to the older boy at the door and was gone.

Callisto wandered through the halls, towards the back of the building. Young thieves and cut-purses lounged about, chatting about their latest exploits – real or imagined. Voices died down. They stepped out of the way as she approached. Even in a den of thieves, Callisto stood out.

She was one of the older youths. She was also one of the few girls among them. It was more than that which made them step away when she walked by, however. She

A WOLF BEFORE THE STORM

had never fit in – whether by choice or circumstance even she no longer knew.

Atreus was standing next to Theia at the edge of the rickety stairs leading up. He smiled at her as she approached. They were the youngest of the pickpockets in the band. They often worked together and were never far apart. Were they siblings or cousins? Callisto wasn't certain. Everyone here had a private story. The details could change with the seasons.

Callisto ruffled Atreus' hair as she passed. "Off from watch duty?"

"My shift was up," Atreus replied. "Pontus had one of the older boys replace me."

Callisto reached into the pocket in her belt, where she had hidden the two silver coins from the inn. She handed one coin each to the two younger pickpockets. "Don't let Pontus know," she added in a low whisper.

Callisto climbed the rickety stairs to the upper loft. Pontus' den was in the rear quarter behind a small carpenter's shop. Not that the shop ever saw much traffic. It was in the wrong quarter of town. Too close to the dockyards to attract business from anyone but the fishermen. It served a purpose, however, and kept the tax collectors at bay.

The stairwell creaked as she climbed it, and the railing swayed when gripped. She knew every rocking step, however, and climbed it nimbly. Reaching the upper loft, she scaled a ladder to a little alcove. It was too short to stand up in. But it had a small, shuttered vent at the end which looked out over the rooftops. Her own little window. Her own private space.

She collapsed onto the mattress in the corner, lying back and listening to the sounds of the surrounding building. From here, she could hear the seagulls squawking in the dockyard, trying to steal their share of the catch. A dull thrum of chatter filtered from the floors below. The roll of wagons on the street. Another, ordinary day – for everyone else.

She was hungry. Maybe later she'd go down to the kitchen to see what fresh goods had been bought or snagged. Her muscles were still tense from her leap across the alleyway. She was sore, but in a stretchy sort of way. She leaned back, remembering. From the moment she had lowered herself onto the balcony of the inn, she had felt . . . alive. Heart pounding. Ears listening.

Callisto relaxed, drifting into sleep. Her dreams began, as they often did, with the day's events. The feel of the lock and pick beneath her fingers. The rush of the chase as she had bolted through the hall. Reliving the moments. Adjusting her response.

As her sleep deepened, however, her dreams turned to a familiar theme. A voice she remembered from her childhood. A voice, and a cry.

"Grandma!"

The woods, dark. A howl in the distance. The chilling instant she had first known: there were monsters in this world.

Chapter 3

Dear grandma,

I did well. Pontus won't say it, but I know I did. He's paying for another day of lessons with Erebus.

I've learned so much. Not just about locks or how to palm a coin in my hand. How to defend myself. How to escape a pursuer. Where to kick and how hard.

Erebus has been teaching me with knives, too. I had written you about it before. I'm always afraid someone might find my letters. He shows me how to use a dagger, how to throw a knife. I'm dead accurate at twelve paces! For the past few weeks, he's been teaching me how to use a saber, as well. A real sword! Like the foreigners wear.

I'm sure Pontus wouldn't approve. He thinks I'm just a burglar, a lockpick, a stupid girl. He tells me I could never survive without his connections.

Can you imagine, yah-yah? Seeing me with a weapon in my hand?

* * *

Callisto started out early the next morning, a youthful spring in her step, a satchel across her shoulder. Training was a privilege she looked forward to – an opportunity to become something more than just a common pickpocket or cutpurse. It was a privilege she had fought to maintain, even if paying for the training meant she became further indebted.

The route to her trainer's studio led through the eastern edge of Centrola. Fishermen were loading nets onto their boats. The cool morning air carried the cries of gulls and the salty scent of fish. Callisto watched the gentle bob of the boats on the docks. The sun was bright and the wind steady. It would have been a beautiful day to be at sea.

She enjoyed the stroll. A chance to glimpse at lives so different from her own. The fishermen on their boats. The sons and daughters helping to prepare the nets.

She turned down a side-street, heading away from the docks again. The shadows cast by the buildings were long at this early hour. Here, away from the dockyards, the streets were largely deserted.

"What have you got there?" Crius asked, stepping into her path. He was tall for his age. A good head taller than Callisto. The pale beige of his tunic and trousers hid the grime of the street – at least until someone was close enough to see how worn his clothing was. Three other boys followed behind him, a mischievous grin on their faces.

"Something for Erebus," Callisto replied. She moved to the side, trying to make her way around them. Crius stepped into her path again.

"Maybe I should deliver it." Crius stepped closer, reaching towards her satchel.

Callisto's hand shot out, gripping Crius by the wrist. She pulled him forward, stepping to the side. Her foot slid across his ankle as she pulled him off balance. He stumbled forward, and she twisted his arm behind his back.

She bent his hand backwards, placing pressure against his wrist. Crius yelped.

Callisto continued to spin him around, keeping him between her and his friends. His head facing away from her, doubled over. Her hands firmly gripping his wrist –

bending it back. She kept her eyes fixed on his friends. They had halted, mid-step.

"Go ahead, another step and I'll break it." Callisto eyed them warily. The three of them stood with their usual, stupefied expressions. "Tell them to back away, Crius." She applied more pressure.

"Owww! Back off, guys! Back off!"

Crius' friends each took a step backwards. Callisto edged around them, her grip on Crius firm. When she had shuffled past, she released her grip, giving him a shove. He went stumbling towards his friends.

"Owww! What kind of girl are you?" Crius turned, rubbing his wrist.

"One who doesn't answer to you."

In an instant, there was a knife in Crius' hand. Even his friends seemed to be surprised by how quickly he had produced it.

"You don't really want to be drawing a knife on me, do you?" Callisto's stance was wide. She was already calculating exactly where to strike to disarm him. How much damage she would inflict.

"No, he doesn't."

Callisto was surprised to hear Erebus' voice behind her. She glanced back. Erebus was standing at the entryway to his studio, his hands leaning on his walking stick.

Despite his advancing age, and the cane he rested against, Erebus still radiated strength. His curly grey hair and beard, streaked with darker bands, were neatly brushed. His muscular shoulders and arms emphasized his working lifestyle. His cold stare was fixed on Crius.

Crius returned the knife to its hidden sheath. "We were just talking."

* * *

Callisto followed through with the motion, her eyes fixed on the target. The knife whispered as it whipped through the air, landing squarely at the center of the painted circle. Four blades, all within the center ring.

"Very good," Erebus said. "You're becoming more consistent, from any side or angle – and from either hand."

"Thank you, master." Callisto walked towards the target to retrieve the throwing knives.

"Let's try something different. You can return the daggers to their case."

Callisto pulled the daggers from the wooden target. The leather of their grip was soft in her hand. Their blades were finer than a fighting dagger, and they lacked the cross-guard. But they felt so natural when she handled them, like an extension of herself.

As she replaced the daggers into their wooden case, she was curious as to what he would have her do. She knew she'd be asked to sharpen any blades later.

The floor of the studio was bare, except for a row of benches at the edge of the room. It had once been a workshop, and the floor still bore the scores from long gone tables. The walls were adorned with swords and knives of different types. Spears and pole arms, as well as an assortment of daggers, hung beside them. Others were housed in wooden boxes which lined the walls or rested beneath benches.

She inhaled as she snapped the case shut. The scent of leather. The salty air floating thought the windows. This was her refuge. A place where she could prepare herself, better herself. Become more than just a pickpocket or cutpurse. How to pick a lock. How to enter and exit without being seen. How to wield a blade.

"Have you thought about what you'll do once you've paid off your debt?"

"I'll be free," she replied.

"What then? Is it enough for you? Is it all you want?"

A WOLF BEFORE THE STORM

She turned to him expectantly, wondering what weapon he would choose from the training rack. She was his best student. She knew it. And not just at picking locks.

She was surprised to see him on one knee, reaching to retrieve a wooden box from beneath a bench. The cover was inlaid with a snarling wolf design carved from a darker grain.

A wolf? It could mean many things. This was Bateria, after all. The box was more elaborate than the simple wooden cases which housed most of his collection.

Erebus held the box in one hand, gripping his cane to pull himself up. She resisted an urge to come to his aid. She knew he wouldn't appreciate it. The movement betrayed his limp – the injury which had forced him to become a trainer, rather than a practicing thief or weapons master. He placed the long, flat box on top of a bench, unlatching its cover.

Callisto froze when she saw the blades. Not one, but two of them. Long blades, with a forward curve to their cutting edge. Their grips were a black leather, with snarling wolf heads carved into each hilt. The blades gleamed silver in the light.

"Do you know what these are?" Erebus asked.

"They're *kopis*," she said. He was watching her, studying her reaction. "A blade with a forward curve."

"They're a matched set, forged from a silver-infused ingot – from a time when monsters stalked the land. It's a lost art, knowing precisely how much silver to add without sacrificing the strength of the blade. Go ahead, see how they feel."

Callisto took a blade in each hand, testing their weight. Why was he asking her to practice with these? These of all weapons? The silver handle tingled where it touched her skin. She tried to maintain a neutral expression. Act as if the request were nothing out of the ordinary. Pretend her mind wasn't screaming, knowing she was holding weapons forged for the express purpose of killing werewolves.

She stepped back to the center of the practice floor. She could feel his eyes on her. She practiced swinging the blades, slowly at first. They were heavier than the daggers she often used, but lighter than a saber. The forward curve gave them extra momentum whenever she swung downwards. It was like swinging an axe rather than a sword.

Callisto swung the blades through a series of figure-eights, practicing techniques to block and disarm her opponents. Periodically she would lunge forward in a thrust, envisioning her blade plunging into an adversary. She began to relax, finding her rhythm.

"That's right," Erebus said. "Like you did with the daggers. Feel the weight of the blade and follow through."

Callisto ran through more complex combinations, routines intended for facing multiple opponents.

"Few swordsmen are equally adept with both hands," Erebus continued. "It is a rare talent. Invaluable, whether you're a thief, hired sword, or paid assassin."

Callisto's stroke faltered. "I'm a lockpick and a thief. Hardly a hired-sword or assassin."

"Don't make it sound so far-fetched. You have a natural talent with weapons, not just at picking locks. The protection and resources of the guild could be invaluable."

She resumed her routine, trying to regain her focus. "They'd hardly accept a girl."

"I'm merely suggesting possibilities. You have an exceptional talent, Callisto. Your sight and hearing are sharper than any lockpick I've ever trained. Your skill with a blade no less."

"Why would they take someone like me?"

"You wouldn't be the first woman who was accepted into the Assassin's Guild. With a letter of recommendation from a first-blade, they'd have to accept you as an apprentice – girl or not. From there, it'd be up to you to rise through the ranks."

"What first-blade would ever recommend me?" Callisto picked up her tempo, her blades whistling with each stroke.

"I winter in Polonia, as you know. The center for both the empire and the Assassin's Guild. I could make . . . inquiries, if you'd like."

Callisto completed her practice pattern, returning to the ready position. "I'm no assassin."

"You're a fine lockpick and an expert pickpocket, Callisto. But to handle a sword or dagger as fluently as you? In either hand? It's a gift."

"I've never killed. I'm not sure I could."

"The empire has killed a part of each of us. It's up to you to decide what to do with that. You're more dangerous than you realize. With your combination of skills –"

The door to the studio swung loudly open, startling Callisto from her thoughts. Pontus stepped in. She stood there, blades in hand. She could almost see his mind at work, slowly processing what he saw. A flicker of surprise, or was it fear, passing through his eyes? "You're training her with swords?"

"*Kopis*," Erebus replied calmly, both hands resting atop his cane. "The girl has a natural talent."

"I pay you to train her as a thief, not a sword fighter."

"Even a thief sometimes needs to fight their way out. The girl should know how to defend herself."

Pontus shook his head, regarding them both. "You're mad. She's a lockpick, not a weapons master. Callisto, get your things. We're going. We'll talk about this later."

Callisto hurriedly replaced the two curved blades. She laid them carefully into their cloth-lined carrying case, her eyes on their wolf-head designs, wondering how many werewolves had died beneath these same weapons. She pinned her hands to her side as she realized they were trembling.

Had anyone seen? What would Pontus think? Would he forbid her from training? She couldn't stand the thought of giving up this part of her life.

"I could make introductions," Erebus insisted. "I'll be in Polonia for the winter. She's more than just a lockpick. With her combination of skills, she could pay off her debt in a fraction of the time."

"I have my own plan for how she's going to pay off her debt."

Chapter 4

Dear grandma,

I have to pack quickly. Pontus is taking us somewhere. I don't know where. You don't need to worry. I keep my letters hidden, in the pocket I sewed into my blanket.

Erebus had me practice with kopis today. Two at once. I know I did good. The blades felt so natural in my hands. I just couldn't get over –

Have to go. I'll write more later.

* * *

"Where are we going again?" Callisto had packed her belongings into a single sack which she carried in her left hand. A couple of changes of clothing, a bar of soap, and her worn, lightweight blanket. Her letters to her grandmother, scribbled onto whatever scraps she could find, were folded away in a pocket she had sewn. A knife was hidden in her boot.

"We're going to see a business partner of mine," Pontus replied. "Never you mind why."

Outside of the storefront was a carriage. Some of the older boys were already loading trunks onto the luggage rack. Carriage fees were expensive – too expensive for Pontus to waste precious silver for anything closer than a day's walk.

The carriage driver was a thin, worn-looking man. His bedraggled grey beard and cloak matched those of the old horse which drew the carriage. A harsh gust of wind would probably have pushed him over. Trust Pontus to find the cheapest coach in town. The driver strained, struggling to pry open the warped carriage door. He all but fell backwards as the latch sprang free.

"Get in," Pontus said.

Callisto looked around in confusion, realizing for the first time no one else was joining them. "Shouldn't we wait for the others?"

"There won't be any others. Get in!"

Callisto climbed up, taking a seat on the hard wooden bench. Pontus took the seat across from her, muttering his complaints about the "Stupid girl!" and all he had to put up with. The door slammed shut behind them.

The cabin was sparingly apportioned, even as carriages went. A minor nobleman or even a well-to-do merchant would expect to travel on a cushioned bench. A more refined client would insist on an elaborate cabin with a freshly varnished finish – the kind which made her nose wrinkle from its thick lacquered scent. Callisto had seen them up close during previous jobs. Those coaches were like mobile houses, insofar as she was concerned.

The carriage jerked into motion as Callisto watched through the windows on either side. The storefront disappeared behind them. They were traveling towards the northeast. Possibilities rolled through her mind.

If the city's authorities had been onto them, they wouldn't be leaving in a coach. It was too conspicuous. They would also have been leaving with more than just the two of them. Why then, were they leaving?

"Is it far?" she asked.

"We're going to meet a business partner of mine." Pontus fixed her with his gaze. "While we're there, you are not to speak unless spoken to. Understand?"

"A partner? Where?"

Pontus regarded her in silence for a moment. "We're going to meet an old friend of mine in Aridia."

The surrounding geography ran through Callisto's mind. Places, names – most of which she only dimly knew. "That's just a village," she said at last.

"About a day's journey to the northeast."

A business partner? Pontus had no regular partner other than himself. At least not for any length of time. There had to be a specific deal involved. A big deal, if it would make him drop everything on a moment's notice.

And why was she there? Unless he needed her skills. A burglary? It had to be. She was easily the best lockpick in Pontus' band. Perhaps the best in all Centrola.

Pontus opened a package on his lap, drawing out a folded pastry. He proceeded to eat his meal, the juices dripping down his lips and onto his beard. Callisto could detect the scent of shellfish, together with an assortment of herbs. He must have bought it from a baker's stand while she was upstairs collecting her things.

Her stomach growled. Even a dried, salted fish would have been better than nothing. She regretted not having found something to eat when she left her training class. Pontus had been in such a hurry to go. A day's journey? It was already late in the day. It'd be dawn before they arrived.

* * *

Callisto shook the sleep from her eyes. It took her a moment to remember where she was.

It was dark. Pontus had drawn the curtains down over the windows on either side. She couldn't tell just how dark it was, or what time it might be – although she knew it was still night.

The carriage rocked and swayed, jostling whenever it went over an uneven patch in the road. Pontus was asleep, snoring noisily on the bench across from her. Sleeping soundly enough. Maybe she could risk raising the curtain to see where they were. Slowly, tentatively, she drew the curtain back.

The twisted trunks of rugged forests swept past, silver moonlight illuminating their leaves. It must have been after midnight. Rugged hills were visible in the distance. The outlines seemed vaguely familiar, stirring memories from her childhood. Happier times, before all of this.

It had been so long since she had been outside of the city. The dangers of being caught outside, in the open – without alleys or wagons or crowds to disappear into – had been drilled into her.

The forest, nonetheless, drew her in. The trees, the brush, the chirping of insects. Like a warm memory, wrapping her in its folds. A part of herself she had forgotten.

Callisto's mind wandered, recalling sights and sounds. Faces from her past, voices from a lifetime apart. A time when she hadn't lived on the city's streets. A time when the forest and its mystery embraced her – full of promise, not tragedy. Memories which beckoned her.

How long had she sat there, staring? The carriage jostling and swaying beneath her? She caught a glimpse. Just a glance. A figure. Near the edge of the road.

Had she seen it? Or merely imagined it? Was it real, or just a dream? A shadowy figure. Amber eyes, glowing golden in the moonlight.

Out of the darkness, a mournful howl arose. A wolf's howl.

Chapter 5

I remember, yah-yah. All the things you shared with me. The scent of the forest. The clear waters of the streams. I remember, and those memories haunt me.

* * *

The sound of the wolf's howl rose and fell, a plaintive note upon the wind.

Callisto yanked the curtain into place, jerking herself away from the window. Her heart was pounding. She slid away from the carriage door, the hard cabin wall against her back.

Memories rushed through her mind. People and faces she had not seen . . . not since that day. The voices of her brothers. A kind face still etched into her memory. *Yah-yah!*

The carriage lurched down the road, teetering like a handcart pulled by a drunken porter. Pontus snored noisily, oblivious to everything she had heard. She, however, was wide awake. It felt like pins and needles, prickling against her skin

She was no longer in the city. These were the lands of a distantly remembered past. Lands not yet fully tamed. Lands where werewolves could still be imagined in the shadows of the night.

Seconds stretched into minutes. Minutes into hours. Her breathing deep, labored, as if preparing for the fight. Her body tense, listening.

The howl was not repeated, and it was not answered. But she couldn't shake its memory. Couldn't fall asleep. Hours drifted by, as the dark sky turned light, painted with the red stain of dawn. Her heart beat loud against her eardrums.

With a final lurch, the carriage came to a stop.

Voices outside. Someone unloading trunks from the back of the carriage. Pontus groggily sat up. He rubbed his hands across his face and eyes. "Are we there?"

* * *

Callisto stared at the plate set in front of her. She was unused to being seated at the table. Not when Pontus was meeting with a client or business partner. Grape leaves, wrapping a combination of rice and vegetables, had been laid out – three to a plate. She could smell the savory mixture of herbs, the nutty scent of the rice, her mouth watering. She hadn't eaten since the morning before.

She wasn't sure if all three had been intended for her. Was she supposed to take one and pass it along, like they would in Pontus' den?

But no, they were setting identical plates in front of Pontus and their host, Cetus.

Cetus was slightly younger than Pontus, his dark beard and curly hair just beginning to show signs of grey. His estate was on the outskirts of Aridia, on a hilltop overlooking the village below. It had a low wall surrounding a central courtyard. The surrounding hills were covered with orchards and vineyards.

Callisto had seen men like Cetus before. He was a thief, just as Pontus was. His eyes betrayed him. The constant shifts and schemes going on in his mind. The nervous twitch of a hunted man. This thief, however, was more accomplished than Pontus had ever been.

His clothes were individually tailored, with brass buttons and patterns stitched into the edges of his vest and sleeves. Even his house servants wore uniforms. Their matching vests had been cut from a pale cloth. In Centrola, the wealthier merchants had preferred darker fabrics for their servants. Darker clothing hid the stains and required less frequent cleaning.

Of course, there was also Taras. He stood behind Cetus, near the entryway – a broad, immovable mountain of a man. His massive arms nearly burst from beneath his white shirt. He remained there, immobile, a bodyguard befitting a prince of thieves. There was no movement in his dark mustache or eyebrows to betray whatever thoughts might lurk behind his eyes.

"Tell the girl to eat, Pontus," Cetus said. "A starving burglar is of no use to either of us."

Pontus nodded in her direction, and Callisto picked up one of the grape leaves, biting into it. A rich mixture of spices exploded into her mouth. So, this was how the wealthy ate! Not the bland, oil drenched grape leaves she was used to – but a blend of subtle spices which complimented the nutty flavor of the rice. Callisto could remember similar scents floating from the manor kitchens she would sometimes pass by – or rob from.

She hungrily devoured all three of the rolled leaves, licking her fingers as she finished. She looked up. They were watching her! Pontus and Cetus were only halfway through their first grape leaf. Had she done something wrong? A servant, wearing a white shirt and vest, came and took her plate, a smirk across his face.

"This is the lockpick who opened the box?" Cetus asked.

"She's the best in Centrola," Pontus replied.

Callisto sat a little more erect, wiping her fingers and lips on the cloth napkin. It was rare for Pontus to offer praise.

"Of course," Pontus continued, "her table manners befit her origins. You can't take the gutter out of the street rat."

Callisto stiffened. The words stung – but were true. She was little more than a gutter rat. She had been reminded of it often enough.

"Perhaps," Cetus replied. "But the lockbox was believed to be impenetrable. The priests who were transporting it weren't entrusted with their own key. They won't realize anything's missing until they're back in Trevio. Now, about the package you recovered, do you have it with you?"

Pontus withdrew the leather pouch from his vest, pausing momentarily before handing it across the table. "Do you know what it is?"

"I know who's paying for the information it contains," Cetus said, standing and reaching for the pouch. Pontus reluctantly released his grip.

Cetus unfolded the leather flap, drawing out the parchment pages. He examined them, first sorting through, then reading from the beginning. His brow was furrowed intently.

"Have you read through the documents yourself?" Cetus asked.

"Yes," Pontus replied.

"What about the girl?"

Callisto was unused to being asked her opinion on anything. "A little," Callisto replied. "Something about a Gnotrix? It talks about letters and a map. It was signed by someone named Herrick."

"Observant," Cetus said. "Gnotrix was a famous mage who lived over two hundred years ago. Herrick was his pupil. These pages were allegedly pilfered from Herrick's journal. They describe Herrick's plans to retrace the final journey of Gnotrix, just before he disappeared into the east."

"Someone is willing to pay money for these? Good money?" Pontus was practically salivating over the prospect.

"Not necessarily for these notes, but for something else they contain. Herrick mentions a series of letters he received from Gnotrix. Letters and a map. Gnotrix, you see, was the last known Arche-Mage. A wizard of immense power. He made a pilgrimage to seek out the secrets of the great mage Xythox. That name, I presume, you've already heard?"

"Everyone's heard of Xythox," Callisto said. "He was the mage who conquered Bateria and waged war on the fae."

Pontus scowled at her. Callisto realized belatedly she had spoken out of turn.

"Quite so," Cetus said. "How well can you read, girl?"

"I can read," Callisto said. "Well enough. My grandmother taught me."

"Why does it matter whether a thief can read?" Pontus said. "She's expected to rob whatever we need, not write about it."

Cetus put the papers down. "Because, my able partner, what we need to steal is described in these notebook pages. It'll be located in the Imperial Library of Polonia."

"The imperial city?" Pontus replied. "What could there be in a library which could be worth so much?"

"If these pages are correct, then the original letters and map, as sent by Gnotrix to his apprentice, would have been left behind in Herrick's study when Herrick set out on his journey. He set out in search of his esteemed master. It was a journey from which Herrick would never return. When he disappeared, Herrick's books and notes were collected by the authorities and deposited in the library. They should still be there."

"We're trying to find his books on magic?" Pontus asked.

"Any tomes on magic have doubtless disappeared or been destroyed. It's the letters from his master which we seek."

"Then we need to have the lockpick sneak in and snatch those letters."

"It's not so easy. The library is vast, and librarians from centuries past may have organized the collection differently. There are no standards for such things. Moreover, no artifacts can be removed from the library. Scholars come from across the empire to access the archives and copy notes from the volumes. We'll first need to determine where the letters are located. Only then can your burglar break into the library to retrieve them."

"These letters are worth something?"

"Anything tied to Gnotrix or Xythox is worth a fortune, to the right buyer. We're just lucky you intercepted these documents before they made their way to Trevio."

"How much of a fortune?" Pontus was leaning forward, his arms on the table.

Cetus regarded him guardedly. "A king's ransom, to the right buyer."

Callisto thought Pontus might drool on the table. "What's our next step?"

"Tomorrow, we leave for Polonia. Once there, we need to get your burglar properly dressed. We'll have to see to those table manners as well."

"The burglar? Why should we care what she wears?"

"No one is going to allow a street urchin to paw over the imperial archives. We'll need to get her dressed like a scholar, with a letter of introduction and an imperial permit giving her access to the library. I know just the forger to provide them."

The servants had returned, bearing trays heaped high with meats. Steam rose from the platters. The scent of roasted lamb wafted through the room. If they continued to feed her like this, she'd gladly follow to whatever strange city they might send her.

* * *

A WOLF BEFORE THE STORM

Night had fallen. Pontus and Cetus had spent all day planning, staying up late as they debated the details of their journey. What they would take. Where they would stay. Who would handle the sale and how they would divide the payment.

Callisto had retired to a guest room on an upper floor. It was a broad room, with a soft bed – softer than any she could remember sleeping on before. At least not since . . . not since the day her childhood had ended.

Callisto stood on the balcony, leaning out, gazing across the moonlit landscape. It was a half moon, in its waning phase. The surrounding orchards were lit in the bright silvery light. It all seemed like a dream.

Rich meals, savory herbs, pillows filled with feathers instead of straw. Was this how the wealthy lived? Even the fabrics she touched were finer, softer than any she could remember.

And then there was the countryside. The sounds of frogs and insects floating on the breeze. The scents of earth and blossoms. All of it awakening her senses.

She took it in. The silver light on the leaves. The gentle sway of branches in the wind.

She had almost forgotten about the wolf's howl from the night before. Almost.

Her attention was distracted. A shape moved across the crest of a nearby hill – a shadow moving between the trees.

Was it a bear? It didn't move like a bear. A dog? Too big for a dog. It rose onto its hind legs, its amber eyes reflecting the moonlight. It was looking, searching, scenting the wind. Looking at her.

She knew, her breath caught in her throat, refusing to release. Yes, of course. This was Bateria, after all. A werewolf. There was no other thing it could be.

Chapter 6

I remember the howls, yah-yah. I remember the final plea in your voice, telling me to run. I ran. But I could never forget the sound, then or now.

* * *

Callisto drew away from the balcony, backing into her room. She glanced around, looking for something, anything she might use as a weapon. She had a small knife which she kept hidden in her boot. It wasn't much of a knife, and it wasn't silver.

She could hear the wolf scramble over the courtyard wall. Dogs barked from the direction of the servants' quarters and stables, below. There was a scraping of claws against stone. The werewolf was climbing. It was being drawn to her. She had nowhere to go.

Maybe the wolf wasn't after her. Maybe it was just looking for opportunities. A sheep which went astray. A foal separated from its mother. A street rat leaning over a balcony.

But she knew, even as the thought crossed her mind, that it wasn't true. When the werewolf's eyes had peered at her, she had been certain: it had found her.

It must have caught her scent. It knew what she was. There was no sense in running. No point in crying out. There was nothing anyone could do. Silver daggers wouldn't be lying around in open drawers.

The wolf crept over the balcony railing, the hair on its shoulders bristling. It inched into her room cautiously, on all fours. Its eyes fixed on her. Its nose twitching as it scented the air.

"I wasn't sure." The wolf's voice came as a low rumble from his throat, as if unused to human speech.

"I didn't mean to intrude," Callisto said, crouching low – her hand hovering over her boot, over the handle of her knife. "I didn't know this was your hunting ground."

The wolf raised itself onto its hind legs. He was in a half-wolf, half-human state. His snout had grown shorter since he had entered the room, making it easier for him to speak. He was rather scrawny for a werewolf – gangly, as if he were not yet fully grown.

"You don't know who I am, do you?" The wolf's amber eyes stared at her.

"Have we met?" Callisto had crept closer to the door. A couple more steps, and she could be racing down the hall – for all the good it would do her.

"Tell me you don't know."

Callisto paused; the scents of the night carried on the breeze. The scent of olives ripening on the trees. The aroma of grapes being pressed into wine. The musty scent of the wolf.

"Makednos?!"

"It's good to see you too." Sarcasm dripped from the werewolf's voice.

Callisto stepped forward, her open hand slapping across the wolf's snout and nose.

"Wha? Owww!"

"Stupid wolf! Don't you go scaring me like that!"

"What did I do?" The wolf was covering its muzzle, cowering backwards towards the balcony.

"I thought I was in a strange wolf's hunting range. I was about to stab you."

"No wolves hunt in these lands. Not anymore. Our hunting grounds have been pushed north."

"What are you doing here?" Callisto asked. She made no attempt to disguise her annoyance.

"I should ask you the same."

"What does it matter? It's not like anyone came to look for me."

"What are you talking about?"

"When they came! You stupid wolf! When the hunters came."

"I was told you were dead."

"Sorry to disappoint you."

"Callisto! We thought you were killed!"

"I wasn't. I can't say the same for *yah-yah*."

"She was my grandma too."

"No one came. Not when the inquisitors arrived."

"I was told no one survived."

"Well, I did survive. Alone. Left to fend for myself on the streets." Callisto stood, leaning over her brother, anger flashing in her eyes. "Alone in a world where you and I shouldn't exist."

"We didn't know," Makednos pleaded, backing onto the balcony.

"Well, you do now."

"Why didn't you come back?'

"Come back? I was captured. An indentured servant, fighting for every crust of bread. All they had to do was turn me in. One whisper, one word in the wrong ear, and the inquisitors would have had me."

Makednos' rear foot came up against the railing.

"I caught your scent a day ago," he said. "I couldn't believe it was true – I had to know."

"So, it was you I heard from the carriage."

"You can come home now, Callisto. Whatever happened before, it's done."

"Done?!" Callisto's hand had fallen onto a chair, her fingertips tracing against the fabric of the lightweight shift which had been set out for her. It was little more than a servant's smock, yet its fabric was softer than any clothing she had worn since coming to Centrola. "No Makednos, it isn't over. But it will be. I'm on the cusp of something big. Of paying off my debt. One more job. One more big job. And I will be free to make my own rules."

"You're not coming back?"

"To the father who couldn't be bothered to come looking?!"

"We thought you were dead."

"Maybe I was, to him. . . . You still haven't explained what you're doing here."

"You know, a wolf has to stretch his legs."

"You had an argument with father again, didn't you?"

"I might have." Makednos flashed his toothy grin.

"You always were the reckless one. How long have you been on your own?"

"A week, maybe more."

"Some things never change, little brother." Brother. It felt odd to say the word out loud, after so many years. She was still angry. But it felt oddly reassuring. Something constant. Something familiar. A family? Somewhere out there. After so many years on her own.

"You could come with me."

Callisto shook her head. "I already told you. I have a job to finish. A debt to clear."

"Callisto –"

"Goodbye, Makednos."

The werewolf watched her, contemplating. Then turned and climbed over the balcony railing, disappearing into the night.

Callisto shut the balcony door behind him, latching it shut.

* * *

The morning sun shone down brightly, as Pontus' last trunk was loaded onto the back of the carriage. It rocked as the trunk was jerked into position and strapped in place.

"We're going without Cetus?" Callisto asked.

"He'll be joining us in a day or two," Pontus replied, stepping into the coach. Callisto followed, gripping a bag with travel rations for the road. She wasn't looking forward to the hard seat or long ride, but at least there would be food this time.

The door slammed shut behind them and the whole carriage swayed. The driver snapped his whip. The crisp hoofbeats as the horse trotted off. The carriage bounced roughly down the road as Callisto stared out the window. Watching, as the estate receded into the distance.

There was no sign of Makednos, or that he had ever been there. She wondered if she would ever see him again. Maybe . . . once she had paid off her debt and could begin life on her own terms.

* * *

It was three more days by carriage to the city of Polonia. They stopped to camp at night, the forests and hills giving way to orchards and tilled fields.

Callisto was half drowsing when the city came into view. The first sign came as the road became less rocky and the ride smoother. Perking up, she leaned towards the window.

The city walls of Polonia were taller than those of Centrola. Taller, and whiter. The houses, visible on the raised, terrace-like hills had been bleached white in the sun.

Pontus took notice. "Sit down. We'll be there soon enough."

"You've been to Polonia before?"

"Years ago."

"It's so big."

"Twice the size of Centrola. Twice the riches, and twice the risk."

Chapter 7

Dear grandma,

The city is so big! I could see it from a distance, rising from behind its white walls. So many new places to learn. So much opportunity.

I'll be free soon. You'll see. It's been building inside me, this whole year now. I'm not so little anymore. I don't want to live this way forever.

I'll be free soon. Free to live my own life. My own terms.

* * *

"The washroom is on the ground floor. I can let out both rooms for two drachmae a night."

Callisto heaved Pontus' chest up the end of the stairway and through the hallway door. The steps groaned beneath her. Sounds of porters moving goods drifted from the warehouse below. Rough-sawed planks made up the floorboards, and the scent of sawdust permeated the air. The warehouse must have recently received a consignment of lumber for shipment. Cheap lumber. Softwoods, by the smell of it.

A pair of small rooms opened on either side of the hallway. Pontus was standing in the larger of them, a scowl on his lips as he made a show of inspecting the premises.

The warehouse's keeper was a rotund woman with a head of grey, wiry hair and shadows beneath her eyes.

From what Callisto had gathered, she managed the warehouse on behalf of a wealthy landlord. She lived in a corner of the warehouse's lower floor.

Judging from their broad, unfinished doors, these two rooms were likely built as extra storage space in the loft. There was no stove or other form of heat for the winter months. She doubted the landlord, whomever they were, was even aware these rooms were being rented out.

"The rooms are small," Pontus said, stroking his beard. "Winter will be on us soon enough. One and a half would be a fair price."

The woman looked him up and down. "This is the warehouse district. I take it you don't much care for any questions or . . . visits from the tax authorities? It'll be two. First week's rent is due up front."

Pontus grunted, opening the purse from his belt to count out the coins. Callisto dropped his chest at the foot of the bed, then carried her little sack to her own room. She dropped her satchel and blanket on the bed. The room was smaller than the one she had enjoyed at Cetus' estate. But was larger than anywhere she had slept in Centrola. The bed was plain, but clean, with a worn trunk at its foot.

"Hurry and wash up," Pontus said.

Callisto rushed down the stairs, her clothing in hand. She wanted to clean off the dust from the road and knew she didn't have much time. The washroom had a metal tub, with water drawn by a handpump from a cistern outside. It was cold, and the soap was harsh against her skin. Pontus would not wait for her to heat it up, however. Nor would he spare any silver to pay for logs and a fire to warm the water.

A cold draft came from the shuttered window. The air smelled of salt and fish, reminding her of Centrola. A familiar feeling. Familiar . . . was that what home felt like? Maybe. Maybe it was what home felt like for others. For Callisto, however, the two could never be the same. The warehouses, the city streets, the docks and the boats – these were where she lived. Nothing more.

She cleaned herself as quickly as possible, her skin and hair still wet as she rushed to join Pontus at the rear entrance. He was waiting, his hands and face freshly washed.

"Keep up, girl. We have a lot of ground to cover."

The two of them started down the alleyway, heading in the direction of the dockyards. Someone was shouting.

"Out with you!"

It was a woman's voice. Callisto glanced around. It didn't seem to be directed at her.

"You can't just throw me out! Don't you remember your own son?!" There was a thin, scruffy looking lad with a scraggly bearded chin. He was standing in the alley beside a worn bedroll.

"I remember well enough, Andros! You've stolen your last obol from me! I've let the rooms out to someone who'll be paying for rent!" It was the warehouse's keeper – the one who had negotiated with Pontus for the two rooms. She tossed another bag into the alley after him.

The young man backed into the alley, flashing Callisto a smile as she and Pontus passed.

"Don't come back until you've got a drachma to you name!" his mother called out.

Callisto made sure to ignore him as she followed Pontus' lead. She had no intention of getting involved in their private affairs. Judging from his unperturbed reaction, this scene had played itself out before.

"We're going to make a circuit of the city," Pontus said, seemingly oblivious to the whole exchange. "You'll want to remember the major streets so you can navigate for yourself. Pay attention. I won't be showing you twice."

The city of Polonia was arranged on a series of hills, straddling the Varda River. The eastern side of the city, where they were staying, contained the principal merchant district, including fishing docks as well as dockyards for trading vessels. The roads through the city were the typical tangle of twisting streets and alleyways she had come to expect after living in Centrola.

The imperial city, however, was on the eastern side of the river. Pontus had to pay a ferry to bring them across. The shallow boat was carrying a merchant and his wagon, as well as a group of men who likely lived on the western shore and entered the imperial city to find work. They appeared to be masons, Callisto decided, judging by the tools on their aprons and belts.

The ferry crossed the river on the northern edge of the city, providing a view of the dockyards to the south. Callisto stood at the edge of the boat looking out. Oarsmen rowed hard to bring the boat across the broad river, their foreman counting a cadence as their oars stroked.

The tall masts of the imperial navy dominated the eastern shore, the empire's pennant with its sunburst pattern streaming from their heights. Farther to the south, visible in the distance, was a rocky island jutting from the sea. Another imperial flag flew from its tower.

Row upon row of masts arose from the dockyards on either side of the river, like a thicket of trees. On the western shore alone, the merchant and fishing docks numbered more than twice as many tall vessels as their counterpart in Centrola could host.

"Have you ever been to the imperial city before?" the ferry's captain asked her. He was a deeply tanned man with a white beard and leathery skin. He stood at the rudder, adjusting as the oarsmen stroked against the river's sleepy current.

"No, never," Callisto replied, counting the masts of the imperial navy. Did she count eleven tall masts? There were more smaller ones.

"It will be a real treat, then. Emperor Bessarion has more than doubled the size of the imperial navy since ascending the throne. Between him and his father, the imperial city has been expanded twice over."

Callisto's eyes roved across the dockyards and towers, and the impressive display of imperial might. "What about the island, the one to the south?"

The grizzled captain followed her gaze. "That would be the fortress of Burcsteli. It goes back to the founding of the city. These days, it's the home of Master Zenodotus, the Imperial Historian."

The ferry drew up to a small quay. Dockside workers lowered planks into place, and the trader's wagon rolled off. Pontus and Callisto followed.

"They've expanded the imperial city since I was here last," Pontus said. "Most of the buildings near the docks are new or refurbished, but the Imperial Library should be much the same."

The first thing which struck Callisto were the streets. The city streets of the eastern half of Polonia, much like those of Centrola, were paved with an assortment of raw or rough-hewn stones. The stones which comprised the streets of the imperial city, however, were all fully dressed. There were few gaps for weeds or grime to collect. They were so clean, also. So clean they looked swept. As if someone had been assigned the absurd task of sweeping them clear of sand and debris on an ongoing basis.

It was a city built to impress. Storefronts, when they passed through the artisans' district, had great glass windows and colorful, carved and painted signs. There were no open-air stalls here. No farmers or fishermen hawking their harvest. Instead, there were windows displaying baked goods, sugary confections, carved metalwork, and vests and dresses adorned with shiny buttons or flowing frills.

Callisto had seen such things only in passing, in the wagons or rooms of wealthy merchants or government officials passing through Centrola. Never had she imagined such finery so openly on display for all to admire.

"Are you done gawking, girl?" Pontus' expression was compassionless as always.

"Yes, sir," she responded. She felt underdressed, walking through these streets – like a beggar outside the gate to a religious shrine. "Aren't they afraid of thieves stealing everything? In Centrola, they keep their finer goods behind the counter."

"The imperial city is patrolled. It's mostly for show, but the punishment for thievery is . . . well, you can guess. Come along. The academy district is just ahead."

Pontus led her to a broad concourse – two streets running side-by-side with a garden-like meridian between them. Tall buildings rose on either side, with people going in and out. Some were dressed like lords and ladies. Others wore simpler garments: a navy-blue skirt or grey vest with dark trousers.

"The Imperial Academy is on our right," Pontus said, speaking in a low voice. "The Imperial Library is across from us."

The structure was larger than any library Callisto had ever imagined. It was a sprawling expanse surrounded by an iron barred fence and gate. There were stairs leading up to a great, double-doored entrance. The white stonework accenting the corners of the structure seemed to glow in the brilliance of the afternoon sun. Marble columns framed the entrance.

Two wings branched off from the central entryway, each with an open upper floor featuring a balcony and colonnade. The wings on either side were at least three flights tall, with the tower above the central entryway at least five.

"That's a library?" Callisto responded, breathlessly. "Is it used for anything else?"

"It's used to impress," Pontus replied. "You should know by now. Half of what the wealthy do is all about who they can impress with their ostentatious waste. The library, however, houses archives which attract scholars from neighboring kingdoms and city states. Which is why the collection is guarded so carefully."

A pair of women were approaching the gate, leading up to the central entrance. They wore matching dresses with long white sleeves, and each had a pale grey scarf covering their hair. They were clutching books against their chests. They paused to show the guards a slip of parchment before proceeding inside.

"Two guards at the gate," Callisto said in a whisper. "More inside, I would guess."

"To be expected," Pontus replied. "Entry requires imperial permission, usually paid for handsomely. Scholars are searched before they exit to ensure no artifacts are stolen."

"Those two weren't dressed like locals," Callisto observed.

"Foreign scholars," Pontus said. "It's not uncommon for an apprentice or servant to be sent on behalf of a more seasoned master from abroad."

They stopped speaking as a young man crossed their path. He had short, dark wavy hair, and wore a white shirt and grey vest, with dark boots and trousers. Handsome and well dressed, Callisto decided. Probably from a well-connected family. He was carrying two books in his arms, heading towards the entrance.

"The young man," Callisto whispered as he passed through the library gates. The guards barely glanced at his pass. "He's a student at the Imperial Academy?"

"Either that or in the employment of the library," Pontus replied, his eyes constantly on the lookout for anyone who might hear or observe them.

Callisto glanced up and down the outer metal fence. "It's not close enough to gain entry from a neighboring building. The only way in is through or over the fence."

"We'll get you in," Pontus said. "I know a number of forgers who can get you a pass. You'll have to find what we're looking for on your own and then smuggle it out when you're done."

Callisto couldn't imagine how many rows upon rows of books and records a building of such size might contain. Just finding what they were looking for would be challenge enough.

As they watched, another pair of scholars exited the library, opening their satchels for the guards to inspect as they exited. "This is going to take some doing," Callisto commented.

"That's why you're here. I promised Cetus you were best suited for the job. Don't disappoint me."

Pontus continued his tour of the imperial city, leading her away from the library before they drew attention to themselves. Neither of them were dressed as if they had any business being there.

There was a row of impressive residences which Pontus averred were the homes of noblemen and imperial officials. Houses with steps and columns at their entrance, some with their own outer wall and courtyard. Callisto was shocked to imagine structures so vast might be used to house a single nobleman and his family.

The dock-side district of the imperial city had also grown since Pontus had last been there. Barracks had been constructed to house the burgeoning army and navy. The sunburst seal with its rays emanating from a central circle was on display everywhere. There was a tramp of boots as soldiers were marched through drills behind the walls of their compound. Patrols were common, armed with spears and carrying swords. They usually traveled in groups of two or four.

Not far from the docks were the official embassy and guild headquarters representing foreign kingdoms and trade unions from abroad. The pennants which flew above them were new to her.

Circling back towards the wagon ferry which had brought them to the eastern shore, Pontus led her past the Imperial Palace. The emperor's halls and quarters were housed in a vast structure, inside a walled enclosure. The towers and parapets were visible from the concourse outside.

A portico ran the length of the wall, proudly displaying the banners from the different houses and localities which had been added to the empire. Callisto recognized the banners from some of the southern, island principalities which had only recently been incorporated – securing trade routes to the south. People passed bye, some ignoring the banners and tapestries, others pausing to admire the captured foreign weaponry on display on the wall above.

It all seemed pompous and gaudy to Callisto. As they passed through another archway, near the entrance to the armory, however, Callisto saw them.

It took a moment for her to realize what she was looking at. When she did, the reality struck hard – like a blow to her stomach. There was a burning in her throat. Her meal from hours before unsettled and ill digested.

They were hung from the wall above her, placards proudly proclaiming their places of origin. Tens, maybe hundreds. Their bushy tails hung down. Sockets where eyes had once been were open and vacant. Stretched hides on display for all to see. Werewolf hides.

She knew what they were. She didn't need the placard to tell her. They were too large, and the proportions were all wrong for them to be from ordinary wolves. They were a testimony to the empire which had rid itself of her kind, hunting them down like vermin. The last vestiges of the campaign had occurred barely a decade before. Hanging before her, they were a macabre reminder of what would happen to her, should she ever be caught.

Pontus continued leading the way, seemingly oblivious, as Callisto lowered her eyes, suppressing the urge to run and disgorge the contents of her stomach. She did not dare to look. Who could say whether she might recognize the name of a place or village? She didn't want to know. Her grandmother's hide might be staring down at her from above.

Chapter 8

Dear grandma,

Do you see me? Do you see what I've become? If you do, do not judge me too harshly. The city streets were more jungle than any forest I might have run to.

* * *

"She isn't going to be scouring the library looking and smelling like a street rat." Cetus had joined them two days later, setting up shop in a private suite at an inn in the imperial city. He had been accompanied by one servant from his manor staff, as well as by his personal bodyguard, Taras.

"I already commissioned the papers to gain her admittance to the library," Pontus replied defensively. "It set me back some sixty drachmae – sixty silver coins!"

"With or without papers, they won't admit her if she doesn't look the part." Cetus sat in a large, upholstered chair next to a desk, scribing down a note.

"Here, take this," Cetus extended his hand, holding the parchment out to Pontus. "It's a note to a seamstress I've worked with before. Her address is in the imperial city. Have the girl outfitted for three dresses."

"Three?!"

"Have you even seen the Imperial Library? It will take weeks, just to learn her way around the building. She'll have to gain the trust of the archivists. And she'll need to look the part of a scholar's assistant."

Pontus looked at the scrap of parchment. There was an address on the reverse side. "This had better be worth it."

"Do you think I would be here if I thought we were squabbling over a sack of silver coins? The expense will be inconsequential after we collect the bounty. Get the girl some soaps while you're at it."

"I use soap!" Callisto protested. She had scoured herself earlier the same day.

"Peasants' soap, maybe. Get her something from the vendor around the corner. Something which smells of fragrant oils, not sheep's fat and ashes."

Pontus wore a sour expression, but he obligingly exited, Callisto trailing behind. It was a short walk, three streets down, with Pontus scowling the entire way.

The address led them to a shop with a sign over the entrance labeled, "Needles and Bows." A giant needle had been carved into the sign, as if stabbing a thread through the words. The shop was at the edge of the merchant's district, near several larger, imposing storefronts with bolts of fabric and tailored suits and dresses visible through glass windows. This shop, however, had only a single door with a sign above it. There was only a small window with no display – impossible to peer through.

Pontus pulled the door open. Inside was a narrow shop crowded with dresses hung from wooden rods. There was barely enough room between the racks to see to the back of the store.

The dresses ranged from practical, but elegant, to the more elaborate, with frills and needlework patterns. Callisto resisted the urge to touch them, still smarting from Cetus' comment about her "peasants' soap." The fabrics had been dyed in deep, vibrant colors, some of the dresses shining like silk in the dim light.

"Hello?" Pontus called out tentatively.

"Do you have an appointment?" came a woman's voice from the back. "I'm much too busy to be bothered without an appointment."

A petite, plump woman emerged from around a corner in the back of the shop. She was shorter than Callisto and seemed to be bursting from her too-tight frock with its flowing sleeves and low neckline.

"You'll need an appointment," she added in an officious manner. "I'm busy until at least next Tuesday."

"A friend of mine, Cetus, sent us," Pontus replied, holding up the note.

The woman snatched the note from his hand, a scowl on her lips. "Cetus, you say?" She read the note over with an intensity which surprised Callisto. Surely there were other seamstresses in town if this one was busy.

"You want to make her look like a scholar?" Her eyes looked Callisto up and down. "Turn around girl, let me see you."

Callisto turned. She wasn't used to being the subject of attention. It made her feel stiff and stick-like, turning in a circle to be examined like a fish at the market.

"There's not much to her. Should be able to cover her bones easily enough. Three sets? That'll be sixty drachmae."

"Sixty?!" Pontus looked like he had swallowed a bad olive, pit and all, and was ready to toss the entire offending bowl against the nearest wall. "How can it possibly be sixty?!"

"You're right. It's a rush job. Make it eighty."

"Eighty?!"

"Be back in an hour with the first half as a down-payment." She gripped Callisto by the hand. "This way girl, we'll have you fit to raid the Imperial Academy in no time."

"Eighty?!"

"Be back with the first half in an hour," she told him sternly. "I'm sure Cetus won't be pleased if he hears you've done otherwise. You want the girl to pass for being a scholar or not? The dresses will be delivered in four days."

The woman dragged Callisto to the back of the shop, Pontus still standing dumbstruck at the entrance.

The rear of the shop was cluttered with wire forms and wooden dummies, atop which dresses were in various states of assembly. Colorful bolts of cloth were lined upon shelves in the back, the room brightly lit with oil lamps.

Six other seamstresses, most of them around Callisto's age or younger, were busily sewing at tables. They glanced up at Callisto as she was dragged through by the shop's owner, a couple sparing her a knowing smile.

"Stand up straight." The little woman held out a length of string with which to measure Callisto's chest and arms. "Hold out your arms. No, not like a yard arm on a sailing ship. Out at an angle. Haven't you ever been fitted for a dress before?"

"No ma'am."

The little lady stretched out a length of coarse twine from Callisto's neck to her shoulder, then down her arm. She marked measurements on the twine with a chalk as she went. She stretched another length about her chest. "Becoming a young woman, I see."

Callisto blushed. She was confounded by the attention. For as long as she could remember, she had worn whatever she could purchase for an obol or two. Sometimes she had worn the cast-offs of peasant girls or older thieves who had outgrown them. Never had anyone bothered to measure her for something as mundane as clothing.

"You have a name, little Miss?"

"Callisto."

"I'm Danae. How'd you get involved with the likes of Cetus and that scrawny man?"

"I . . . I'm paying off a debt."

A couple of the young seamstresses glanced up at her from their work. Being an indentured servant was all too common, Callisto knew.

"There's no shame in it," Danae said. "Although to be owing a debt to the likes of those scoundrels . . ."

Danae wrapped the twine around Callisto's hips, marking down another notation as she worked.

Callisto's eyes wandered, suppressing her anxiety at being touched and prodded. Her eyes fell on a dress in a corner, only partially complete. The color had caught her attention. It was a deep, rich shade of red, in a fashion intended for a woman, not a girl. What lady or merchant's wife might the dress be intended for, she wondered?

"Do they always dress you in rags like these?" Danae asked.

"Yes, ma'am," Callisto answered, briefly wondering what it was like to live the life of a lady, or even of a shopkeeper's daughter. Wearing fitted dresses rather than worn cast-offs.

* * *

The streets of Polonia were in shadow, as Callisto walked back towards the tiny flat where Pontus had arranged for them to stay. He had sent her out to pick up additional items, including the soap which Cetus had insisted she use. He had carefully counted out every drachma he handed her, making sure she knew he expected to see the proper change when she returned.

She was still lost in thought, wondering what it was like to wear tailored dresses and to scrub herself with real lady's soap all the time – not just when playing a role. If only she didn't have to pretend. If only she didn't have to hide who she was.

There was a sound ahead of her, something moving in the alley ahead. She slowed her steps. A figure stepped from the shadows.

"You shouldn't walk alone at night." Andros, the warehouse keeper's son.

"I get by just fine, thank you." Callisto continued, keeping her distance, watching for any more movement in the shadows.

"My mother doesn't usually let out rooms to girls." He stepped closer, blocking her path. Movement – a flash of metal. There was a blade in his hand. "I've never seen a girl with such short hair before. Are you a real girl?"

Callisto glanced up and down the alley. Alone, with no weapon, facing a boy wielding a knife.

Chapter 9

"Is this how you always find your girls? In dark alleys, with a knife in your hand?" Callisto moved cautiously forward. She needed to ensure Andros was really alone before she committed herself. It wouldn't do to have another of his friends jumping out from the shadows.

"I can have plenty of girls." He was directly in her path now, the small knife in his hand waving.

"Out of my way, Andros."

"I think I'd like a closer look at you first."

Her first kick caught him squarely in the groin. He was lighter than the sparing partners she'd practiced with. She nearly lifted him from the ground.

His eyes were still wide with disbelief and pain when she gripped his wrist and twisted. He dropped the knife almost immediately.

She really wanted to break something, leave him with more than just scrapes and bruises. Pontus, however, would probably be angry if they lost the rooms they were renting because she couldn't control her anger.

Still gripping his wrist, she swept both his legs in a single, fluid motion, sending him face-down onto the stones of the alley pavement. She was gripping his arm, her knee in his back as he coughed and sputtered.

"Get in my way again, and I'll make sure you crawl back with more than just a passing limp." Her voice was a growl in his ear. "Don't ever mistake me for some common gutter rat."

She released her grip, leaving him lying in the alleyway, still wheezing. Her steps were brisk – pounding out her anger as she proceeded toward the warehouse and flat.

* * *

"Repeat it again. What's your name? Where were you born?" Cetus had been drilling her for over an hour, making sure she had memorized the details behind the persona whose name appeared on her forged paperwork.

"My name is Mira," Callisto answered, putting as much conviction as she could into her voice. "I was born in Lynxios, north of Bateria."

"What is your business in the imperial city?"

"I am employed by the honorable Lord Larkin, of Southfold. I am researching subjects of historical significance."

"Is this really necessary?" Pontus asked. "She knows all this by now."

"She needs to be able to answer without hesitation," Cetus replied. "We are relying on her ability to pass herself off as an apprentice to a master archivist."

"But why Southfold?" Pontus asked. "Why not say she's from Centrola?"

"There are unlikely to be other researchers from as far away as Southfold. If we claimed she was from Centrola or elsewhere in Bateria, they'd wonder as to why no one had heard of her or her sponsor. By claiming she was born in Lynxios, on the other hand, we can explain why she speaks with a Baterian accent – but is currently employed by a nobleman overseas."

"It seems like a lot to go through, just to get someone inside the library."

"If it was easy to pilfer rare documents like these, then other thieves would already have done so – for sale to wealthy collectors here or abroad."

There was a knock at the door. Cetus' personal attendant opened the door and bowed. "Tailors have

A WOLF BEFORE THE STORM

arrived, your lordship. Dresses, I believe." Was there a twinkle of amusement in the attendant's eye?

"You had them sent here?!" Pontus replied.

"Of course," Cetus said. "You can't have the girl leaving a flat in the western warehouse district, dressed like a scholar. She'll need to come here to change before entering the archives each day."

"Don't forget," Pontus added, "this stupid girl is my apprentice! She's working off the debt she owes to me."

"Of course, of course." Pontus turned to his attendant. "Have the dresses brought up to the spare room. Let's make sure they fit. We don't want to wait until tomorrow. Have a bath drawn for her as well. I wouldn't want to get the clothes stained before she has a chance to wear them."

"I thought she just bathed, two days ago," Pontus said, looking at Callisto accusingly.

"She will need to bathe at least every other day, if we expect her to pass as an archivist's apprentice. I told you this would be easier if you'd rented a flat in the imperial city."

"Imperial city flats demand imperial city prices."

Cetus' servant returned, leading a pair of young women carrying a box between them. The one was probably younger than Callisto. They looked around the suite with interest, their eyes falling upon the crystal glassware and brandy decanter, as well as the well stuffed chairs.

"In the servant's room," Cetus directed.

It was several minutes before Cetus' attendant had heated a bath for her. The tub alone was more extravagant than any Callisto had ever bathed in – although she had seen their like in some of the inns in Centrola. It rested on four legs, shaped to resemble clawed feet, and was coated with a white enamel finish.

Callisto locked the door behind her, before casting aside the peasant's garb which she usually wore. Scented oils had been added to the bath, filling the air with a light floral fragrance. Callisto lowered herself slowly, absorbing the water's warm embrace. It was hotter than she'd expected! She allowed herself to grow accustomed to the warmth, before leaning back to douse her hair.

Only after she had soaked in the waters and warmth, did she reach for the bar of scented soap at the edge of the wash tub.

Callisto set to scrubbing her skin vigorously, as if trying to wash away years of grime – making up for all of the cold baths or grimy street heists she had been through. Only after her skin was reddened from the effort did she allow herself to climb out of the bath and wrap herself in a towel.

"Are you done in there yet?!" she heard Pontus say.

"Almost!"

Callisto opened the lightweight box which had been deposited on the bed in the servant's quarters. The dress which greeted her was simple, but tasteful, with a white shift featuring long sleeves, and a pale beige dress which went over it. There was intricate needlework across the bodice and hem.

She ran her fingers across the fabric. It was almost silk-like beneath her fingertips – or what she assumed silk must feel like, never having handled it herself.

Callisto quickly donned the shift and wiggled her way into the dress. There were hooks and loops which secured it. More than she was accustomed to. She maneuvered the last of them only with difficulty. Brushing out the folds of the dress, she admired her reflection in a mirror. A real mirror! Tall enough to see herself from head to toe in a single glance.

She had never worn clothes tailored to fit her before. They accentuated her hips and chest, making her appear a couple of years older than she was. She could probably have passed for sixteen, maybe seventeen, she decided.

There was a matching white scarf, which she placed over her head and tied about her chin. It hid how short her hair was. Danae had thought of everything.

Yes, she decided. She could get used to dressing like this. When she finally finished this job and paid off her debt to Pontus, she wanted to dress like a woman from a wealthy merchant's family. Maybe even pass for a nobleman's daughter. No more cast-off rags unfit for a discarded sack of vegetables.

"Callisto?!"

"Coming," she said. She reached into the box. Yes, two more outfits, just like the one she was wearing. Danae's seamstresses had been busy in the past few days. But . . . no. There was also something else, in the bottom of the box.

Callisto's heart skipped a beat. Rich red fabric, accented by goldenrod thread. The wine-red dress she had admired at Danae's dress shop! Could it be?

Callisto felt a warm pressure at the back of her eyes. Moisture trailed down her cheeks. No one had ever given her a dress before. No one had ever given her anything she hadn't paid for or stole. Not since her grandmother had died.

Chapter 10

Dear grandma,

Tomorrow will be my first day in the library. The first day in a new dress, wearing a new name. So many changes. So many things I might be or become. I promise, yah-yah, I won't forget myself through it all.

* * *

The guard let the two girls in front of her proceed. Callisto stepped up, her imperial pass in hand.

"I haven't seen you before." The guard at the gate scrutinized her slip of parchment. He was a younger sentry, with dark hair and a trimmed beard. Callisto recognized the markings on his shoulder: two stripes. They denoted an enlisted soldier in his second year of service. A shield-bearer, not an officer.

"I arrived a week ago," Callisto replied, keeping her voice cool and confident.

"Where are you from?"

"I am apprenticed to an archivist from Southfold, under the patronage of the honorable Lord Larkin. I was born in Lynxios."

"Lynxios, eh?" The sentry glanced at the guard shack for a moment. The senior officer on duty was busy with the driver of a wagon, directing another pair of guards to open the cart for inspection. "I'm not familiar with the signature on this document," the guard said, turning back to her. "I'll need to have the foreign office verify it."

"Verify?" Callisto asked. What was he really after? She had seen some impressive forgeries in her time. The embossed seal alone should have convinced even the most senior official.

"If you come back in the afternoon, I could verify the proper tolls and duties have been paid. They have been paid, haven't they?"

Paid? It was a bribe he was after.

"If you have any doubt," he continued. "I could just collect the fee here. Make sure it goes to the right place."

Callisto seethed. It was an impeccable forgery. Fee indeed!

"Oh no, I wouldn't want to distract you from your work," she replied, her voice taking on a honey sweet tone. "Perhaps we should ask a more senior officer to verify for you. Excuse me." She took a step towards where the officer on duty was reviewing the bill of lading for the wagon.

The guard stepped into her path. "That won't be necessary."

"Oh, but I insist. I wouldn't want you to have to spare precious time from your other duties, would I?" Callisto took another step, as if to go around him.

"No, really. That won't be necessary," he handed the imperial pass back to her. "You may proceed."

Callisto allowed a sly smile to trace the corner of her lips. "Thank you, kind sir." She took the pass and proceeded towards the library entrance. She hadn't survived as a street rat all those years without knowing when to call a bluff.

Ahead of her, the double doors of the entrance opened into an atrium with a central desk. Scholars and archivists milled about, some carrying books and others pushing carts loaded with records. It appeared to be a receiving point for visitors or records amassed for storage. Callisto stood for a moment, taking it all in. Balconies above looked down upon the entryway. High overhead the ceiling soared, resembling a canopy of tall trees.

Signs pointed the way to various sections in the imperial collection. Medicinal records were prominently identified with an arrow pointing towards the eastern wing of the building. Several men and women seemed to be congregating in that direction. It also housed the foreign documents collection.

Another set of signs pointing left, towards the western wing of the structure. The historical collection, the signs read. The western wing appeared to also house records of imperial rulings and pronouncements.

"I apologize for how rude the guard was at the gate."

Callisto turned, surprised to hear a voice from behind her. It was a young man, with dark wavy hair, dressed in a white shirt and grey vest. He had dark boots and trousers. The same young man she had seen the other day? When Pontus had showed her around the city? She thought so but couldn't be certain. There was an emblem on the left side of his vest, depicting an old-style oil lamp lit beneath the imperial sunburst.

He was clean shaven, with soft-brown eyes. Gentle eyes, she decided.

"I'm sorry," Callisto said. "Were you speaking to me?"

"At the gate," the young man answered. "I noticed how rude the guard was, trying to extort money from a foreign scholar. At least, I presume you're a foreign scholar." Was he blushing? "You handled the brute well . . . I'm Phaeton," he added at last.

"I'm Mira," she said, remembering her cover story. "You're a student here?"

"I work here. I'm a journeyman archivist. You're here as a student?"

"I'm here on behalf of his honor, Lord Larkin, of Southfold. I've been sent on a research topic that's of interest to him."

"I could show you around the collection. What are you here to research?"

"Records from the early imperial era, during the first century of the empire."

"Really? I don't meet many girls interested in the historical collection."

* * *

Phaeton gave Callisto a tour of the library's halls. As the sign had indicated, the historical archives were in the western wing. "The first floor contains the oldest documents, dating back to the earliest werewolf wars and the foundation of the empire. If you're looking for documents from the first century, they'd be on the first floor. The second and third floors contain more recent additions."

Callisto listened attentively as he explained how the files and tomes were organized. His help was invaluable. And she was secretly grateful for the young man's bashful glances and blushing attention. In Centrola, she had seldom merited attention from young men – certainly not men of Phaeton's social standing. When she did, it had usually been because she hadn't been fast enough lifting their coin purse.

"You said your father was a nobleman?" Callisto asked.

"From a lesser family. Just a small estate in the west. I'm the youngest of three brothers, so I don't stand to inherit much. Outside of the family name, that is. My father arranged for me to become an apprentice, and then journeyman to a senior master of records in the capital. It's not an exciting role, but it's an important one."

"Oh? I thought archivists were just people who couldn't control their addiction to reading." She couldn't resist teasing him, if only a little.

"That too," he chuckled. "But mostly I'm sent to retrieve records on specific topics. Sometimes from the legal rulings, sometimes from the medical volumes. I don't get to spend as much time in the historical wing as I'd like. What about you? Do you like it? Reading, I mean?"

"I like to read stories from the past. They help remind us of who we are today."

Phaeton showed her each of the floors, stealing furtive glances in her direction. Was he flirting with her? Was this what it felt like? The men whom she dealt with were usually more direct and crass.

By the time they finally circled back to the first floor, Callisto's face was tingling. She was certain her cheeks had been stained scarlet. She was unused to the attention. She had always been a plain girl. As a thief in Pontus' company, she was often mistaken for a boy. She rarely dressed in a feminine manner. Even when she did, it had always been as a means to blend-in, not attract attention.

She set her notebook on a table, drawing ink and a quill from her satchel. She was distinctly aware of his eyes on her. "Thank you for the tour," she said with a shy smile. She kept her head down, focused on the desk. She was afraid to meet his eyes.

"I'm sure we'll run into each other again," Phaeton replied, taking his leave. He made his way towards the stairwell – with several glances back. Callisto waited until he had gone, exhaling deeply as she regathered herself. Guards fishing for a bribe she knew how to handle. Cute young men who blushed when they spoke with her – she didn't.

The collection was expansive, if a bit eclectic. The wooden shelves, arranged in neat, identical rows, provided

A WOLF BEFORE THE STORM

only a thin veneer of order. Beneath that façade was a chaotic reality.

One side of the first floor was reserved for imperial edicts and records. The other side was a mix of Baterian records from the same period. Some were bound into books, while others were sealed in tubes or packed into sleeves – piled on top of each other on rows of shelves.

There were accounts of traders and travelers. Reports from garrisons on the edge of the empire. All compiled together with what appeared to be little organization. Cetus had not been exaggerating when he had suggested it might take weeks to find the documents they were looking for.

Where to begin? It made sense to start with the earliest documents, dating from just before and leading up to the founding of the empire: the first of the werewolf wars. That's what Phaeton had called them. She knew the stories well. Still . . . she couldn't help but to peruse the shelves with an air of nostalgia. The accounts she had been raised on were probably very different from his.

She shuffled through the first shelf of records. Many of these early volumes appeared to be correspondence from remote outposts. Descriptions from a time when the werewolves had ruled Bateria on behalf of the warlock, Xythox. An era when humans were the subjects of feared and brutal beasts which could shape shift from human to wolf – or anywhere in between.

Flipping through the records, she recognized the depictions of the werewolves in these accounts as bloodthirsty beasts. The descriptions of the war to overthrow them were equally, if not more bloodthirsty.

Callisto knew the stories. Knew the outcome. Xythox had ambitions to rule a vast empire and the werewolves were only pawns in his larger scheme. He had challenged the magical kingdom of the fae far to the north, and the war between them would last decades. The outcome, however, was inevitable. Wounded by the broader conflict, the werewolves had lost their tenuous grip over Bateria, and out of the ruins the empire had arisen.

The accounts she thumbed through documented the systematic extermination of the werewolves from the empire. They were driven into hiding, then hunted by the Office of the Inquisitor.

There were accounts from each of the towns. Tallies for the places and number of wolf pelts collected. A slow, remorseless march to oblivion. Callisto knew these tales. She had lived them. A last member of a scattered, dying race. She thumbed through volumes, picking up one, perusing it, putting it back. Many were simple, dispassionate tallies. How many sheep had disappeared. How many wolves had been killed.

Others were more detailed. Descriptions of the inquisitors' methods. How they ferreted out werewolves in their human form. Hot irons. Silver knives. Callisto shuddered as she put another volume back. Apparently, not much had changed in the past three hundred years.

One tome caught her eye. It was different from the rest. The texture of its dark leather binding was rougher than the others. She drew it from the shelf. There was no labeling on the outside. It must have been worn off with age.

She opened to its title page, and her breath caught in her throat. Lore and Legends from the Werewolves. Not of the werewolves. Not about them. But from them.

Callisto looked around. She was alone, at least for now. This corner of the Imperial Library was deserted – apparently of less interest than others.

She took the volume back to the table where she had laid out her notebook, sitting down to peruse more closely. Memories flooded through her mind. Her grandmother's soft voice. A fire flickering in the hearth. Stories she had heard, but never seen in writing.

The pages of the tome were coarser than most of the others, the lettering in some places faded. It was all so familiar. She flipped slowly through, remembering. Famous names. Werewolf leaders who had come and gone. Legends and prophesies of the times to come.

"What are you doing here?!" A woman's voice, coming from behind!

Callisto froze, horrified. Why hadn't she heard someone approaching? She had been too caught up in her own thoughts, she realized. Her own reminiscing. It could all be over at once. She had been caught. Reading a book of myth and legend. Myth and legend as related by her own kin.

Chapter 11

Dear grandma,

There are some truths which do not change with time. Wherever people are, they judge. Without knowing and often without compassion. It has been the same everywhere I have gone. I'm sure I have been guilty of it too.

* * *

It was a young woman wearing a white blouse and navy-blue skirt. She had a grey vest and wore a frown across her lips. A floral fragrance, heavy with lilac, floated through the air. Her uniform was typical of others which Callisto had seen in the archives. The academy students appeared to wear them. This girl, however, wore dangling earrings, each sporting a tiny, sparkling stone. Like the heavily scented perfume, it was an item which few could afford.

"Excuse me?" Callisto said innocently. She needed time to regather herself. She was still angry she had let someone sneak up behind her.

"I asked what you were doing here."

"I'm here as a researcher, on behalf of the honorable Lord Larkin of Southfold."

The blonde girl gave a dismissive snort. "What would a nobleman from Symru want from the archives of Bateria?"

"Oh, Mira! I see you've met Cassandra." Phaeton was waving at them from the other end of the hall, walking towards them. He quickly closed the distance. "Cassandra, this is Mira. She's been engaged by a patron in Symru to collect records from the first century of the empire. Mira, this is Cassandra. She's a student at the Imperial Academy."

"She still hasn't answered my question," Cassandra insisted. "What sort of research would a nobleman from Symru be paying for?"

"My patron has a fascination with the legends and lore of the early empire." Callisto fell into the backstory she had rehearsed so many times before. Her heartbeat had slowed now, and she was beginning to think more clearly.

Cassandra leaned over her shoulder. "Lore and Legends from the Werewolves?" Her voice was a sneer. "What stories could those beasts possibly have?"

"Actually," Phaeton said, "the legends said to be common among the werewolves are very similar to those of northern Bateria and the countryside. They share a lot of traits."

"You're not trying to compare stories from those filthy beasts to the cultural history of the empire?"

The condescending tone in Cassandra's voice infuriated Callisto. Filthy beasts? Did she have any idea what the Imperial Inquisitors did? Talk about beasts indeed!

Phaeton took a step closer, glancing across Callisto's shoulder from the opposite side.

"I'm just saying the two communities were in close contact for centuries. They share many of the same stories and traditions. Like the story of the great destroyer, in the chapter Mira has open now."

"You can't really compare peasant folklore and nature spirits to the order and traditions of the empire." Cassandra had phrased it as a statement, not a question.

"What's so bad about folklore?" The words were out of Callisto's mouth before she had a chance to pause or think them through.

"You would ask a question like that," Cassandra said. "You're from a northern province, aren't you? Judging from your accent."

"Lynxios," Callisto replied – in keeping with her cover story. The towns and villages of her childhood were just a little further south. Not that she would be sharing those details with this girl – or anyone else.

"Even worse," Cassandra said.

"I'm surprised to hear you say that," Phaeton said. "Many of the peasant traditions are much older and more deeply rooted than the established religion and temples we know today. The story of the great destroyer, for example, goes back to the oracle Pythia, who lived in the wild lands a century before the empire was established."

"You Phaeton, of all people, should know the importance of relying on official, state-sanctioned sources." She turned her attention back to Callisto. "I'll break it to you now. Not all sources are equal in the eyes of the empire, and that's doubly true when you're a woman." She turned, walking brusquely away.

"Is she always like that?" Callisto asked, after she had gone.

"No. Sometimes she's worse," Phaeton smiled.

Callisto tried, unsuccessfully, to suppress a giggle – covering her mouth as she did.

"Cassandra is a second-year student at the academy. She has a reputation for doing and saying whatever she believes will advance her standing. Whether with senior officials, or at the academy."

"You're telling me she says what she needs to get ahead."

"Sort of. She's the youngest daughter from one of the lesser noble families. Sort of like I am."

"But you don't lord it over everyone. Not like she does."

"She's ambitious," Phaeton replied, thoughtfully. He glanced around to make sure no one was within earshot. "She's not satisfied with becoming a minor clerk in the imperial bureaucracy. That's where most graduates end up. Granting permits or assessing taxes. It's no secret Cassandra dreams of something . . . bigger. Some say she has a habit of living beyond her means."

"I noticed," Callisto replied, wrinkling her nose. "Her perfume. I thought someone had drowned an entire lilac plantation."

Now it was Phaeton's turn to chuckle.

"I've only encountered a few noblewomen who could afford such a luxury." Callisto thought through the exchange, turning over Phaeton's words in her mind. "Did you really mean what you said about the peasant traditions being older and more deeply rooted?"

Phaeton regarded her, as if there was some inner debate going on in his mind. When he spoke again, it was in a soft, lowered voice. "I had a teacher who used to share all of the old stories with me. He had a passion for Bateria's history. All of it. Not just the most recently ascendant."

"I grew up hearing stories like those. Stories of the destroyer. How the spirit of the wild lands could never be tamed. How the life force of the lands and forest would one day rise-up, and exact retribution on the despoilers of the land."

"Stories of a great battle and judgement day are common to both the werewolves and the peasantry of Bateria – as well as several other cultures."

"What else did your instructor tell you about the legends of the re-maker?"

"Re-maker?"

"It's another name the destroyer was known by in northern Bateria." Callisto silently chided herself, realizing she might have revealed more than she had intended. She had never heard the destroyer being described in quite this fashion, as the re-maker, in the time she had lived in Centrola. For all she knew, it was a tradition unique to her werewolf kin.

"I've heard the term once or twice before, although it's not commonly used. Traditions suggest there would be a great battle, a time when men would die by the thousands and werewolves were gnaw on the bones of the slain. When the bodies of the dead would be lit in a great fire, visible for leagues."

"And in the aftermath, the northlands would become a wilderness ruled by the re-maker, who will give them over to the wild beasts of the forest. A place where men will fear to tread."

Phaeton smiled. "Sounds like you know these stories well."

"Those stories, and their era, are part of the reason why I'm here." Callisto silently congratulated herself for her quick recovery. "My patron has a fascination with the period those stories came from."

"My former teacher knew those stories well," Phaeton continued, "A time of judgement and destruction presaged by the raising of the dead."

"Not the dead, but the undead. At least in the stories I was told. The undead, raised by the poison of human greed. Whatever happened, to this teacher of yours?"

A cloud of pain passed over Phaeton's eyes, and she regretted having asked the question.

"His interpretations of Bateria's history were . . . unpopular. He was retired. Forcibly."

"I'm sorry," she said in a soft voice. There was an innocent, lingering sadness in Phaeton's expression.

"He used to say the stories and writings of our past should belong to all the people of Bateria. Everyone should have a say in what we discard or keep, not just the select few." Phaeton recovered, a sad smile tracing across his lips. "What I was never clear on, from the stories, was what or who the destroyer was. Was the destroyer an individual, or a force of nature – a cataclysm which simply happens."

"In the north, the destroyer was always spoken of as an individual. As a single person or presence. Some spoke of him like a parent or guardian, presiding over the wounded wilderness. That's how he was regarded by the werewolves . . . and also among the people of northern Bateria."

* * *

Callisto was weary as she made her way back to her flat. She had already stopped at Cetus' inn, changing into her plain street clothes, before making her way to the warehouse district on the western shore.

Cetus had grilled her regarding the arrangement of the library and where the documents they were seeking might be tucked away. He had listened intently, confirming his earlier assessment that it would take weeks if not months to find the documents they were looking for. He seemed unperturbed, however, by the duration and complexity of the task. That she had infiltrated the library and gained the trust of a journeyman archivist had delighted him to no end. "I'll make some inquiries and find out what I can about this nobleman's younger son," he had told her. "You never know what information might prove useful."

"Where's Pontus?" she had asked.

"He said he was attending to some business or another," Cetus had replied in an irritable tone. "He would do better to focus on the business we already have at hand."

Had she seen a smile flicker across the lips of Cetus' bodyguard, Taras? She hadn't been sure. He always stood at the side of the room; his expression unreadable.

Now, trekking back to the warehouse where Pontus had rented their rooms, she had a sense of dread. The excitement of the day had worn off, and she was not looking forward to repeating the events in detail yet again. The sun had dipped below the horizon, staining the western sky in shades of orange and red. She wanted to sleep. Time to herself to rest and recover from the day's events.

When she finally climbed the warehouse steps and reached the hallway which connected their rooms, Pontus was waiting.

"Where have you been? The library should have been closed hours ago."

"Cetus demanded a detailed description."

"What did he expect? He said himself it would be days before you found anything."

"He wanted to hear it for himself. He said it would be weeks, not days."

"You're late, and I have a job for you."

"I thought infiltrating the library was my job."

"I have another one. A target of opportunity. Tonight."

"I thought finding these documents, whatever they are, was going to pay handsomely. A year's worth of small jobs."

"Tens of years' worth, to hear Cetus talk. But my coin purse needs to be refilled – now. And I know just the place to find an unsuspecting payoff."

Chapter 12

Dear grandma,

I don't have much time to write. Pontus has me going out on another job. It's a rushed burglary. The kind he should know better than to do. The kind likely to run into an unexpected mistake.

* * *

Callisto crouched, keeping her profile low against the roof of the warehouse. The building was right on top of the dockyards. The masts of merchant ships stood like barren trees in the moonlight. From across the eastern shore, over a hundred yards away, lanterns winked from windows. Their yellow light glittered across the waves and ripples of the sleepy river.

Unlike the warehouse loft where she and Pontus were staying, this warehouse was well guarded. Whatever cargo they had unloaded was under constant surveillance. Callisto had nearly stumbled into a patrol as she had scaled the outer fence.

Here on the rooftop, she waited. Listening to the sounds of the night. The lap of the waves. The rocking of boats in the harbor. The footsteps of the guards on their rounds.

She really hated these rush jobs. Pontus knew the importance of casing out a target in advance, just as well as she did. Why he had insisted on performing this job with so little preparation was a mystery.

She had figured out the rhythm of the patrols now. There were four of them, each with two sentries. They were armed with spears and had swords at their sides. She could hear the swing and jostle of the scabbards as they walked. The tap of the blunt end of their spears against the paving stones. The leather straps which held their armor in place groaned as they moved. Their footsteps were sluggish, reflecting bored disinterest. Bored and confident. Only a fool would attempt to steal whatever was being housed inside. She tended to agree with them. This was a foolish heist.

Callisto was dressed in a dark shirt, trousers, and boots. She had a hood drawn over her face to prevent the moonlight from giving her away. A garter cinched her trousers tight against her skinny legs. She had taken every precaution she could to hide in the shadows. If they had waited for a night with no moon, or had a chance to case out the site more thoroughly, it would have made her task easier. But no, Pontus had insisted this couldn't wait. So here she was, trying to figure out the guard rotation as she went.

She waited for the guards to circle to the other side of the building, then lowered herself over the eave. Her hands gripping the roof's edge, she hung there, swinging herself until she had enough momentum to swing through an open window onto an upper floor.

She stretched her body out as she slipped through the opening, then curled into a ball. She banged blindly into boxes and bags. The corner of a crate stabbed into her shoulder. She'd be feeling that bruise for hours.

She rolled to her feet. She had made more noise than she had intended. She remained where she was, listening, silently cursing Pontus and his insistence on completing this robbery without planning and preparation. He was going to get her killed with his impatience and greed.

She was in a storeroom, its floor crammed with crates and bags ready for shipment. Empty wooden boxes had been stacked against the far wall. The room swelled with a mixture of odors – some faint, others more insistent. The aroma of spices, leather, fish and raw coffee beans filled the air. There was a steady sound coming from further inside. Sound, and light.

Callisto moved cautiously forward. She had wrapped her boots in cloth to muffle her steps, but she nonetheless stepped carefully – testing each floorboard to ensure they didn't creak before committing her weight. There was a door ahead, partly ajar. Light filtered in from the next room. And there was a scent – another scent, floating in the air. A human scent, damp with sweat from the late summer day. It was too fresh to be left from the porters. Could it be from the guards outside? No. It was too immediate. There had to be someone closer, someone inside the warehouse with her.

She halted at the doorway, listening before opening it. There was that steady sound again. Like an old tree moaning as it bent in the breeze. Snoring? It had to be. Hopefully she had only one guard to deal with.

She gently pushed the door open. It began to creak! She halted. The snoring sound remained steady. She had been lucky so far. Luck, however, could be a fickle partner.

Gripping the door she lifted it ever so slightly – relieving weight from its hinges. She continued to push. The groaning sound had ceased. When it was opened wide, she stepped lightly outside.

She was standing on a loft, near a railing, overlooking the lower warehouse floor. There were multiple boxes, crates and sacks lined up along the walls. In the center of the room, lit by a dirty lantern, was a stack of items loaded onto a wooden pallet – exactly as Pontus' informant had said it would be.

A guard reclined in a chair near the edge of the room, snoring loudly. He wore some sort of uniform, with a red patterned tunic. There was a sword at his side. His hands were folded over his generous belly.

It was his face which drew her attention, however. His hair and beard had been trimmed to flare-out at either side, his dark hair contrasting sharply with his fair skin. It was not a style she had seen in Bateria. He must have been a foreigner.

There was a set of stairs at the far end of the loft which led to the ground floor below. Crossing the length of the warehouse, however, would take time. It would also invite more opportunities for squeaking floorboards. Instead, Callisto swung herself out, over the railing, descending on a sequence of ladder rungs loosely fixed to a column. She dropped the final few feet to the paved floor. The guard's snoring remained steady.

She approached the pallet of chests and boxes cautiously, keeping an eye on the sleeping guard. He reeked of cheap alcohol. There was a shiny brass pendant on his uniform, featuring the snarling face of a screaming monkey. Now that she thought of it, the trim of his hair and beard bore a striking resemblance to the monkey pendant. Another foreign religious cult? It had to be.

The chests and boxes bore various seals, most of which Callisto didn't recognize. She was looking for one chest, which she had been told had a large red stone set into its lid.

The contents of the pallet had already been strapped securely into place. If Pontus' sources were correct, the pallet and whatever valuables it contained were due to be shipped out by wagon in the morning. She worked her way around the pallet, hoping Pontus' sources had been correct. When she saw the wooden trunk, she nearly gasped out loud.

The gemstone in the lid was the size of a goose egg, its rich red color evident even in the lantern light. The chest was three feet long, and two feet deep and tall. Its wooden lid was set with multiple gems, in hues of red and white. Patterns depicting strange trees and animals had been carved into its lid.

The chest was breathtaking in its arrangement of gems and artistry. It was almost a shame to leave it behind. It was too large and unwieldy, however, for her to make off with easily.

The clasp featured a keyhole in the center, set into the mouth of another screaming monkey. She had seen monkeys a few times before. They were sometimes brought by traders from southern shores, to be sold as pets or curiosities for wealthy noblemen or clergy.

It appeared to be a simple enough lock. She drew her collection of tools from the satchel, unfolding her pouch. She selected two stiff tools, each with a sharp bend.

Callisto slid the first one into the keyhole, pressing and feeling her way. A little turn, a light pressure, and she had engaged the latch. She could hear it shift against its bolt. She inserted the second, bent rod, maintaining her pressure on the latch as she turned. A moment later, the clasp sprang open.

Callisto kept her eyes on the sleeping guard. His snores snuffled, before settling back into their rhythmic pattern.

She swung the lid up and open, her eyes greeted by an intricately carved statue of a monkey. It was seated, its hands holding up a glittering bracelet in one hand, a large ring with a ruby in the other. A heavy necklace hung about its neck and shoulders, strung with carved golden plates adorned with red and white gemstones.

It was easily the gaudiest jewelry she had ever seen. Even the wealthier merchants, clergy and officials she had encountered would have been uncomfortable wearing such a collection of heavy stones and thick golden charms.

The monkey, meanwhile, had been carved from a darker, wood-like substance. She could see brackish veins running through it, although she couldn't be sure if it was wood or some sort of stone. It had a faint, odd odor about it. It reminded her of a bog, where matts of wood and plant matter were slowly decaying.

She wondered briefly if she should take the statue with her but quickly decided against it. It was too large to fit inside her sack and too cumbersome to carry. Besides, she wasn't sure if Pontus would know where to resell it without arousing suspicion. Snarling monkey statues were not in vogue among the wealthy these days. It was the jewelry she had come for.

Callisto replaced her tools in her satchel. She plucked the bracelet and ring from the monkey's hands and dropped them into her sack.

Her eyes darted between the chest and the sleeping guard. She had a sense something had changed. Something had moved while her attention had been on her satchel. Had the guard shifted slightly? She couldn't be sure. He was still snoring loudly enough.

She reached behind the monkey to lift the necklace from its shoulders. It blinked. Blinked!?

With a screech, the carved monkey came to life – leaping out of the box.

The monkey's jaws snapped in the air, its fingers clawing against her hands as it strained to reach her throat. From the corner of her eye, she saw the slumbering guard beginning to stir.

She struggled to maintain her grip on the animated statue. Gone were any thoughts of gold or jewels. This would be a fight for survival.

Chapter 13

The jaws of the enchanted statue snapped in the air, screeching its protest as it strained to reach her. It was all she could do to keep her grip on the smooth, wood-like surface. How could anything so small be so loud?!

Its eyes, once just another part of its wood-like carving, had become a glossy black. Its long canines, like the rest of its surface, appeared to be carved from a dark, wood-like substance.

The monkey squirmed, twisting free from her hand. Callisto jerked her head aside as it lunged. There was a stab of pain as its teeth dug into her shoulder. Its fangs had only just missed her neck.

Driving her nails into the smooth surface, she twisted around, swinging the statue. She swung it up, then down – slamming it into the stone floor of the warehouse. There was a sharp crack as the head broke off. The monkey ceased to move.

She was startled to see nothing resembling blood inside. Just shards, like bits of shattered pottery, scattered across the paved stone floor. Its insides shared the same wood-like grain of its surface.

She rolled onto her knees – and someone grabbed her arm from behind. The sleeping guard! The screaming monkey had awoken him.

"Thief!!" The guard's yell came from just above her. He towered over her slight form. The grip of his fingers like a vise around her arm.

Callisto spun, pivoting about her seized right arm. Ignoring the pain in her shoulder, she drove her left hand into her opponent – just below the sternum. Her fingers sank deep.

The guard released his grip and she spun free, just in time to avoid the meal which the guard regurgitated onto the floor.

He was nearly twice her height. For the time being, however, he was doubled over, heaving his stomach onto the stones. His head was at her level.

Callisto sent a kick across the guard's face, putting the force of her body into it. Her foot landed squarely across his jaw. He tumbled backwards, blood trailing from his lip. His head struck the ground as he fell.

She stood poised, ready to deliver another blow. He made no move to rise.

She didn't know how long he would be unconscious, and she didn't have time to wait and see.

She scooped up the golden necklace from the scattered remains of the monkey statue. Her shoulder was still bleeding from where it had bit her. She heard the door to the warehouse swing open with a slam. The other guards!

She didn't wait to see how many were rushing in. She raced up the ladder to the loft. She was already there, before they could reach their disabled sentry.

The loft shuddered. A poorly aimed spear slammed into the wall above her head.

Callisto raced through the dark storage room, towards the open window. Her heart was pounding in her ears. She leapt out, grasping the eave, and swinging herself up, over and onto the roof.

Her shoulder burned in protest. She couldn't see how deep the wound was – but there was no time to inspect the damage.

"Where'd they go!?"

"The loft!"

Damn Pontus and his short-sighted greed.

Callisto was racing across the roof, heading for the far end – to where the warehouse was closest to the outer fence.

"Do you see them?!"

"He's out cold!"

More shouts. She needed to make her escape while they were still searching inside.

At the edge of the warehouse, she glanced only briefly to ensure there were no guards waiting below. Swinging herself over the eave, she slid down a drainpipe and raced towards the fence.

The fence was formed by iron bars, weathered and rusted, with spikes at their tips. She didn't have time to use a rope. She gripped the cold iron, pulling herself up. She tried to use the soles of her feet to gain traction. But the cloth she had wrapped her boots with to muffle her steps was too slippery. She had to pull herself up on the strength of her arms alone.

Her shoulder protested every movement. She strained to haul her body up, and over the top of the fence. More shouts from the guards. Footsteps, running. They still hadn't realized she was nearly over the fence.

At the top, her trousers caught on the metal spikes. Voices, drawing nearer. They'd reach her in seconds! She pulled her leg free, tearing her breeches, and slid down the outside.

Her shoulder was still painful and stiff. Even with the recuperative powers of a werewolf, it would be hours before it was fully healed.

She was outside the compound, however. In the dark, she would have the advantage. Her eyes didn't need lantern light to see. Bleeding and aching, she disappeared into the night.

* * *

"You risked being captured, risked our asset, just to steal some trinket from a warehouse?!"

Cetus was lecturing Pontus when Callisto stepped out of the servants' room where she had been changing. She was tired, and sore, but at least she was clean. She was wearing a fresh dress, ready for her day's journey to the library.

Cetus and Pontus turned to regard her as she stepped out.

"Are you well enough to travel, girl?" Cetus said. "I heard you had a nasty gash."

Callisto rubbed her shoulder. The wound was hidden beneath her dress. It was still sore, although barely visible. In another day it would be completely gone.

"It wasn't deep," Callisto lied. Anyone else would have been nursing a wound like that for weeks.

"My servant said the shoulder of your smock had been torn and was covered in blood."

"She's well enough to work," Pontus replied. "That's what's important. Send her on her way. The sooner we can find those papers, the sooner we can be out of here."

"We're not done. It was reckless. You risked our lockpick to steal a trinket."

"It was no mere trinket."

"It pales in comparison to what awaits us when we recover the mage's hidden records. We cannot afford further diversions."

"It was an opportunity I could hardly have passed up."

"There will be no more diversions! Are we agreed?"

Taras had moved from his usual spot near the door, positioning himself a couple of steps behind Pontus. He was surprisingly quiet for such a large man. His hand rested on his dagger.

Callisto doubted Pontus was aware of his peril. Should she warn him?

Cetus shook his head, a barely perceptible "no." Taras took a step back. Had Pontus noticed the gesture, Callisto wondered? He had come dangerously close to becoming a sheath for Taras' blade.

Pontus still hesitated. Just why, Callisto couldn't fathom. The necklace alone, gaudy as it was, must have been worth more than a year's worth of heists in Centrola. Was he letting pride get in his way?

"Agreed," Pontus said at last. He turned to her. "What are you waiting for, stupid girl? I told you to get along."

Chapter 14

Dear grandma,

I keep imagining it, imagining being free. Free to make my own choices. What to say. Where to go. What to do. I imagine it, but each day I wake up here again.

* * *

Callisto bent over her notebook, scratching out another row of shelves. Her writing had grown neater, she had to admit. But she had as yet found no documents bearing the names of either Gnotrix or his apprentice, Herrick. She was systematically marching through the stacks, combing through shelf by shelf, volume by volume. She had to ensure she missed nothing.

"Hello, Phaeton."

She had grown used to having him dropping by each afternoon. She had been sure not to allow herself to become so distracted that someone might surprise her. Not like on the first day.

"Having any luck?" Phaeton asked, walking up from behind.

It was nice, she had to admit, having someone pay attention to her. In Centrola, she had been just another street rat.

"Not yet. There are so many records to sort through."

"At least they're letting us continue doing our jobs. I'd hate to think of what might have happened."

"Why wouldn't they?" Callisto looked uneasily into his eyes. Rumors and gossip were the lifeblood of a thief's network. In Centrola, she had known where to go for the latest news. In Polonia, she felt isolated – exposed.

"You heard about what happened at that dockside warehouse, didn't you? The one someone robbed two days ago?"

"No." Callisto kept her response as emotionless as possible. Inside, however, she was trembling. Was this the same warehouse she had raided?

"Some religious cult was planning to deliver an extravagant gift to the emperor. Jewels and an enchanted statue they say. But thieves robbed them before they could deliver their gifts."

Callisto was certain her eyes betrayed her shock. What had Pontus plunged her into?

"It seems this cult was attempting to negotiate exclusive rights to scour the Imperial Library for records on some enchanted artifact or another."

"Sounds like some very valuable items to go missing."

"That's what everyone's saying. The cult's emissary complained about the thieves to the Imperial Guard. Told them it wasn't safe to do business in Polonia. There were too many officials taking bribes or looking the other way."

"That's pretty bold of them."

"I'll say. Emperor Bessarion got word of the accusations. He was so angry he refused to ever meet with the cult's leaders again." Phaeton seemed highly amused by the story, a smirk on his lips as he retold the details.

"He rejected their emissary?" Perhaps her luck had taken a happy turn, after all.

"Emperor Bessarion took their complaints as a personal insult. He ordered the cult's delegate expelled from the imperial city. Banned them from the eastern shore."

"Sounds severe."

"That's Bessarion for you. The cult leaders kept protesting how they were the victim of a professional band of thieves. Their complaints only made Bessarion angrier. We're pretty lucky it turned out that way."

"How so?"

"If Bessarion had granted their request, then you, me and all the other students, archivists and researchers would have been asked to vacate the library. They'd be making room for the cult to paw over the collection."

Callisto felt the chill of realization pass through her. Their entire plan had nearly come crashing down. It was only dumb luck Pontus had learned of the jeweled shipment and had ordered her rob it.

"Hey, no need to look so upset. It all worked out. Bessarion sent them packing. Told them to never insult his capital again. Bet those foreign cultists are plenty steamed now."

* * *

"We were exceedingly fortunate," Cetus said. "We should have known there would be others seeking the same things we are."

"You should have known. I have an instinct for scoring a find." Pontus was inordinately pleased with himself in his fresh new shirt and vest. He wore a silver belt buckle, with a golden chain around his neck.

Callisto stood at the edge of the room, already having changed into her street rags.

"It was pure luck, Pontus," Cetus replied. "We can't afford to be too confident. There will be others looking to collect, just as we are."

"Yes . . . We'll have to be watchful."

"More than watchful. There can be no more robberies we don't all agree to."

"Of course."

"I mean it, Pontus. We cannot risk drawing attention to ourselves. Nor can we afford to lose our lockpick for a few baubles."

Callisto always felt invisible during these discussions. She was the lockpick. The "stupid girl." A tool. Nothing more.

"They were not baubles."

"No more, Pontus. Are we agreed?"

There was a pause before Pontus replied. "Agreed."

He turned, as if realizing she were there. His face was red with embarrassment. "Let's go, girl. Be quick about it."

Callisto followed Pontus out, trailing him down the stairs and outside. They traversed the streets wordlessly, heading for the river and the western shore. He may have said nothing, but she could tell he was still seething from the conversation.

He paid the ferry master curtly, then pounded out his frustration against the cobblestone streets when they reached the other side. Callisto had to step up her pace to keep up. Pontus was walking ahead of her at a good clip.

He was angry. She knew his moods well enough by now. He resented anyone having power over him, all the more so that she had been there to witness it. She would need to stay out of his way tonight – and likely the next day too. He could be unpredictable when his ego was bruised.

He turned down an alley and she followed. Why, she wondered? It was a different route than they usually took. Less lit and more vulnerable.

Abruptly, she was shoved against the wall of a building. Pontus' hand gripped her arm tight, his nails digging into her, his other hand on her shoulder.

"Don't act so smug, girl! I still own you!"

"I didn't do anything."

"You've been acting too much above yourself!" He squeezed her harder for good measure, shaking her by the shoulder. "Don't go thinking those fancy dresses make you anything more than a street rag! You're going to be paying me back for every dress. Don't forget. I'm the reason you're still alive. I made you. All those years of training were at my expense. Just one word, one whisper, and your hide will be stretched across the wall, just like the others."

Pontus shoved her to the side, and she fell backwards. She had let him shove her. She knew it would go better if she didn't resist. It had been this way for years. Ever since he had found her alone and hungry. Ever since she was little.

Pontus continued towards the warehouse. Callisto climbed to her feet, brushed herself off, and followed behind – at a distance. She could have argued with him, could have pointed out how the last heist alone was worth more than a year's worth of jobs in Centrola. She could have argued, but it wouldn't have done any good. She just needed to complete this job, this one job. Then she would be free of him forever.

Chapter 15

Dear grandma,

I've been searching the library for weeks now. It's not the sort of work I'm used to. Tedious in its own way, unexpected in others. When I open the cover of a book, I can never be sure of where the pages might carry me.

Sometimes what we seek is not what we find. And what we find, is not always what we expected it to be.

* * *

Callisto replaced another volume, completing another shelf, and reached for the next tome below.

The real problem with the imperial archives wasn't so much their lack of organization, as it was the result of competing organizational methods. Different archivists, across different decades, had arrived at their own opinion regarding how the collection of official reports and unofficial stories might be arranged. Some had tried, and failed, to organize by regions of the empire. This had proven impractical as the empire had continued to add towns and villages, and as the administrative boundaries had shifted between them. Others had tried to organize volumes by shared themes: agriculture, taxes, or the administration of justice. All these competing organizational methods now overlapped in a cacophony of volumes, with little consistency between one row of shelves and the next.

She thumbed through the next volume. A census ledger, from the look of it. But from which decade? Maybe she could find records of this Herrick in it – if she were lucky. Maybe identify his town or towns of residence.

The steady tap of shoes against the polished floor brought her attention back to her surroundings. Someone was crossing the aisle from the center of the library. She knew the pattern. An almost angry pounding of footsteps as they walked. Cassandra.

Callisto glanced around the corner. She was marching towards the section where Callisto was standing, her lips pursed tight in concentration. Her gate was purposeful, determined.

Callisto lowered her eyes. She needed to focus on the task she had been sent to do, not involve herself in the ambitions and maneuverings of the students, nobility, and scholars.

Cassandra's footsteps halted, mere feet away.

"Where did that Phaeton boy get to?" she asked.

Callisto glanced up. The scent of Cassandra's flowery perfume hung in the air.

"I haven't seen him," Callisto answered, keeping her tone even.

"Come now, surely he must have been here earlier. He's always hanging around this quarter of the library since you showed up." Was there a smirk on her lips?

Callisto was startled by the suggestion, her eyes betraying her surprise. "I'm sure you're mistaken. He hasn't been around here since first thing this morning."

"Don't play all innocent with me. Every woman knows how to make the most of her assets. It's a man's world, after all – and we're only allowed to go so far on our own."

It took a moment for Callisto to realize her mouth was hanging open in a wide "O". She had never imagined herself as being notably feminine. She certainly didn't believe Phaeton had more than a passing curiosity for her.

Cassandra, however, continued speaking without skipping a beat. "You needn't worry about me. He's a cute enough boy, but I have my eyes set on a bigger prize. I just need Phaeton's help finding the records Master Zenodotus is seeking."

"Master? What records?"

"Master Zenodotus, the Imperial Historian. I've been working with journeyman Neilos to collect records from the last round of the werewolf wars – a decade ago."

"I . . . I wouldn't know where to look." Callisto had avoided perusing the more recent records on the upper floors. She had no reason to – and was afraid of finding places and names she might know.

"Of course you and I wouldn't. That's why I need Phaeton's help. Zenodotus is preparing an official record of Emperor Bessarion's conquests, beginning with the final campaign to stamp out those beasts." A knowing smile crossed Cassandra's lips. "There will be many eligible noblemen in attendance when the volume is presented in court – and I intend to be there."

"I suppose that makes sense." The words had left Callisto's lips before she realized how they sounded. How could she be so thoughtless? The last thing she needed was to make an enemy out of Cassandra – or any of the other scholars or archivists.

Cassandra, for her part, appeared unperturbed – continuing as if nothing out of the ordinary had been said. "Don't delude yourself into thinking they will ever let a woman rise to a role of prominence in the empire. It doesn't matter if you're born as a peasant churl or to a lesser noble family. Just because you can read and think for yourself, doesn't mean they'll ever accept you. There are only so many master scholars recognized by the empire – and all of them are men."

* * *

It had become overcast during the day, the evening sky turning prematurely dark. The wet air seemed to cling to Callisto's clothes and skin as she made her way through the city streets towards the warehouse and room they stayed in.

Her mood was as gloomy as the skies above. Cassandra wasn't really her friend. But she wasn't an adversary either. The two of them were both caught in the machinery of an empire which would never accept them as anything other than what they had been born as.

Peasant churl? Maybe she was. Or more likely, something even lower in the social hierarchy of Bateria.

She could still hear Pontus' words ringing in her ears. She was a slave to his will. Her only hope was to finish this job, whatever it was Cetus had her looking for, and pay off her debt. She was certain this job would be big enough to pay off whatever she still owed Pontus for sponsoring her training and upkeep as a lockpick and thief.

But . . . she was no closer to finding the records she had been sent to recover. After combing through a third of the archives from the first century, there was no sign or mention of either mage. The answer had to be there – somewhere in the remaining two thirds of those stacks. But where?

She stopped. She had been so lost in thought, she had almost missed the warning signs. The streets were vacant, but the breeze carried the scent of men. She could smell their sweat, the musty odor of their damp clothes in the humid air. There were four of them. Their scent radiated from the alleyway on either side of the road ahead.

She inhaled, letting her predatory instincts clear the fog of the darkness. Four men, definitely. One she recognized. Andros.

Callisto turned, circling back the way she had come. Was Andros lying in wait for her . . . again? Had he brought friends this time? How would he even know where she spent her days? Had they known to be lying in wait on her here? On her way from the imperial city?

She retraced her steps, two streets and an alleyway away, before disappearing into the shadows. She waited, listening. No one had followed her.

She circled around to the next parallel street. Staying in the shadows, using wagons or crates for cover, she circled around to the opposite end of the alleyway where she had first caught their scent. She paused, listening and scenting the air. There was no sign of anyone keeping watch on this end of the alley. She peered cautiously around the corner.

For ordinary humans, the alley was dark, its shadows a murky shroud. To her eyes, however, they were brightly lit in the reflected light from the windows and lanterns of the adjoining street. She could make out two figures at the far side of the alleyway. They were crouched behind wooden crates arranged to shield them from view.

Two men on this side of the street. Probably another two in the alleyway opposite. A pattern for an ambush. Who were they expecting to rob?

It was already dark, in a part of town the wealthy seldom frequented. They were unlikely to find a rich purse to snatch. They were at the edge, between the warehouse district and the textile mills – with its weavers and tailors. Hardly a prime site for scoring a payoff. Had they been meaning to intercept her? It didn't seem likely.

On the one hand, what Andros and his lackeys were up to was really none of her business. If they wanted to waste their time robbing some fisherman of their bread, who was she to stop them? It wasn't like she was some paragon of virtue. There was no reason for her to get involved. Still . . . she had to wonder.

Staying in the darkest shadows of the alley, Callisto crept closer. She had evaded enough imperial guards over the years to know how to go about her business: moving in furtive bursts from shadow to shadow; pausing to ensure she hadn't been detected; moving forward again, a little at a time.

Empty boxes and crates had been stacked up outside the back entryways to the shops on either side of the alley. They provided the cover she needed. She crept closer, until she could hear them whispering.

"Someone's coming," one of them said.

"This is it!" Andros' voice!

From where she was crouched, Callisto couldn't see who might be approaching on the road. At this hour, no less? Maybe she should just turn and go. She only had a small throwing knife on her, after all. Still, she was curious.

Andros and his companions moved into the street, two on either side, boxing in whomever had been traveling at this late hour. Callisto drew up behind them, taking advantage of the same crates they had been hiding behind moments before.

Two young women, apprentice seamstresses by their appearance, had been cornered by Andros and his companions. They wore simple dresses, locks of blonde or red hair visible from beneath their scarves. Fear etched in their expressions.

Seamstresses? This was Andros' scheme? They were going rob a couple of obols from apprentices working late?

"A blonde and a red head, what did I tell you?" Andros said. "Just what the master ordered."

"Going somewhere, girls?" One of the men leered from the other side of the street, a knife ready in his hand.

"Maybe we could have our own fun first."

The girls' eyes followed the motion of the knife in horror. Finally, Callisto realized what was happening. Andros wasn't after a couple of obols.

A memory sparked in her mind. A time when she was younger. A lecherous hand. Her claws erupting from her fingertips, raking across skin and bone.

The tone in their voice. The look in their eyes.

Callisto did not think before stepping from the shadows. It wasn't pity which moved her. It was something else. Something deeper. Something angry.

All the pain she had been through. The taunts. The insults. The missing years. Her missing family. It all came crashing through in an instant. She didn't remember having stepped from the cover of the alley – yet there she was.

Callisto's foot connected with Andros' gut. He was already doubled over when she gripped him by his hair. He hadn't seen her. Hadn't noticed her slipping from the shadows. Not before she drove his skull into the pavement.

The companion closest to him, on Callisto's left, barely had time to register what had happened. She gripped his knife hand by the wrist. A punch to his throat, a kick to the groin. He was already going down when she brought the heal of her boot across his face.

The two seamstresses fled, their wails resounding from the deserted streets. No one so much as cracked a window. No one dared to get involved. Not in this corner of town.

Callisto turned to face the tallest of the four. He towered over her, a long, evil looking dagger in his hand. "Bitch!" he snarled as he lunged. He was bigger. Much bigger. Probably thought he was stronger, too. He was wrong.

Callisto gripped his knife hand at the wrist, guiding his thrust past her head, letting him over-extend his lunge. She followed through with the heel of her other hand, striking him squarely at the side of the elbow. There was a sickening crack as his joint twisted in a direction it was never intended to bend.

Still gripping his wrist, Callisto brought her fist into the man's jaw, pushing upwards with her legs, lifting him with a force no human should possess. He fell to the ground, out cold.

Three of them were down and the fourth had fled, his footsteps racing down the alleyway. But she was angry. Angry for every time she had been mistreated. For every human who had ever crossed her. Every insult or jibe which settled beneath her skin. Everything and everyone she had ever lost.

Callisto stood in the street, her chest heaving from the exertion, her legs spread in a ready stance. There was still time to chase down the fourth would-be assailant. Still time to vent a little anger before she returned for the night.

"Had enough fun beating on the street scum?"

Callisto turned to see a figure standing beneath a lighted window, a box tucked beneath his arm. His hands rested on a cane. Erebus.

Chapter 16

Dear grandma,

If I learned anything from my early years with my brothers, it was never to shy away from a fight. If they were stronger than me, I had to be craftier. If they were older, it didn't mean I had to agree with whatever they said. I might win or lose. But no one was going to stand up for me if I would not.

* * *

"Master Erebus," Callisto bowed, stuttering. "I did not . . . I did not expect to see you here."

"I winter in Polonia, you may recall."

"Winter is still weeks away." Callisto felt awkward standing there, her chest still heaving from her exertion. Her hands were bloodied from her foes, three men lying on the street.

"I came early." The grey-haired master thief stepped towards her. "Pontus told me you'd be along shortly. I was hoping we might speak in private." He glanced up and down the street. "We should go. Someone will be along soon enough to clean up this mess."

Callisto fell in behind as Erebus led the way. Despite the questions percolating through her mind, she didn't dare to speak – at least not until spoken to. Master Erebus had always cautioned his students how force should be exercised with restraint. Leaving opponents dead or bloodied drew the sort of attention a thief seldom sought.

"You've been practicing your skills?" Erebus asked.

"Some, master. I don't have anywhere to go for formal training. Not since coming here."

"I will have to show you where my winter workshop is. From what I hear, Pontus has kept you busy."

"Yes, master."

"I do not doubt those street rats you pummeled deserved it, but I will caution: one of the traits of a true assassin is self-control."

"I'm not an assassin, master. I'm a street thief."

"You could be. If you want to be treated like a professional, you need to behave like one."

"Yes, sir." Callisto wanted to add how Andros and his friends really did have it coming to them but decided against elaborating further.

Erebus led her through the streets, his cane tapping against the paving stones. They were heading for another corner in the warehouse district, one farther from Pontus' flat.

"Where are we going, master?"

"To make some introductions. Someone I need you to meet."

He turned into an alleyway, stopping when he reached a door. A rear entrance. He knocked twice.

"It's late!" came a voice from inside.

"The moon is still bright," Erebus replied.

Callisto was about to object that there was nothing bright about the overcast alleyway – but thought better of it. The door opened, and Erebus entered. She followed closely behind.

A young man with a straw-like beard stood guard at the entrance. It was unlikely any human visitor would have been able to detect the sword at his hip in the dimly lit room. Callisto wondered at what they might be guarding in a warehouse like this.

Lantern light came from ahead – a broad receiving area, where the floor had been cleared of carts, bags and crates. Two men were waiting, although Callisto's ears could detect the breathing of at least two others in the shadows. A rough circle had been drawn on the floor in chalk, spanning some two dozen feet across.

"Is this the girl?" the older of the two men asked. He was tall, with a full beard and mustache. He wore a dark cloak over his shoulders, secured with a gold chain and clasp.

"She's skinny," the younger man added. He had a dark, trimmed mustache and wore a sword at his side – a long saber.

"This is her," Erebus answered. "I am requesting she be officially recognized as my apprentice." He drew a parchment from his vest, holding it out. Callisto couldn't read what it said. There was a signature on it. Erebus' signature?

"Not so quickly," the older man said. "We need to test her first."

Surprise flickered across Erebus' brow. "Since when has this been part of the process? She's been out of practice for the past month. Pontus has her on some thief's errand."

"If she were properly trained, it wouldn't matter. Xystos?"

The younger man unclasped his cloak, leaving it draped over a sack. He drew his sword and stepped into the circle.

"This is irregular! My word should be more than enough." Erebus' voice was low, hovering over a growl. He had drawn himself up, feet spread, balance forward – his cane not quite touching the ground.

"If she's ready, she's ready. If she fails, you can bring her back in a year." The older man remained implacable, his features betraying no hint of emotion.

"Don't worry," the younger man said, stepping into the center of the circle. "I won't leave too much of a mark."

Callisto glanced between the two strangers and Erebus. Was this some sort of test?

"I'm ready," she said. There wasn't a thief at Erebus' studio whom she couldn't defeat – handily.

"You said she has skills," the older man said. "Let's see it."

Erebus' shoulders sagged. "Very well. But the match is to first blood only!"

"Of course," the older man replied.

"A cut or two might improve her appearance," the younger man added.

"Master Erebus?" Callisto asked. It didn't seem like he had anticipated this.

He turned to her. "I'm sorry, Callisto. It seems the rules have been changed. I expected this to be a simple exhibition of weapons skills – not a match."

"If you think she's not ready, say so now," the older man said.

"She's ready," Erebus said. He set the box he had been carrying down on a crate. Callisto inhaled sharply, recognizing the carrying case. It was inlaid with a wolf's head design.

Erebus opened the clasp. The silver blades gleamed golden in the yellow lamplight.

"Your own blades, Erebus?" the older man said.

"One or two blades makes no difference," the younger man replied. "She'll be going home bloodied."

Erebus nodded in Callisto's direction. "Take them, lass. And remember what I told you about control. The bout is until first blood only."

Callisto stepped tentatively forward, her hand grasping the black leather of the handles. She could feel the silver where the hilt brushed her fingertips. It tingled. She suppressed a shiver.

She tested the weight of the blades in her hands, the forward-leaning arc – axe-like in their movement. She nodded at Erebus, hoping his trust in her had not been misplaced.

She stepped into the chalk circle. Xystos immediately lunged. She barely had time to parry his thrust and spin out of the way.

Chapter 17

Dear grandma,

I remember when I was young, following my nose down the trail of an unfamiliar scent, getting lost before I had realized how far I had gone. For a moment,, I would be afraid. But only for a moment. Back then, I could always find my way back to you. Can I still find my way today, now that you're gone?

* * *

"What? No bow?" Callisto backed away and into the center of the chalk circle. The young man sprang forward again, and she brought her left blade up to parry.

"This is a street fight, not a tournament," Xystos replied, his body in a low crouch. He was shifting his stance, swaying to either side – keeping her guessing as to which direction he would pounce.

"Step out of the circle, and you're disqualified," the older man said.

Callisto tested the weight of the kopis in her hands. How the weight and curve of the blades added momentum behind each swing. She flexed her wrists. She was reminded again of how much heavier they were than the daggers she used to us. But they were also lighter than the wooden truncheons Erebus had her spar with many times before.

Xystos lunged, his thrust whistling past her shoulder as she batted it out of the way. He was fast, this one. Fast and skilled. They circled each other, Xystos' blade tracing circles in the air as they each looked for an opening.

"Few swordsmen can be equally effective with weapons in both hands," the older man said.

Xystos lunged, a dagger appearing in his left hand. Callisto barely had time to move out of the way before swinging her blade to counter. A sly smile crossed the younger man's lips. He was full of surprises, this one.

Callisto pivoted, then lunged forward in her own attack, each blade a blur of motion as she tested for weakness. If she could just force an opening, force him to make a mistake . . .

"She's little more than a stick," the older man said. "I doubt she'll have the stamina to keep up for long."

As if on cue, Xystos launched himself at her, his dagger parrying, his saber slashing. He put more force into it. The crash of metal against metal resounding loudly across the warehouse walls.

Callisto tried to meet his show of force, letting her blades fall in rapid succession. She shoved aside each slashing attack.

Why had he resorted to such hasty attacks, she wondered?

Metal crashed on metal.

And with such force? Was he trying to wear her down?

Another slash, another parry. Xystos brought each blade to bear.

Probably. His strategy might have worked on another girl – any other girl. She, however, was something else altogether.

Xystos made a sudden, lunging thrust. Callisto barely spun out of the way in time. She turned her body to the side. Her blouse tore as his saber cut through the fabric. It was inches from slicing through her chest and heart.

"Got her!" Xystos crowed triumphantly.

"There's no blood," his master frowned. "The match continues until the first sight of blood. Or until your opponent dies."

Dies? What kind of sparing match was this?

Xystos shifted his attack again, the swings of his sword becoming more methodical. He'd swing with his saber, then with his dagger, striking hard – trying to draw Callisto out, trying to create an opening. Every two or three strikes would be followed by a thrusting attack, aimed at her head and face.

Was he trying to kill her?!

"Is this really necessary?" Erebus said, the strain evident in his voice.

"You said she was ready," the older man replied.

Another crash of swords, another thrust which narrowly missed her cheek. Why couldn't she come close to landing a thrust? He was faster than any opponent she had faced before, offsetting the advantage in speed she had usually relied upon.

Her animal instincts were taking over. The scent of his sweat was in the air. His heartbeat pounded like horse hooves on the run. She listened for the rhythm of his breath. He'd draw in deeper before each lunge. Was it something she could use?

"Your apprentice lacks control," Erebus said with a growl. "There's a difference between holding a blade in either hand and being able to use it equally in both."

Was Erebus giving her a hint? Callisto didn't have time to dwell on it. She could only hope she understood his intent.

She switched her pace, going on the offensive, batting at his sword and dagger with swift slashes and deft thrusts. She could match his pace, blow for blow. She charged in, then drew back, keeping him too preoccupied for his own thrusts to be effective.

Given time, she might have worn him down like this, precisely as he had hoped to do to her. He might even suspect this was her strategy. But it wasn't.

She intentionally focused her slashes and thrusts against his right sword arm. Charging in, then pulling back to draw him out. She needed to keep him occupied, frustrated.

She imagined the slashing attack she had in mind. She imagined the path of the blade, the feel of its impact. She visualized precisely how deep she intended to cut. How deep, and no further. Just as Erebus had counseled.

Another thrust, another parry on his right flank. She heard him draw a deeper breath. He intended to lunge!

He lunged into a counter thrust, just as she had expected. This time, she stepped to the right – striking his left side.

Her right blade whistled through the air, catching the dagger in his left hand. She wrenched it free with the force of her blow. Pivoting, she brought her second blade to bear. It sliced across his left eyebrow, leaving a trail of blood.

Xystos stepped backwards, his hand pressing against his forehead, attempting to stem the bleeding. He held his saber firm in his other hand, prepared to meet her attack.

Callisto stood, her lips drawn back in a snarl, her feet spread in a ready position. Both blades were poised to meet whatever might come next. First blood had been drawn. She was ready to spill more.

"Match!" the older man barked.

"She almost sliced my eye!" Xystos growled.

"You let her," his master replied.

"She won your little contest, Memnon," Erebus said, beaming. "Although I must say, the rules for the appraisal seem to have changed since I was an active member."

"We had to be sure, Erebus," the older man replied. "It's been a long time since you accepted a contract. We had to answer the skeptics."

Xystos was still trying to staunch the bleeding from his brow. Blood stained his white shirt as he donned his cloak single-handed. Callisto maintained her distance, weapons still in hand. Had she missed something in their conversation? Contract? Had she heard right?

"We are in agreement, then?" Erebus said, leaning against his cane. "My petition has been approved?"

"Yes," the older man replied. "You are free to continue her training as a member of the guild. Whether she ever becomes a third-blade will depend on her."

Memnon gave a curt bow, turned, and exited. Xystos followed.

"I'll take those," Erebus said, retrieving the two curved swords from Callisto's grasp.

"What was this all about?" she asked, bringing her breathing under control.

"The sparing match? Something they cooked up to convince themselves they could trust my judgement."

"Guild? You mean –"

"Yes, the Assassins Guild."

"I thought I needed a letter of recommendation from a first-blade. Is this why we came here tonight? To obtain a letter from this Memnon?"

"No, Memnon was here to accept my letter. Women have been admitted into the guild before, but it's rare. They also apparently didn't accept my word on the matter. Must have thought I'd gone soft in retirement." Erebus wiped the blades clean with a cloth, placed them in the box, and snapped the latch on the carrying case shut.

"You recommended me? Then you'd have to be –"

"A first-blade? Yes, I am. Or was. Before my injury." Erebus led the way out. "You will report to my studio every Sunday for training, after you have fulfilled your duties for Pontus."

"Does Pontus know?" The possibilities rolled through Callisto's mind. An assassin? A member of the guild? The payment a trained killer could ask for was far more than any lowly thief could command. But still . . . she was no trained killer.

"About the guild? No. You are never to speak of this. As far as Pontus is aware, I have my own job lined up for you. Something I'm preparing you for – for after you complete his little robbery."

The prospect was both exciting, and daunting. She had never thought about what would happen to her, where she would go, after she was freed from Pontus' service. An assassin? Did she have it in her? To kill for a price?

She looked down at her fingers. They appeared small, fine boned and pale in the shadowy light. Her fingers were still sore from the pummeling she had inflicted on Andros and his friends. She realized, with reluctance, Erebus had been right. She could kill, if need be. She had nearly killed Andros. Only Erebus' admonitions about control had kept her from doing the same to Xystos.

An assassin? Maybe it was what life had prepared her to be, after all.

Chapter 18

Dear grandma,

Every day has been a struggle, here in the city. A struggle just to live. To find food. To stay alive. I know you told me to believe in something more, yah-yah. You told me there was still magic in this world. Something wonderous if we just take the time find it.

I know you told me. I just don't know if I believe it anymore.

* * *

Callisto had just set her satchel down. Staff and scholars were still shuffling in, the light of the morning sun shining high above from the windows facing south.

"Mira? Mira!" Phaeton was rushing towards her from the other side of the hall.

"Hello, Phaeton. Is something wrong?"

"You have to come with me," his hand lightly gripped her elbow. There was an excitement and intensity in his eyes.

"I just came. I haven't even had time to set up."

"There's no time. It might not be there if we wait."

He led her towards the entrance of the Imperial Library, and out towards the street. She was grinning despite herself. His enthusiasm was infectious.

"Phaeton! We'll have to go through the guards and gate again."

"I can get us through."

Phaeton waved his pass in front of the guards at the entrance. The guard nodded and waved them through. To Callisto's surprise, they didn't bother to search her satchel this time, as Phaeton rushed them past.

"What's this all about?"

"I tried to convince my father to come see it, but he has no time for such things."

Phaeton was leading her through the early morning streets, towards a district of shops. She recognized it from the tour Pontus had given her. These shops were known for imported luxury items. Many of them were still opening as they rushed past.

Callisto had to break into a broken trot to keep up with him. Phaeton was making a beeline for one shop.

"Phaeton?"

"Quick, in here! It's still early, so there won't be any crowds yet."

The storefront had a broad glass window, its display set with leather and wooden goods of all shape and description. Tables and chairs were carved from richly grained lumber. There were shiny metal tubes with glass covered ends. Musical instruments hung from hooks. It was an assortment of goods, large and small.

As they entered, the scent of seasoned wood, rich lacquers and incense assaulted her nose. Some were scents she knew, others she was unfamiliar with. It was a cacophony of odors, resembling a band of instruments – each playing a different tune at the same time.

Phaeton, however, seemed oblivious to the exotic scents. He was intent upon marching towards the glass-covered counter at the back of the store. An elderly proprietor with a receding hairline and wiry eyebrows nodded as Phaeton approached. "Well met, young journeyman. Is your father well?"

"He has been," Phaeton replied with an eager smile.

Callisto stepped up behind him, still bewildered by Phaeton's urgency in dragging her to this strange shop. There was an array of clocks and other fine, mechanical metalwork on display on the wall behind the counter. Gnome-made. They had to be. The detailed workmanship and tiny features were unmistakable. Was this what Phaeton had wanted to show her? She had to admit, it was an impressive collection. They had to have been imported from either Trevio or Alencia.

"I heard you had a special shipment last night," Phaeton said, his voice low. "Something fae-made?"

The shop keep gave them a knowing smile. "Your father does keep abreast of the manifest." He bent down, unlocking a glass cabinet, and removing a box from within. It was an octagon-shaped, wooden enclosure, painted in a bright finish with stylized embellishments along its edges. Callisto had seen similar boxes in the curio cabinets of the wealthy. They were used to house imported artifacts or other rare items for the entertainment of guests. The wealthiest could have entire rooms devoted to such extravagances. Everything from stuffed and mounted animals, fish, or birds to mechanical contraptions, or works of art.

The proprietor set the box on the top of the counter. He undid a clasp on the front, opening the box like a clamshell. It swung open along a vertical hinge, the two sides parting to reveal a padded interior. Between them, at the center of the box, was a forested tableau sculpted in porcelain.

The detail and colors were exquisite, with individual leaves sculpted on the branches of tiny trees. A stag and small animals stood beside a stream portrayed in clear glass. Callisto imagined it would have fetched a small fortune at any market in Centrola. She had never seen its like.

Phaeton crouched, bringing his eyes on level with the porcelain figures, motioning Callisto closer. It was a beautiful work of art, yes. But she didn't understand why he had insisted they rush to see it. She had hoped to make good progress this day.

The proprietor tapped lightly on the treetop at the center of the scene – and what had once been a finely crafted porcelain sculpture came to life. The stag with its stilt-like legs stepped forward, walking up to the stream, bending its head down to drink. A hare raced from brush to brush, its tiny nose twitching. A squirrel scrambled up a tree, its ears cocked. Even the water, once a fixed glass-like surface, moved as if it were water flowing over rocks and around obstacles.

"Fae magic!" Phaeton spoke breathlessly, as if his voice might shatter the spell. His eyes were fixed on the enchanted scene.

"I can hear the faint sound of the brook." Only after she had spoken did Callisto realize how closely she was bending over the miniature scene.

"Fae items like this come to Polonia only rarely," Phaeton replied. "The Feyfell hasn't let outside visitors in for centuries. Can you imagine? The magic to produce this? It makes you wonder what else they could do."

"During the Xythox wars, the fae would make themselves invisible." Callisto's eyes were on the stag. It had raised its head as if scanning for danger. Could it sense them standing over it, she wondered?

"They can do that?" Phaeton looked up at her, the wonder still mirrored in his eyes.

"That's what I was told." She had probably said too much, but with Phaeton's eyes staring into hers, she couldn't help but add more. "During the Xythox wars, the captain of the fae army once made a raid deep into Bateria, together with a squad of fae warriors. They infiltrated, invisible, into the court of the Alpha-Were."

"Alpha-Were?"

Oh . . . she had said too much. But there was no turning back now. "The Alpha-Were is what the werewolves call their leader. The wolf chief who's head over all the packs. The Alpha-Were's bodyguards fought fiercely, but the fae infiltrators, they . . . they killed the Alpha-Were and escaped."

"That was bold."

She shouldn't have said so much, but the way he looked at her, like a child being read a story. She just couldn't help herself.

"It was bold. Bold and treacherous. The successor as Alpha-Were, Rog-En-Airden withdrew the werewolves from the Xythox Wars. He made a truce, to spare his people more bloodshed. A truce which guaranteed the fae would never return to these lands."

"I had never heard of the Alpha-Were before."

Blood was rushing in Callisto's ears. She was sure she had to be beet red in that moment.

"Yes, well . . . it's one of the stories they used to tell in the northland."

Chapter 19

Dear grandma,

You used to tell me to be grateful. I try to be. I try to remember your voice and your words, reminding me not to feel sorry for myself. Reminding me, no matter how bad things might be. There are always those who have it worse.

* * *

"You'd better not be holding out on me girl!" Pontus gripped her wrist, his nails digging into her skin.

"What would I be holding out?" Callisto had already changed into her dress, her hair covered beneath a scarf. All she needed was her shoes and satchel and she'd be ready for another day scouring the archives.

"You've been taking your sweet time!" Pontus snarled. "If you're thinking of selling off whatever you find –"

"Pontus! Let the girl go!" Cetus said. He was seated in his chair, watching the exchange from the other side of the room. "We all knew the Imperial Library could take weeks to search."

"Just making sure she knows where she stands." Pontus replied, releasing her. "Don't be taking too long."

Callisto rubbed her wrist. It still hurt, even though she knew any marks would heal. She had noticed a new gold ring on Pontus' smallest finger, too. She had felt it digging into her.

Cetus and his henchman, Taras remained at the far end of the room. Cetus was sipping from his cup, the heavy, sweet scent of the coffee grounds filling the room. Taras was his usual, stoic self, standing near the entrance.

"Keep your focus on the bigger prize," Cetus said. "Impatience breeds errors."

* * *

Callisto checked off another row of shelves as complete. She had been systematic in her search, taking notes and marking off each stretch of shelves. She had covered over half of the historical archives with no record of the wizard Herrick or his mentor, Gnotrix.

The bruises where Pontus had, yet again, gripped her, were long since vanished. Nonetheless, she could still feel his nails digging into her. A phantom memory lingered. What if they didn't find what they were looking for? What if it wasn't there?

Callisto's quill paused. She was being watched. She could hear someone breathing, somewhere behind and on her left. She didn't turn her head, inhaling the air, testing the scent.

She relaxed and continued to write, a smile crossing her lips. "Hello, Phaeton."

"I never can sneak up on you, can I?" Phaeton had stepped forward to stand at her left elbow.

No, no one had crept up on her unawares. Not since that first day. He watched her scribe a couple of notes alongside the label for the row of shelves she had just completed.

"Will you be taking a break for lunch today?" he asked.

"No. I'm fine. I had breakfast."

"You don't stop to eat?"

"I'll have something when I get back tonight. I'm used to it. We didn't always eat so well, growing up in the north." She hadn't eaten so well in Centrola sometimes, but she wasn't about to volunteer that.

"Oh yes, I'd forgotten how different it must have been. The untamed lands. I've heard travelers say they're crawling with werewolves."

"They exaggerate. The werewolves largely keep to themselves, at least these days."

"There was a story, a couple of years ago, about a woman whose body was washed ashore. There were scar marks across her back and shoulders. People said a werewolf must have dragged its claws across her skin. Her hair was also missing. Her scalp torn clean off."

There was a sad, almost tragic note in Phaeton's voice.

"Did you know her?" Callisto asked.

"Not personally. I was an apprentice at the time – not yet a journeyman. She was an academy student. She was an assistant to Neilos, one of the senior journeymen in the history bureau. I think I saw her once or twice. She had beautiful blonde hair. It was really long – halfway down her back."

Callisto debated whether to say anything. Phaeton's tone was so melancholy.

"It doesn't sound like werewolves to me."

"Really? Why not?" He glanced up, as if surprised to hear her voice.

"Werewolves would have no need for her scalp. Wolves hunt for food, or to protect themselves – and their territory. Only humans take trophies from the things they kill."

"I hadn't thought of that," he reflected. His expression turned brighter again. "Didn't you say the werewolves have their own chief or leader? An Alpha-Were who rules over all the packs?" There was such a boyish enthusiasm in his voice whenever he spoke about myths and legends – werewolves included. Callisto wondered how he would react if he actually came face-to-face with a real one.

"They do, although the title meant more in generations past. As I mentioned, they mostly keep to themselves.

Whether they have a king, or emperor, or Alpha-Were hardly matters to most. They're just trying to live their lives."

There was a pause. She could tell Phaeton was searching for what else to say or ask. She could hear it in his breathing, the way he shifted his stance. Despite herself, she was unable to resist a smile at his expense.

"Are you finding . . . you know . . . what you were looking for, I mean?" he stammered out.

"Not really," she sighed. "The records my patron is looking for are probably too obscure to be readily located."

"What is it you were sent to find?"

Now it was her turn to hesitate. Did she dare say what she was seeking? Out loud? "I'm looking for records from a wizard named Gnotrix, and his apprentice, Herrick. Herrick lived in these parts during the first century of the empire."

"A wizard? They might have stored records like those in the archive for magic."

"There's a separate archive for magic?" The thought had never occurred to her.

"It's in the vault, below. Most students or archivists aren't permitted there, but . . ." He glanced around. "I suppose I could show you, just this once. No harm in admitting where they are."

Callisto gathered up her notebook, quill and ink and followed him. Phaeton led her down a flight of stairs, to a barred gate. Lanterns had been lit on either side.

He drew a ring of keys from his belt, unlocked the gate, and took a lantern from a sconce at the side. The hallway within was dark, and unlit. A scent of leather bindings and ink drifted from inside.

"We can't be here if someone else is using the archive," Phaeton whispered. "But if it's just you and I, it's probably alright."

Within, Phaeton led her through a short hallway, to a second door, and drew out another key. There was another door to their right.

"What's in there?" Callisto asked in a whisper.

"That's were they keep enchanted artifacts, or so I've heard," he answered. "I don't have a key for that door, but I do have access to the archive for magical books and scrolls."

He turned the key, leading the way inside. Taking a long, tapered candle from a shelf, he lit the wick from his lantern, then used it to light another pair of lanterns on the wall.

As lamplight flooded the room, Callisto's eyes lit up. Shelves stood, row upon row.

Whereas the Imperial Library on the floors above projected an aura of discipline and order, this collection conveyed a sense of claustrophobic chaos. Books and scrolls filled every free space, spilling from the shelves from floor to ceiling. Everywhere she looked, there were volumes and notes crammed into every available corner.

There were no windows to let light in, the unvarnished shelves dark with age. They seemed to have been constructed on the premises, in a haphazard mix of smaller and larger sizes.

Callisto ran her fingers across the edge of one. A light layer of dust stirred into the air. These records appeared to be infrequently used.

"There are so many of them." Her voice was an astonished whisper.

"This is where they store volumes from famed seers, magicians and sorcerers. Some are notebooks, some are recipes for potions, others spell books."

"You can cast spells with these?"

"That's what they say. If you're magically inclined. Most of the volumes were written in obscure languages or were hidden in code. It's not as if just anyone can read and understand them."

"You've tried?"

"I'm not supposed to, mind you." Phaeton had lit a third lantern. "When the second emperor founded the library, they thought they might harness the power of the mages and fae. None of the emperor's advisors, however, were ever able to interpret any of these works."

He was perusing the shelves, counting down. "One, two . . . the sixth shelf on the right," he said out loud. His fingers searched across the row of books. They halted, resting on a thick volume bound in a rich, burgundy hued leather.

Callisto had followed him, watching and listening intently. He slid the volume from the shelf.

"Mostly, these archives go unused now. It requires special permission to access them. Permission is seldom granted. Like I said, most of the volumes here were intentionally obscure. But a few of the books, like this one, record events or legends as written by purported wizards, seers or sages." He handed the book to her.

It was large, and heavy. She turned to the title page: Prophesies of Pythia.

"The same Pythia who foretold the destroyer?" Callisto asked.

"The same." Phaeton was grinning boyishly down at her as he turned the pages of the volume. He was standing close, his chest brushing against her shoulder. He smelled of cloves. "I can't let you take the volume out of here, but it doesn't hurt to let you see it. This copy is unique. Supposedly written by Pythia's personal recorder. An original copy transcribed while she was still alive. It's one of my favorites from this collection."

Phaeton's fingertip scanned down the page, reading aloud when he came to a certain passage.

"The oracle of Pythia of Bateria. A vision has taken hold of me. How hast man railed against the wilderness, pillaging what he has no right to possess. Record how I have foreseen it. When the greed of men has pushed north, pressing hard upon the wellsprings of nature, when the undead have arisen from lands despoiled, a great destroyer shall be awakened, a remaker of worlds.

"I have seen his coming, casting a shadow, terrible and great. The destroyer comes as a storm out of the north, winds with the imprint of neither human nor fae. The redolence of spring rivers and woodland waterways shall follow on his heels. The spirit of the wild lands brought to life. His wrath upon those who have despoiled the land."

He glanced at her, smiling – inordinately pleased with himself. He had such a boyish enthusiasm. Like a puppy dragging a wineskin across the floor – too delighted with his find to understand or care what it was.

"Men will die by the thousands, their bones gnawed by werewolves and the beasts of the forest," Callisto continued. The words were written before her, but she could have recited them from memory. "The bodies of the dead lit in a great fire seen for leagues. The lands of the north shall become a wilderness ruled by the destroyer, who shall give them over to the beasts of the forest. It shall become a place where men will fear to tread. For a great truth shall be revealed: Some wild things cannot be tamed."

Callisto allowed herself a small, sad smile, looking up at him. "I knew the story well. My grandmother would tell it to me."

"Maybe someday, as my teacher would say, these works will be available for everyone to read and interpret."

Chapter 20

Dear grandma,
There has always been something special in the night. Shrouded in black, the moon on my shoulders, the night as my cloak. These are the moments I can be myself, yah-yah. My fate in my own hands. A creature of the night.

* * *

"Why didn't you find this before?" Pontus scowled at her. They were in Cetus' suite. Callisto stood to one side, with Pontus and Cetus at the other. Taras stood next to the entrance, as impassive as always.

"We knew it would take time to discover the Imperial Library's secrets," Cetus countered. "Time to win their trust. It was an investment towards a bigger reward."

"She'll have to go back there tonight," Pontus said.

"For many nights, I am sure. This is why I asked you to bring your lockpick for this job and not a simple cutpurse." Cetus turned his attention towards her. "Do you think you can open the locks to this chamber?"

Callisto shrugged. "From the key, it looks like it's a simple lever-tumbler lock. Nothing special. Nothing as sophisticated as the lockbox was."

"Good, you should start tomorrow night."

"Tomorrow?! Why not tonight?" Pontus asked.

"We will want her well rested. She'll need to leave the library an hour earlier each day to give her time to eat before changing and returning to the archives at night."

"Each day? You're still planning on her going to the library?"

"It would look suspicious if she suddenly stopped appearing. People might inquire as to her whereabouts. More importantly, there may still be valuable information to gain from this boy, Phaeton. She should continue to come here each morning. She'll spend the day completing her survey of the upper archive, then switch into thief's clothes to return at night. I can arrange to find quarters for her in the imperial city, closer to the library."

"No! She's still my lockpick, remember?! She owes me the debt! She must report back every night."

Cetus sighed. "It will give her less time to peruse the mage archives. She'll only have two, maybe three hours each night, before returning to your flat."

"Why so few?" Pontus' impatience was showing. Was that a new gold chain on his wrist, Callisto wondered?

"The lockpick needs some sleep, Pontus. We can let her start her daily routine an hour later, but we still need her well enough rested to avoid making mistakes. As I said. This is an investment. It will take time to deliver. It would be easier if we found her quarters on the eastern side of the river."

"No. Out of the question."

* * *

The booted footsteps of the guards padded lazily against the paved walkways. The leather of their armor strained and groaned with every step. Callisto wondered if they were aware of just how loud they sounded to ears as sensitive as hers. It had been easy enough to figure out the pattern of their patrols.

The outer grounds of the Imperial Library were broad, and there were too few guards to cover all the pathways at once. She had only to wait for the latest pair of sentries to pass out of earshot.

As their footsteps receded, Callisto launched herself at the outer fence, gripping the heavy iron bars and pulling herself up. She scaled over the top and slid down to the flagstones, landing in a low crouch. She was clad in a dark, nearly black outfit, a satchel with her tools slung over her shoulder and a dagger at her waist.

She paused to listen. There was no change in the movement of the guards. No voices interrupting the chirping of insects in the night. She moved forward. The decorative stonework at the corner of the Imperial Library would afford easy handholds.

She scrambled up, the stones cool and hard against her fingertips. One flight, two. She topped the third floor, not daring to look down, pulling herself onto the roof.

The roof tiles were smooth. They might pose a challenge, she realized, should it rain. Would she have to use her claws then? Maybe. Tonight, however, they were dry. It was a short walk to where the eave hung over an upper balcony.

She had made sure she was on the shadowed side of the library. From the ground below, she would be nearly invisible to human eyes. Kneeling at the edge, she grasped the eave, swinging and lowering herself onto the upper balcony.

She approached the balcony door, keeping to the shadows. It was unlocked during the day. Scholars would sometimes come to sit in the open air while they read or studied. At night, however, she could not be so certain.

She squeezed the latch, and the door opened. She listened. The interior was lit by lanterns, but there was no sound of movement. Had they neglected to lock the upper doorways? They had probably never counted on someone like her, stealing in.

Callisto slipped inside, shutting the door behind her. She crept down the hallway.

Coming to the end of an aisle, she spotted a lone figure at a table a dozen yards away. She froze. He was hunched over a table. He had the uniform of an imperial archivist – much like Phaeton's but more elaborate. He must have been a senior member of the staff, intent upon some task.

Callisto moved silently past, making her way to the stairwell which spiraled down.

The lanterns which had been there before were absent. To Callisto's eyes, however, the dim lighting was no obstacle. She approached the lock, drawing out her collection of picks from the satchel. She drew out a round metal rod, with what looked like a flat plate attached at a right angle – almost key-like. The round rod, however, had been ground in half – with a hollowed-out trough down the middle.

She slid a heavy, bent wire down the hollowed trough and inserted the two of them into the keyhole. She turned the heavier pick until she felt it engage against the cam. Maintaining light pressure, she adjusted the wire rod. She could feel through the tips of her fingers as it engaged each lever. She raised the lever plates, one-by-one, listening for them to click into place.

One lever plate. Two. On the third one she heard a softer click. Probably a false gate – intended to jam the lock closed if an inexperienced lockpick attempted to open it. She adjusted her wire a little more, listening for it to slide past the false gate and into its open position.

Four levers. Five. The tension rod turned, and the bolt slid open. She pulled the gate. It grated noisily. She would have to bring oil with her on her next visit. She waited, but no one appeared to have noticed in the empty, cavernous halls above. There were probably several noisy doors or gates scattered throughout the archives. She proceeded to the inner door.

The lock for the inner door proved to be no more troublesome than the outside gate. Once inside, Callisto took a moment to extract a flint from her pouch – lighting an oil lamp. She could see well enough to navigate in the dark, but not if she was going to be reading.

She re-locked the gate and door behind her, securing them in case a sentry came to check. Locked inside, she brought out her notebook, quill, and ink. She would have to catalogue the collection just as she had for the texts she had explored on the floors above. There were fewer of them, but these volumes promised to be more esoteric. She was no mage, and it would take time to understand how the collection had been arranged.

She set eagerly to work.

Chapter 21

Dear grandma,

The forests, the streams, the howl of wind and kin – these still fill my dreams. I feel so far away from that life, living on these city streets. I wonder what of me is still the wolf-child you used to know.

* * *

Callisto rubbed her eyes, trying to shake the sleep from her mind. Daylight poured in through windows high above on the walls, illuminating the archives. It had been over a week since Phaeton had showed her the magical archive below, and the combined days and nights of searching records had taken their toll.

She was tired enough she almost missed the soft footsteps on the floor behind her.

"Hello, Phaeton." She struggled to keep her voice even, hiding her tired tone. She had learned to recognize the distinctive pace and pattern of his steps. "Keeping up with errands?"

"I have a few record requests I was chasing down today, so I thought I might stop by to see how you were doing." He leaned over her shoulder. She had been tabulating her observations. Short comments were arranged next to columns of numbers. "Taking lots of notes?"

"I've been starting to draft my report for my patron. I've pretty much exhausted the records on this floor. I'm just organizing things."

"Maybe your patron will give you another assignment. In the library, I mean." He couldn't hide the hopeful tone in his voice.

"Maybe," Callisto smiled. "Although," she flipped through the pages of her notebook, "I did have one question. I found a scrap of parchment, like a card, located on one of the shelves. It was sandwiched between two volumes." She pointed to the notations on her page. "It listed a title, a date, and read: Master Callimachus."

"Oh, those indicate when a volume has been withdrawn by a Master Archivist. Callimachus is the master librarian. It might mean someone has sponsored the production of a duplicate, or it might mean it needs restoration to preserve its contents."

"This happens often?"

"Not too often. The cost of producing a complete duplicate of an entire volume is usually prohibitive for most patrons. They usually just have someone scribe notes or make duplicates from specific pages. Like you're doing. When you see a card like this, the volume will have been withdrawn by either Master Callimachus, who's the Imperial Archivist, Eratosthenes, the Imperial Geographer, or occasionally Zenodotus, the Emperor's Historian."

"Zenodotus? Where have I heard the name?"

"He's the one charged with composing the official history of the empire, remember? It's scheduled to be unveiled at the emperor's thirtieth birthday next year. Zenodotus has been working on it for a few years. There'll be an official presentation with a monument and public display. It's all being assembled on the island fortress of Burcsteli."

"The rock in the harbor? That's where I must have heard his name. Why would he live on the island? It looks like a prison, not a home for a sage."

"It's hard to say. The island certainly gives him seclusion. Zenodotus has been collecting artifacts and specimens from the werewolf wars, and the island was where some of the last captives were held. He's been looking to restore or expand the collection for the official celebration. Maybe that's why he chose to reside there."

"Expand? The last round of the werewolf wars was a decade ago."

"They still trap or kill an occasional werewolf in the north."

"It's been years since I'd heard of such a thing. Sightings maybe, but none killed or captured. They've grown far more elusive."

Phaeton glanced over his shoulder and lowered his voice, turning more serious. "Emperor Bessarion launched the last werewolf war at the beginning of his reign. Sort of how he cemented his claim on the northern settlements. Rumors have been floating that Zenodotus is intent on adding another trophy to the collection in commemoration of the emperor's birthday."

The image of the stretched wolf skins hanging from the walls of the Imperial Armory plunged through her consciousness. It was a memory she had attempted to block out, and which now left her cold and pale.

"You needn't be so concerned," Phaeton said. "No werewolf would dare enter the city walls. They're no threat to us here. But there have been sightings on the road, just north of Polonia. They say sheep have fallen prey, even among the emperor's flocks."

"Sounds more like a rumor than flesh and blood. Could have been peasants, poaching from his herd."

"Maybe. But they're treating these reports seriously. They say the howls are bloodcurdling. They've summoned an inquisitor out of retirement from the east. He's expected to arrive any day now, hunting hounds and all."

* * *

Callisto dropped her pale, day-time satchel at the foot of the bed in the servants' quarters. There was a tray of food awaiting her. She could smell the aroma rising from the meat-filled pastry. The scent of the herbs and lamb made her stomach growl. The thoughts running rampant through her mind, however, left her queasy.

She was a street rat. No family name or history. No one to rely on but herself. Yet here she was wearing a tailored dress, with a full plate of food. Somewhere out there, they would be hunting down her kin. Men with spears, pole arms and hunting dogs.

"Did you find anything new today?" Cetus' voice came from the next room. She usually reported any findings before going to the servant's quarters to change. Today she had been too shaken and had gone to change without stopping.

"Nothing to report," she called out. "Another row complete."

She began unfastening the hooks from her dress. The disguise which allowed her to pass as an archivist's assistant – a common girl. Not a beast to be hated, hunted, and killed.

She didn't know who these werewolves were who had been foolish enough to travel so close to the capital. Maybe an old wolf who had lost their pack. Or maybe a young wolf striking out on their own. She didn't know who they might be. It was really none of her business.

Her black, thief's outfit had been laid out on the bed for her. Her tools were neatly packed into a dark satchel. Even her thief's cloak was less worn and threadbare than what she had grown used to in her years as a pick pocket and lockpick.

No. She didn't know who these foolish wolves were. It wasn't her business. She owed them nothing. But she knew what she had to do.

* * *

Callisto dug her claws in, clinging to the outside of the wall. The stones were cold against her fingers and toes. It was a long way down. She could afford no misstep.

Her boots had been tossed into the sack across her back, allowing her to partially transform her hands and feet. The night air was cool after the heat of the day, but the shadowed, northern wall was cold. She lowered her foot, searching for somewhere to grip in the darkness. Her grip slipped! Chips of stone fell! She caught hold again. Only the insects answered her in the night.

A few moments more, and she dropped the final few feet to the ground. She paused to listen. The guards on the outer wall had been lax. Perhaps she should send a note of reprimand to their commander. The thought amused her. They were strangely concerned with thieves smuggling goods past the guarded checkpoints. No one was watching for a wolf-girl scaling the walls.

The bare earth was soft against her toes, the grass dry this time of year. Callisto focused, transforming her feet and hands. She gritted her teeth. It was a painful process, stretching bones and sinew from one shape to another. Even a partial transformation would leave her fingers and feet sore. It had been necessary, however. Claws retracted, her fingers and toes taking on the fine-boned features of a young woman once more.

She pulled her boots back on before making her way across the fields. Human footprints would draw less attention than wolf tracks.

She wasn't certain of where she was going, only the general direction. Poplar trees marked the edges of arable fields – now fallow. They would be planted again with barley in the months ahead. Before her were hills covered with olive groves and vineyards.

She continued walking, until she came to the edge of the first field, where the taller trees and scrub could afford her some amount of cover – should she need it. A dirt trail wound between the adjacent farmlands.

Her heart was pounding. Nerves? Definitely. Even in the night, even with no one around, she had seldom transformed. Not even partially. The terror of it had been beaten into her. To be a hunted beast. An animal. A hated monster to be killed or tortured without remorse. Her own shadow a thing to be feared.

Tonight, however, she had no other choice.

Leaning against a rock, she slipped off her boots again. Her bare feet pressed against the hardened earth of the farmers' roadway. This time, it was her whole body which would stretch, and ache. Feet, hands, back and jaw. She let out a low growl as the pain built – as if the pain was a thing to be cowed by her claws and fangs.

She had bent over onto all fours. The transformation shuddered through her. Her jaw and nose extended, becoming a muzzle. Claws stretched from her toes and fingers. Dark fur sprang from her arms and hands.

She could see it, her shadow no longer human. Her feet extending, toes touching the ground, heel lifting. Her very existence a hated thing, as her body took on the proportions of a beast. The beast she truly was. Somewhere between human and wolf, sentient yet feral.

She lifted her muzzle to the crescent moon, letting out a long, mournful howl. She didn't know if there would be an answer. But she had to find out. They had to know. She had to warn them.

Chapter 22

Callisto's howl rose into the night, its sound haunting and wild. She held the last note in a wailing arc, her muzzle pointed skyward. The call was everything they said it was. Everything they said about her. Dogs barked in the distance, and peasants shuttered their windows. She was a wolf, disguised as a street rat. A predator. Hated, feared, and reviled.

Callisto sat and waited. From the north, a howl answered in response. One voice, then two. They were distant, but within earshot. It would be several minutes before they would reach her.

She transformed back, her claws withdrawing, her proportions becoming those of a girl once more. Hiding the horrifying beast within.

She would be sore for much of the next day, transforming back and forth so many times. She quickly redonned her boots and laced them tight. There had been two replies, two voices. She couldn't be sure as to who they might be, but she had a good guess. There had been a familiar ring in that wail. But she had to be ready. Her kind would not be the only ones who had heard her howl.

She stood on the pathway, legs apart, hands at her side. She didn't plan for this to be a fight. If it turned out to be a strange werewolf, however, it could easily become one. She waited, the nighttime insects chirping. She waited, until she heard the soft, padded footsteps of two wolves approaching.

Callisto inhaled deeply, scenting the wind. She had been right. She had recognized the howl.

"Makednos."

The lanky, juvenile werewolf stepped out from the brush and onto the rutted dirt path. He was more wolf-like than human, his fur nearly black. He lifted his forelimbs from the ground, transforming into an intermediate, half-human, half-wolf shape – his muzzle becoming shorter to facilitate speech.

"Good to meet you too, sister."

"What are you doing here?" Callisto was speaking to her brother, but her eyes were fixed on Makednos' companion. Even from the shadows, she could tell he was bigger. Much bigger. Fully grown and filled out. Standing on all fours his head came up to her chest. The size of a bear, and far more menacing.

"I could ask you the same," Makednos said.

The other werewolf stepped forward, transitioning just as Makednos had, into a partly human shape. His fingers ended in long claws. Black hairs bristled from his neck and back.

"I already told you. I have a job to complete. One last task, and I will be freed of my debt. Able to decide my own future. What I want to know is, why you are here? It's been centuries since there have been werewolves this close to Polonia."

"We've come to bring you back."

"Back? To where? Grandmother's dead Makednos. I was there. I saw."

"Father sent us."

"The father who left me for dead?! So where is he? Is he here?" The blank expression on her brother's muzzle confirmed what she had expected. "He couldn't be bothered to come for me himself. He had to send you two flea traps instead."

A low growl emanated from the larger werewolf.

"He has responsibilities to more than just to us," Makednos replied. "That's what it means to be Alpha-Were."

"Since when did you make excuses for father? I have no reason to return to his mange-filled den."

"Hold your tongue!" the older werewolf spat.

"Why? Because the Alpha-Were couldn't look after his own family, let alone his pack?"

The larger wolf took another step towards her. Too close.

Pack order was a physical thing. Messages conveyed as much by posture and body language as by words. This wolf, had stepped too close for comfort.

She brought her boot up and down across his muzzle in a crescent kick.

Control. Erebus' words echoed in her mind. She had practiced long and hard. Her kick should be just enough to deliver a warning. Not hard enough for any real damage.

The wolf growled, a trickle of blood trailing across his nose and lip.

"Back-off! This is a family matter." Callisto's voice was low. She stood in a ready stance, prepared to follow with greater force if need be. A wolf with no growl or bite would wind up at the bottom of the pack.

"Irus!" Makednos barked. "She's still my sister."

The larger wolf took a step back, his teeth still barred. "So you say. It remains to be seen." The wolf's voice came as a low growl. "I was sent to keep an eye on you, Makednos. Not bring back some wolf-whelp pretender."

"No one believes I'm alive, even now, do they?"

"Callisto," Makednos continued, "everyone thought you were dead. No one imagined you could have lived."

"I was alive. I clawed and scratched to keep that life. I lived every day, hiding among those who wanted me dead. An indentured servant to a thief master."

"Callisto, please."

"And now, when I'm on the verge of earning my freedom to live among the humans as an equal and not a servant, I'm not going back to being the forgotten daughter of a lesser wolf king."

The older wolf sprang, faster than she would have expected from his hulking mass. His claws dug into her shoulder. She was thrown from her feet, sliding along her back. She had forgotten how large, how strong an adult werewolf could be.

The fabric tore in her tunic. Stones dug into her back. The wolf's snarling jaws were inches from her face.

"Irus! Remember your place!" Makednos' voice cut through the pain. "Let her go! I order it!"

The older werewolf drew back, releasing her. She climbed back to her feet, brushing herself off. She had miscalculated. She would not make the same mistake twice.

"Someone should teach this bitch her place," Irus growled.

Callisto glared at him. "I am still the daughter of the Alpha-Were, no matter how long ago he abandoned me."

"We didn't know, Callisto," Makednos replied.

"He should have! He shouldn't have assumed."

"He sent me to find you."

"He sent this brute too?" Callisto rubbed the wound in her shoulder. Blood oozed from the claw marks and scrapes. It was already beginning to heal, although the tear in her tunic would not so easily mend.

"I was sent to make sure Makednos stayed out of trouble," Irus replied. "Not to take orders from some pretender."

"She's my sister, Irus. I'm certain of it," Makednos said. "A twin never forgets the scent of their own littermate."

"Your father is not yet convinced."

"Whether my father is convinced is the least of your concerns," Callisto replied. "You did find trouble. There are rumors flying all across Polonia about werewolves on the outskirts of the city."

"There are werewolves everywhere in Bateria."

"Not openly, and not this close to the emperor's palace. They're recalling an inquisitor from retirement to track you down. Hunting hounds and all."

"We know how to evade them," Irus said.

"Oh really? You two stink of the wild. I bet Makednos here hasn't changed into a human in years, much less bathed as one."

"More than a decade," Makednos added with a toothy grin.

"You can't wash the scent off so easily. You two need to leave, before they find you."

"We were sent to bring you back," Makednos pleaded.

"I'll return when I'm good and ready. When I can face father without a debt to my name."

"Callisto –"

"I mean it Makednos. I fought long and hard to find a place, a life in the human world. I earned that life. I'm not giving it up now."

Makednos' head dropped. "What will I tell him?"

"Get out of here, Makednos. I'll see father again under my own terms."

She turned without another look back and without waiting for his response. She had done what she had set out to do. She had warned them. If they wanted to be foolish and linger, it was no longer her concern.

She could hear Makednos and Irus making their way through the brush north of the dirt trail, going their separate way. She was relieved they hadn't tried to follow her. They were already too close to the city's walls.

Maybe she had judged her father too harshly. Maybe. But she still couldn't bring herself to forgive him. She had survived by relying on herself. Nothing had happened to change that.

Chapter 23

Dear grandma,

I saw Makednos again. He always was a reckless, stupid wolf. But he's still my brother, even after all these years.

I miss those days. Being part of a pack, somewhere I can be accepted. Somewhere, where I'm not a monster, hiding in the shadows of those who hate me. But how could I go back, knowing you are gone? Knowing I ran when they came for you? I'm still angry father didn't come looking for me. But maybe I'm angrier with myself, that there was nothing I could do.

* * *

Callisto jotted down a series of quick notations. Another row of bookcases catalogued. She had developed her own shorthand to record her impressions and findings. The further she had gone through the archives, from decade-to-decade, the more records there had been – and the less they'd had to say.

The picture which had been painted depicted the gradual growth of an empire, expanding outward from the founding city of Polonia. Records told of governors appointed, taxes collected, and towns being built or conquered.

They also chronicled the gradual push north. The story of civilization pressing against the wilderness. That's how they portrayed it. Counts of wolf pelts collected in the inevitable push against the wild. Werewolves. Her kind. Fewer and fewer collected each year – as they were slowly squeezed out of existence. It was a picture she had never appreciated before. It had not been the task she had been sent to record. It was, however, the reality she had come to understand.

"Hello, Phaeton." She allowed a smile to cross her lips. His footfalls were so distinct. Like a young colt trying to contain itself and breaking into a trot as it neared – eager and clumsy at the same time.

"Hi Mira. I was wondering if you'd like to break for lunch." He stood over her, looking so boyish in his uniform.

"I don't usually have lunch," she replied.

"You can share mine. Really, I insist." Phaeton extended his hand.

"It would take at least hour," she protested, "just to go through the guards at the gate." She was flattered, and self-conscious. No boy had ever taken an interest in her.

"I brought extra today, and I usually eat on the library grounds."

Well . . . maybe it would be okay. She gathered her quills, capping her ink. He was watching her. She felt her face flush. She still wasn't used to the attention. "I have to let the ink dry on my notebook."

"You can leave it here. No one will touch it."

"But someone might –"

"Not here. Not inside the library grounds. Remember? Everyone is screened when they come and go."

Callisto reluctantly set her satchel down on the chair, following Phaeton to one of the side entrances. The door opened onto a pathway through the manicured gardens.

The sun was bright this day, with only a few clouds drifting across the blue sky like tufts of bleached wool. Bright birds flitted between the bushes, their voices chiming as they scattered at their approach. The birds were fatter here, she noticed. When she was young, she would sometimes hunt small birds when she was hungry. They barely made for mouthful.

Phaeton led the way to a bench, lying his satchel on his lap as he sat. Such an ordinary activity, she mused. Sitting down on a bench. It was strange to realize she had never done this before. Sitting next to someone she wasn't trying to rob. What was the appropriate etiquette? Shouldn't she leave some space between them? How much? How close or distant was proper?

For as long as she could remember, she had been trying to disappear into the crowd. Hiding who and what she was, what she was doing. Trying to go unnoticed.

She sat down, leaving a handsbreadth between them. Was that too much? Phaeton drew two pastries wrapped in a coarse linen from his bag, offering her one.

There was a ring on one of his fingers, set with a red stone. She had noticed it before but hadn't had a good look at it.

"It's a nice ring," she said. The words were out of her mouth before she had even considered them. A ring like that would have been a prime target for a pick-pocket – not exactly a topic she wished to bring up. The setting was silver, with a bull's head pattern on either side of the stone.

"Oh, that. It's my family's signet ring, one of two. My older brother gave it to me when I came to live in the city."

Callisto accepted the pastry from his hand, stuffing the end of it into her mouth. The filling was still warm! The lamb, herbs and roots erupted onto her palette in a seasoned mix, their juices spilling onto her lips. She hastily covered her mouth with one hand. She hadn't expected the pastry to be quite so full.

Phaeton was watching her. "My father's cook prepared them. I asked her to send me extra today." He took a bite from his.

"You have servants?" The thought had somehow never occurred to her.

"My father keeps a small staff in the city for cleaning and cooking." He took another bite, and Callisto did the same.

The meat pie was savory, and she was hungrier than she had admitted to herself. The taste of the lamb and spices flooded her tongue, its scent enhancing the flavor. It reminded her of happier days. Younger days.

She wondered what it was like, to live in a house where people prepared food for you. To have no worries about where the next meal would come from or whether there would be a next meal at all.

She continued to eat in silence, letting the sounds of the world around her fill her senses. For once, not listening for the boots of sentries or the wail of the clergyman whose purse had been snatched. Just listening to the sounds of the garden.

Birds. The breeze in the trees. The rolling wheels of wagons just beyond the outer fence. She was seldom outside to appreciate the sounds of the city. Not during the day, and not like this.

"Things were different in the northlands?" Phaeton asked.

"Quieter. Fewer people, smaller houses. Nothing like the streets and walls of the imperial city."

"They say the woodlands of northern Bateria are filled with wild animals. Herds of dear. Wild boar. Werewolves."

"They are, or at least were. The werewolves usually avoid contact with people. They're heard but seldom seen – unless you go out at night."

"You mean on a full moon?"

"They're more active when the moon is full. It makes it easier to hunt. But they're not compelled to change into their wolf shape, if that's what you're thinking."

"Really? I thought they always changed when the moon was full."

Callisto shook her head. "It's not so simple. The transformation takes energy. It's somewhat painful to transform – at least I've heard it is. Most werewolves transform for a reason, whether for play or the hunt. Some prefer to stay in one form or another throughout most of their lives."

"You know a lot of werewolf lore."

"Growing up in the north, you hear a lot of it." Had he edged closer to her? She swore she had left more space when she sat down.

She finished the meat pastry, letting the blend of spices linger on her tongue. "Thank you," she said. "It was very good."

"I usually try to come outside to eat," Phaeton said. "It helps break up the day."

"The gardens are beautiful," she granted.

"Sometimes I'll go outside the gates or catch up on gossip with the more senior journeymen. Like those werewolves everyone was talking about the other day."

"Yes. I can see why hearing wolves so close to the city could be unsettling." Callisto was watching a jay foraging for berries. She was trying to avoid eye contact with Phaeton. He had moved closer again. Their legs almost touched. She did like him. It was hard for her to admit it, but she did. Soon, however, her task here would be complete. She would return to her world. She wondered if she would ever see him again. It would probably be better, for both of them, if she didn't.

The words, the thoughts, knowing she had to leave, came so easily to her mind. So easily, they could only be true. Why then, did it hurt so much to admit them?

"They were captured, you know."

She swung her head around, the chill of his words stabbing through her mind. "Who?"

"The werewolves. An inquisitor and his hounds led a band of soldiers to them. They were captured a day or two ago."

It couldn't be. Perhaps it was just an ordinary wolf. Or maybe it was another werewolf. A different werewolf. Not her brother. Not him.

"I'm sure up north, where you come from, such things were more common. But they're little heard of in Polonia. Werewolves right outside the imperial city! They say there were two of them. Tore through four imperial soldiers before they took them in."

"They were killed?!" Callisto's heart sank. Two? Her stupid, reckless brother. It could only be. She felt the sting of tears at the edges of her eyes. No! Not here! Not now! Why did Makednos always have to be so reckless?

"They were captured. They say it was a bloody mess, but they were taken to the fortress of Burcsteli. They'll want to know what they were doing here, or who was helping them. They're supposed to be executed in another week – if they live that long."

Chapter 24

Dear grandma,

I remember you talking about the importance of kin, the importance of the pack, from my earliest days. How the pack depended on all of us, and how we depended on the pack. I remember. Even after I stopped believing – after the pack failed me. After I was left alone.

If I don't make it back, yah-yah, know that at least I tried. There's still a part of the pack in me.

* * *

Callisto paddled softly, guiding the lightweight skiff as quietly as she could through the water. The silhouette of the Burcsteli fortress was visible in the darkness ahead. Watchfires were lit atop its battlements, and here and there a window was lit by lantern light.

A part of her could scarcely believe she was there. She was supposed to be stealing into the Imperial Library. She was supposed to be picking locks and scouring magical archives, searching for a payoff which would land her taskmasters in villas of luxury. Instead, she was paddling a tiny boat to a fortress island, guarded by armed sentries who wouldn't hesitate to kill her.

She shouldn't care. It shouldn't matter to her. It wasn't her fault Makednos and that stupid brute had been captured. Yet here she was, in a desperate attempt to reach her brother – before the unthinkable happened.

Although she could swim well enough, she was hardly an expert boatman. She was only lucky she had found the small, shallow boat at the edge of an unlit pier. The Imperial Navy was less active in the late fall and winter months. She could thank their lack of rigor and supply of liquor for leaving the upper docks unattended.

This trip was very much unlike her. She preferred to plan a break-in well in advance, taking her time to scout out the territory and observe the rotation schedule for any guards. As it was, she couldn't wait this time. Every day her brother and Irus remained in the island prison was another day they might not see the end of.

She had found the floor plans from the original construction and had a good idea for what she was getting herself into. The fortress of Burcsteli had been built in the first half century of the empire, and its details were easy enough to locate from the library's archives. She could only hope any additions or changes had been minor. The tall watchtower on the southern face looked out towards the sea. It was intended to be the first line in the city's defensive ring. Ballistae and archers' slots adorned the southern face of the rocky island. The northern face on the other hand, the side facing the harbor, was where the island's docks were located.

If well maintained and manned, the island was intended to repulse would-be invaders on wooden ships. Callisto could only hope, in a time of peace and prosperity, the watches would be more lightly manned.

She paddled slowly; grateful the waters were calm. Moonlight glittered across the waves, as she brought the boat beneath the fortifications on the western side of the island. Leaping from the prow, she lashed the mooring line onto the rocks. An overhand knot followed by a half hitch, and the boat was secure.

The rocky cliff of the island rose above her, the fortifications rearing overhead. It was dark, and the cliff face would offer few handholds. No one would be expecting an intruder to scale this – least of all at night.

Callisto slung her boots into the shallow boat, fixing her satchel with her tools over her shoulder. She had a dagger on her belt. She hadn't had time to find another weapon.

Reaching up the cliff face, her fingers extended into claws. Her bare feet stretched, lifting her heels from the ground. Her face was contorted from the pain. It was wearing, transforming like this. With practice, the pain would become less sharp. More of a steady throb. Tonight, however, it was once again a stabbing hardship she'd have to endure.

She transformed her feet and hands, her claws digging into the rock. There were grips, crevices in the rock face, too narrow for human fingers to grasp. She scrambled up the natural cliff face. Loose rocks and stones showered the rocky shore beneath her. She didn't have time to scale the entire cliff in silence. She could only hope the steady crash of the waves would drown out any noise. Hand over hand, scrambling to plant each foot, she raced up the rugged face of the island.

When her claws struck into harder rock, she knew she had reached the stone of the walled keep. The walls were hard, but roughly hewn. There were gaps and pockets where her claws could dig in. She slowed her pace, becoming more deliberate in choosing her hand holds. She needed to make less noise as she approached the battlements above.

From the floor plans she had found in the library, the island fortress of Burcsteli was divided into two sides. The southern side, with its tower and outward-facing fortifications would be on the lookout for ships in the distance. The defenses had been built with opposing navies in mind. The northern side, in contrast, was where most of the soldiers would be housed, near the dockyards which brought food and other supplies. She had positioned herself between the two, where there would hopefully be fewer sentries stationed.

Unless changes had since been made, prison cells would be near the base of the tower on the southern side of the island. She couldn't be sure, however, until she reached the courtyard which divided the two sides of the keep.

As she approached the heights of the battlements, Callisto waited – listening for signs of sentries. The wind was cold, and brisk, heavy with the scents of the sea. She couldn't detect the scent of anyone nearby. She could still make out the steps from a guard shambling along the top of the wall, further to the south. A dull drone of voices drifted from the dockside barracks to the north. There was no sign of movement nearby.

She pulled herself up, and over the edge of the wall. There was a walkway along the battlement heights. Below was a courtyard, partially illuminated by lantern light filtering from the barracks on her left. Above her, the tower loomed, its windows brightly lit. The walkway atop the wall, however, was deserted.

Below her, on the opposite side of the courtyard, was a heavy wooden door, reinforced with iron bands, just to the side of the tower's base. It was exactly where the building plans suggested prison cells should be. She was surprised to see no guards posted outside. Were they really so confident in the sanctity of their island fortress? She could only hope so.

Callisto descended a stairway to the courtyard grounds, moving from shadow to shadow. Her ears were alert for movement. The soldiers in their barracks and dockyards were relaxed, even jovial. She could hear it in the tone of their voices, in the scent of the cheap wine and ouzo being uncorked. Why shouldn't they be? No foe had ever penetrated these walls before. Or at least, none who lived to tell of it.

When she reached the prison cell door, she listened for movement within. Still nothing? They left the prison cells unguarded? This she could scarcely believe.

She drew her claws across the door, making a rasping sound. Then she vaulted onto the low roof, just above the entrance. She waited. Nothing? She transformed her clawed fingers back into a human hand, clenching her teeth against the pain. She needed her fingers if she were to make use of her tools.

If there had been anyone inside, they should have heard the noise and moved to investigate. But there was nothing. No reaction. Not even to open the little window-like shutter in the doorway.

From the floorplans, there should be an area just inside the doorway where two or more sentries could be stationed. Had they really failed to guard their own dungeon?

She dropped from the roof, crouching before the entrance, drawing her tools from her bag. Another warded lock. She had it open in seconds, turning the latch and pulling the door open. She gritted her teeth as its hinges groaned in protest. Lantern light poured out from within.

She had only just pulled the doorway ajar – when she was met by an agonizing scream.

Chapter 25

The cry came from an open stairwell at the rear of the vacant guardroom. Callisto felt the hair standing up on her arms. Makednos! If something had happened to him . . .

She didn't know how she could forgive herself. She had arrived too late! Her little brother. Her stupid, reckless little brother.

Voices echoed from the stairwell. She needed to hide herself. Quickly.

The guard's room was lit by a single lantern, with a table, a small stove, and two stools. There was a rack on the wall which held a pair of pole arms, a stand for hanging cloaks in the wintertime, and a closet at the side of the room.

She opened the closet door and slipped inside. There was an old wineskin hanging from a peg which had gone rancid. She wrinkled her nose in disgust as she pulled the door shut. She could hear two voices approaching from the stairwell. She had to get her breathing under control, or she'd be found.

"Did you see how the beast's flesh smoked as the silver blade was drawn across? Like watching it burn." An older voice, with a certain raspy quality to it. "Just like the accounts describe."

"Yes, I've seen it before." The second voice was younger, deeper. "Even after losing so much blood, the beast still lives. Their powers of regeneration are remarkable. Did you see how strong it was? How hard it was to control? Without two guards and their poles pinning it down, we never could have held it long enough to saw through the hide."

Callisto adjusted her view, trying to spy through cracks in the doorway. All she could see was a glimpse of their backs. One was broader, with dark hair. He wore a dark, heavy cloak about his shoulders. Too heavy for this season. He must have been from farther north. The other figure had wiry grey hair and wore a dark vest over his white ruffled shirt.

Two Imperial Guards followed; the sunburst insignia visible throughout their armor. They were each carrying a long pole arm with a spike and a hook on the end.

"I shall take this to the embalmers in the morning. See what he thinks about mounting it." It was the older voice speaking again. "I have an expert tanner on staff. He mounts all my trophies. You're certain there's no danger from handling it?"

"No. It's the bite you have to be wary of. I've had to eliminate my own men on more than one occasion after they were infected."

"Excellent. If the embalmer's successful, we should add the other before they're led to execution."

The other one? Callisto's heart was pounding, her skin prickled as dark, horrified thoughts raced through her mind. Was her brother alive or dead?

The accompanying guards returned their pole arms to the weapons rack.

"What about the younger one?"

"He's too scrawny to make much of a display." The older, raspy voice answered again.

"It'll give good sport just the same. I've heard you've had experience with . . . setting examples?"

Sport? The scrawny one? Callisto's heart was pounding. She could feel her own claws, as if they were just beneath the surface of her skin, itching for release. She had to bring her emotions under control. If anything happened to Makednos . . .

"Well . . . yes. But those were only common rabble. Not the same as beasts like these. I'll have to show you my private collection and trophy room sometime, master Darios. My assistant does the embalming himself."

Callisto couldn't see the faces of the two men speaking. Their backs were still turned. She could, however, see the discomfort etched into the features of the two sentries as they returned their pole arms to the rack. Their reaction to the mention of a "private collection" had been involuntary, and visceral. Whatever the older man was referring to, even the Imperial Guards found repugnant.

The outer door unlatched and was pushed open. A draft of cool air swept the room.

"Odd. I thought I had locked the door before we went down for interrogation."

"Maybe we should leave a guard in the room."

"It's late. You saw what kind of shape it's in. Neither of them will be going anywhere." He half turned towards the sentries. "The two of you two can return to barracks. I'll be locking up. We can resume interrogation in the morning."

The door was swung shut and latched. There was the sound of a key being inserted, locking it shut. Callisto waited in the closet, counting the seconds before stepping out.

The guard room was dark. They had extinguished the lone lantern when they left. She stepped lightly down the stairwell, heading into the dungeon below. She rested her hand against the stone wall, steadying herself. She had no idea of what to expect.

There were lanterns alight on the lower levels. She could see the glow from below as she followed the spiral stair. The ascending stench left her queasy. A mixture of urine, blood, and death. She could hear the scamper of rats as her bare feet brushed against the cold stone steps. Her sharp ears could pick out a rasping, wheezing sound. Someone breathing.

At the bottom, the stairwell opened into a broad room. A table with chains and leather straps sat at its center. Walls were adorned with whips, knives, and various tools. Poles with hooks leaned against one wall. Prison cells lined the perimeter, each with a narrow window and slot for a food tray.

Suspended from the ceiling, however, were two metal cages. A fur-covered figure rested in each. From one, a smaller, gangly figure stared out at her. The look of fear was unmistakable in his amber eyes. The other was slumped in its cage, curled into a ball like a spider which had been crushed underfoot.

"Callisto?" Makednos' voice was faint, as if unwilling to believe.

"What have they done to you?" She asked, racing to the edge of the room. There was a wall-mounted crank which hoisted the caged on a chain. She tugged at the latch. It didn't budge. She tugged harder, and the crate holding Makednos came down to the floor with a crash.

Callisto winced. She could only hope no one had heard. She didn't have time to rush up the stairs to investigate.

"How did you find us?" Makednos whispered, coming to the bars.

"Word travels." She rushed to the iron enclosure. If anything had happened to him . . . "Are you alright?"

"I got the lesser of it." She could see where blood had dried on his fur.

Callisto brought the lockpicks from her satchel. There was a heavy metal lock on the crate. She'd need her largest set of picks.

"You always were the reckless one," she whispered.

"Don't I know it."

She inserted the par of picks, her fingers shaking as she hurried to free him. The steel of the lock was cold against her fingers.

There was a loud click as the lock sprang open. She flung the door wide, and her brother sprang out – catching her in an uncharacteristic hug. The stiff guard-hairs of his undercoat scratched against her cheek. His body warm, his scent familiar.

He was wounded, but alive. She didn't know what she would have done had it been otherwise.

"Get yourself a weapon from the wall," she said. "I'll free Irus."

"Leave me," the older wolf growled. He was still hunched over in his cage.

Callisto returned to the wall, pressing the latch to release the winch suspending the second cage. She was more careful, this time, to control its descent. It wouldn't do to have another loud crash.

The second cage came down with a jerking motion. The winch released, catching, released, catching again, until finally settling to the ground. Callisto ran forward to pick the lock. Makednos was standing watch near the stairwell.

"I thought I told you to grab a weapon," she said.

"I'm a werewolf. I need no weapon," he replied.

"Lot of good that'll do you. We're surrounded by guards. We won't stand a chance if we're detected."

She finished unlocking the second cage, drawing the door open noisily.

"Irus? Can you stand?"

"I told you to leave! I'm just a burden." He hadn't moved, not even when the cage had jerked to a halt against the floor.

"Is that what my father taught you? To abandon the sick or weak?"

There was a low growl in his voice. "I should claw you for that."

"You can try if you like. Just so long as you get up." She hesitated at the open door. Irus had made no attempt to rise. "Makednos, can you carry him?"

"I said leave me!" He raised his head for the first time. She could see there was fresh blood coating the fur of his chest. It was slick with it. She couldn't tell where it was from.

"I'll get him," Makednos replied, crawling into the cage. He pulled the wounded werewolf across his shoulder, helping him to stand and maneuvering him out the door.

There were marks across both of Irus' arms, their puckered openings still oozing blood and puss. Silver! Callisto knew the signs of a silver-edged blade well enough. Knew how it burned against your skin.

It was Irus' right hand, however, which made her inhale in a gasp. It was missing. Blood dripped from the ragged wound where his forearm had been sawed off. Bone was visible from the bloody stump.

She hadn't been prepared for this. "We have to get those wounds clean," she said. "Wounds from a silver blade won't fully heal if they're not washed."

"You have to get out of here," Irus growled in a low voice. "Or we'll all be dead."

Callisto started back up the stairs. "Follow me," she said. "I have a boat waiting."

Makednos followed with Irus propped against him, their claws scraping across the steps as they climbed. By the time Makednos had dragged the larger wolf up the stairs, she had already unlocked the door to the prison and was peering outside. She glanced back as they shuffled towards the door.

"I'll lead the way. The courtyard is empty but try to make as little noise as possible."

She opened the door, shutting it behind them as quietly as she could. Conversations rose from the dockside quarters of the fortress garrison, but the crescent moon was low in the sky – casting long shadows across the courtyard. Only a werewolf's eyes could have pierced the darkness so completely.

Callisto motioned Makednos to wait as they came to the stairway leading up to the outer wall and walkway. Her ears had picked up footsteps, and she couldn't be sure of how many there were.

She drew her dagger, stalking silently up the stairs. There was a sentry, making his rounds along the walkway above. He was blocking their only way out.

Chapter 26

It was a lone sentry, but it might as well have been a dozen. If he raised the alarm, there would be hundreds descending upon them.

He held a small lantern and was peering over the edge of the battlements towards the sea. Their success or failure, whether they lived or died, all came down to what happened next.

If she waited, the guard would likely continue his rounds. They could lower themselves over the wall as soon as he was gone. Maybe. If he turned around and peered down the stairwell at the courtyard below, they'd be found. The lantern's light would surely give them away.

She didn't have time for what-ifs. Didn't have time, didn't have patience. This was the place which had imprisoned her kin. These were the men who stood guard while her kind were tortured like animals. Their limbs hacked off as trophies for the sick race of men.

The guard was facing outward, his back towards her. She stalked closer. He appeared unaware of his peril. Was he tired? Bored? Did he have a family he was thinking of?

She edged closer. All that mattered now was her life, and the life of her kin. She needed to strike swiftly. Strike somewhere his armor wouldn't protect him. Guilty or innocent, this soldier would pay for the empire's crimes.

Her left hand shot out, gripping his chin and yanking his head back. Her right hand brought the cold edge of the dagger across his throat and artery in one fluid motion. Blood splattered everywhere. He collapsed backwards – on top of her.

His armor was heavier than she had expected. His lantern dropped noisily to the ground. He slumped against her shoulder.

She was angry. Angry for everything her kinsmen had endured. Angry for every silver-edged scar which had ever burned her skin. She clenched her teeth, her lips drawn back into a snarl as she lifted the guard's body upwards. Lifting him up, armor and all, over her head, the strength of an enraged beast coursing through her. The strength of a werewolf.

She tossed his limp body out, over the wall. There was a satisfying splash as it landed on the rocks and surf below. Weighed down by his weapons and armor, his remains might never be found.

She snuffed out the lantern, then tossed it after the slain soldier. She would leave no clues as to what had become of the missing sentry. Let them guess at his fate. Let them think he had deserted his post to go drink in some corner.

Turning, she leaned over the wall to motion Makednos to follow her up the stairs.

"How will we get Irus down?" Makednos asked, as he staggered to the top. Irus' arm was slung over his shoulder, the big werewolf leaning against him.

Callisto was already drawing a length of rope from her bag. "We'll lower him to the rocks below, then climb down after him."

They tied the rope in a loop around his chest. Irus was large, even as werewolves go. It took both of them to lift him over the side, and slowly guide his descent over the wall. Irus provided no resistance, or assistance for that matter. His face was pale, his strength spent.

Callisto and Makednos braced their feet against the battlements, leaning back as the rope uncoiled, lowering the older wolf down.

A WOLF BEFORE THE STORM

"You could grip better if your hands are more human," Callisto grunted.

Makednos scowled but transformed his fingers a little more. "How far to the bottom?" he growled.

"The wall is forty feet, and the cliffside another fifty. We should have just enough rope."

They felt the rope go limp as the last of its coils unwound through Callisto's fingers. She released the line, letting fall over the edge

She swung herself out and over the wall. Claws extended from her fingers as she transformed her hands and feet, finding crevices in the wall's face. She climbed cautiously down the wall, checking to make sure Makednos was following her, albeit more slowly.

"Do you do this often?" he rasped, trying to jam his claws into each handhold.

"What? Save your pathetic tail?"

"No, climb down walls."

"All the time. It's easier if you feel for hand holds. You don't have to jam your claws where there aren't any."

Makednos grunted in response.

Her toes came up against the cold, wet rock. Irus was slumped against the cliffside. His breath came in and out, in a wheeze. The bleeding from the stump where his hand used to be had slowed, but not stopped. If the landing had caused him any additional pain, he made no sign or complaint. She had dragged him across the rocks halfway to where the boat was moored before Makednos joined her. Together they heaved the injured wolf into the boat.

"Where are you taking us?" Makednos asked as she set the oars into their posts.

"There's a shallow beech, just outside of the city's walls. I scouted it weeks ago. There's an abandoned shack once used to cure fish. The scent should shield you from their hounds."

As they pulled further away from the island fortress, Callisto put more strength into the oars. She needed to get her brother safely outside of the city's walls – and still have time to return before Pontus suspected.

Heave. Pull the oar up. Back again. Heave.

Was she really doing this? She hadn't had time to think, just do. Her muscles were aching by the time she felt the skiff slide across the sand.

Leaping out, she dragged the boat ashore. Makednos helped Irus to stagger onto the beach.

"That way!" Callisto hissed, gesturing towards a battered shack. She finished dragging the boat ashore, retrieving a sack and waterskin, before following.

The building appeared to be barely standing. Boards were missing from its roof. Stars peeked in from above. The air was heavy with the scent of salt and fish, their decayed, skeletal remains littering the floor.

"Why would they abandon this place?" Makednos asked, lowering Irus to the ground. "We're almost on top of the city walls."

"It was built too close to the shore," Callisto responded. "A storm battered it pretty bad a few years ago. Another big storm and it will probably collapse."

"We'll be lucky if it doesn't collapse," Irus observed. The large wolf was sitting on the floor alongside the debris, clutching his mangled arm against his chest. "This place stinks!'

"That stink is why nobody will follow their dog's barks if they happen to lead them this way." Callisto drew a water skin from her satchel, reaching out for Irus' wounded arm. "Here, let me see it."

He growled at her, showing his fangs, his mangled arm and missing hand clutched next to his chest.

Callisto handed the water skin to Makednos. "You see if you can't get him to wash it. If he doesn't clean the silver-scarred wounds, they'll get infected and will never heal."

"Are you coming with us?" Makednos asked. There was a sad, plaintive tone in his voice.

"No. If you clean out the wound, it should heal enough to travel by tomorrow night. Don't head north. They'll be expecting you that way. Head west, along the coast for at least a night's travel. Then head north. It should throw them off your scent."

"What about you?"

"I'll return the boat to its dock. Let them guess at how you escaped. I'm already late for my return from my duties. Hopefully I can get some sleep before daybreak. How did the two of you get captured?"

"We were hiding in what we thought was a deserted cottage. Turns out it was a hunting lodge for the lord of the manor. The cleaning servants discovered us. We were surrounded before we knew they were upon us."

"No one will bother you here. They're too afraid of the building coming down."

"I share their fear," Irus remarked with a cough.

"You're still not returning with us? You're staying with them?! After you've seen what they're like?! You're not alone, Callisto. You have a pack."

She paused, considering what had happened this night. All she had been through, all those years. The two of them standing there now. They must have made for quite a sight. A slight girl in a dark cloak, and a gangly looking werewolf youth with bristling hair and wild eyes.

Makednos didn't wait for her reply. His arm reaching around her, his bristly hair against her shoulder and cheek. The musty scent of wolf. His embrace, like a long-lost memory, faded but still remembered.

"Take care of yourself, big sister."

"Stupid wolf." She hugged him despite herself. "I'll return in my own time and place. If I was forgotten this long, a few more months will hardly make a difference."

Chapter 27

Dear grandma,
It's been years I've spent, hiding in the shadows. Trying to go unnoticed. Trying to seem like something other than what I am. I have learned many things along the way. I should know better than most – things are not always as they seem.

* * *

"Your progress has slowed over the past week," Cetus remarked, examining Callisto's logbook.

"It took longer than expected to inventory the last row of shelves." Callisto stood with her hands clasped in front of her. She was dressed in her scholar's uniform, prepared to leave for a day at the archives. Cetus usually reviewed her notebook once or twice each week.

"Slowed? Slowed how?!" Pontus snapped.

"You needn't concern yourself," Cetus replied. "We're still on track to complete our survey of the magical archives within the next three weeks. If the documents are there, we'll find them."

"What if they're not?" Pontus said. "I have a good deal invested already."

"You needn't worry," Cetus replied, sliding the notebook across the table towards Callisto. "We'll all get the share we have coming. More than one party is offering a considerable reward. Everyone seems to be convinced the documents exist. We just have to find them."

* * *

"How ever did they escape?" Callisto asked innocently. She was walking with Phaeton after lunch, making a circuit of the gardens which surrounded the Imperial Library.

"They're saying they had outside help. Probably another werewolf."

"Three werewolves?"

"More, if you believe the rumors." Phaeton glanced around before lowering his voice. "Everyone says they couldn't have gotten past the Imperial Guard without an inside connection. They rotated out the entire guard staff from the Burcsteli fortress and demoted their commander."

"Seems a little extreme, doesn't it?"

"Not in the empire's guard. Emperor Bessarion has a reputation for accepting no excuses."

There were footsteps from the paved walkway, ahead and to their left. A sharp rhythm from someone approaching from a side pathway. Callisto glanced at Phaeton. He didn't seem to notice. Should she say anything?

When Cassandra stepped out onto the main pathway, there was a momentary look of surprise on her face.

"What are you doing here?" Cassandra's eyes were wide with alarm, her gaze fixed on Callisto.

"We were taking a stroll during lunch," Phaeton replied.

"Not you, her. There aren't supposed to be any foreigners about when the master arrives."

"What master?" Callisto was already confused. What did Cassandra care where she went?

"A reception for Master Zenodotus is being held in the east wing, where they have more space," Phaeton said. He turned his attention towards Cassandra again. "None of us were invited, yourself included Cassandra. Besides, Mira isn't a foreigner. She's from Lynxios."

Callisto clamped her jaw shut, biting back her own reply at the mention of her assumed name. That's right. Lynxios. That was her cover.

"Lynxios isn't part of the empire," Cassandra said.

"It was settled by Baterians," Phaeton pointed out.

"But it's not under the emperor's rule. And she's here under the patronage of a foreign nobleman."

"What? You think she's a spy? Or maybe you think she's an assassin? She's as skinny as a starving stray. It's not like she could pose a threat to the Imperial Guard. Or is it the ink in her quill you're afraid of?"

"It doesn't matter what I think. There are officials who will look for any excuse to cover for their own mistakes. Journeyman Neilos has been on edge all week over this meeting."

There was a commotion on the pathway ahead. Groups of armed guards had been arrayed on either side of the walkway leading from the gate to the main entrance, as a party of noblemen were being welcomed by the library staff. A man with wispy hair and a long grey beard was at the center of the group.

One of his attendants, a younger man with dark hair and a full beard, appeared to be searching through the crowd. "Cassandra?!"

Cassandra glanced over her shoulder. "Coming, Neilos!"

She turned her attention to Callisto again. "Stay as far from the reception as you can. There are some who wouldn't hesitate to report a peasant to the guards and have you dragged from the premises."

Cassandra turned, walking towards the welcoming party, the clop of her steps sounding against the paving stones of the pathway. Her lilac-scented perfume wafted through the air as she left, unsettling Callisto's stomach.

"What's she so anxious about?" Callisto wondered out loud.

"Don't take it personal," Phaeton replied. "Cassandra's been trying to gain the attention of the journeymen who report to Zenodotus for some time. Neilos is only the most recent, and most senior."

"Why is the Master Historian even here? Does this happen often?"

"Not often, and not for the reasons Cassandra is thinking."

"What do you mean?"

Phaeton glanced warily around, then began to lead her back, the way they had come – away from the front entrance and the reception. "There have been a few volumes which have gone missing from the archives in recent weeks."

"Volumes?!" Callisto belatedly realized her mistake and lowered her voice. "What sort of volumes?"

"Original editions which have vanished. The kind collectors would pay handsomely for."

"You mean, they're being sold on the black market?" So . . . she might not be the only one scouring the shelves, seeking a pay-off from a wealthy, unknown client.

"It wouldn't be the first time. Cassandra should be more worried about herself."

"What do you mean?"

"Master Zenodotus has a reputation. He had a certain eye for pretty women when he was young. A fondness for blondes and redheads, or so they say. It didn't stop him from having a very low opinion of them, however. As for Neilos . . . he always struck me as a bit too cold. Like a haddock from a three-day old catch. There's not much emotion in him. She shouldn't expect any favors if things go bad."

Chapter 28

Hiding. So much of my life has been about it. Hiding where I come from. Hiding from the people I was sent to stalk. Maintaining a calm outward demeanor. Even when I was screaming inside. Even when I wanted to lash out. Hiding everything, even my feelings. Even from myself.

* * *

"Hi, Mira." Phaeton's voice seemed anxious. She had noticed it for the past couple of days. Had she been incautious? Had he read the tension in her glance?

She had been feeling on edge, ever since Phaeton had revealed how documents had gone missing. It wouldn't matter if she wasn't the one who had been selling them to local collectors – at least not yet. She knew the guards and officials would be looking for a thief in their midst. And she was, after all, a thief. She half-expected guards to appear at any moment to drag her away.

Her greatest shield, she knew, was her own self-confidence – real or projected. Each day she had to reinforce her façade. Brace herself to face the guards, the officials, even Phaeton. She knew her credentials were an impeccable forgery – more authentic than many who might have had legitimate reasons for being there. The possibility of being caught, and the consequences, however, kept her on edge.

"Hi Phaeton," she replied, a faint smile on her lips. "How have you been?"

"I'm good. You're making progress?"

"As good as can be expected. This last row of stacks was a real swamp to trek through."

"Not as glamorous as you thought it would be," he replied with a grin on his face.

"Too many dry reports from appointed governors and ministers trying to impress."

"The stacks can be like that." Phaeton hesitated, his mood turning pensive. "You're nearly done, aren't you?"

"I probably have another couple of weeks to collect my materials. Then I'll have to ask my patron if he has other research he wants me to do." There was no point in leading him on. She only had a few more shelves left to survey in the archives for magical tomes. The archives he didn't know she was searching each nightfall. She still hadn't found what she had been sent to locate. But there was no point in surprising him and leaving a trail when she disappeared.

"What will happen if he doesn't?"

She shrugged. "I guess I would be asked to return to Symru." Or to the miserable life she had known, as a common street thief in Centrola. The thought was not a pleasant one.

* * *

It was dark as Callisto made her way back to the warehouse flat. She had changed back into her threadbare, street rat clothing, her steps slower this night – her mind wrapped up in thought. The prospect of having to leave, of having to move to the next chapter in her life had never troubled her before. When Pontus had moved his operations from one hideout to another during all her years in his gang, it had been only a minor inconvenience. None of those hideouts had ever been a home. They were a place to sleep. Nothing more. Why was it different this time?

True, if she somehow succeeded and found what she had been sent to retrieve, she would be free after this job. Something she had dreamed of for years. The master of her own fate. She could go where she wanted, live how she wanted. It was a mirage which had hovered over her dreams ever since she had found herself as a frightened child alone on the streets.

For the first time, however, she found herself wanting to stay. To live the role she was playing, the fabrication which was a necessary part of the heist. She wanted this fictional life. That, of course, was the one thing she could never have.

So lost in thought was she, she almost didn't notice the figure skulking outside the warehouse. It was only when he moved that she recognized Andros leaning against the wall. He ducked his head, his eyes avoiding her gaze. There was a jagged scar across his brow – where his skin had healed in a stretched-out pattern and his hair hadn't quite grown back. Did he even know it had been her? She hadn't exactly waited to introduce herself, and Andros had been the first to go down.

She eyed him with suspicion. She hadn't seen him for days, if not weeks. Not since she'd pummeled him into the street. He made no movement in her direction. She climbed the stairs outside the warehouse, looking back at the top to see him walking around the corner, exiting the alley.

She had an impulse to follow him, to see where he might be headed at such a late hour. But she was tired and couldn't spare the energy to pound his sorry hide – even if he did deserve it again.

As she opened the door onto the hallway, Pontus was waiting.

"Where have you been?!" he asked.

"I was in the archives, same as every night," she said. She shut the door behind her, proceeding down the narrow hall. She needed to get to her room. Needed to get some sleep.

"Have you found it yet?!" His voice was accusing. She noticed he was wearing a new vest over his white shirt, with shiny brass buttons. He had taken to wearing a lot of new clothes lately, although he still wore the same overcoat – with its hidden pockets and knives.

"If I'd found it, you and Cetus would know."

"Unless you tried to sell it yourself."

"As if I could ever sell anything without you hearing about it."

"You'd better believe you couldn't." Pontus had opened his coat, the handle of his silver bladed knife visible. "Don't think I don't know about what you did on that island."

"What island?"

"The island the wolf was freed from. Don't play innocent with me."

"What could I have done?"

"I'm sure you had something to do with their escape. Just remember, one whisper from me, and it will be you who'll be strung-up in the dungeons of Burcsteli."

Footsteps. Heavy, booted feet on the steps leading up to the upper loft.

"I made you, and I can destroy you. You wouldn't be alive without me." Pontus continued his stream of accusations, oblivious to the approaching footsteps.

She turned just in time to see two figures crash through the outside door. Two men, each with a short sword in their hand, dressed in dark cloaks and boots. Their beard and sideburns had been brushed to flare out from their face. Flaring out – like a monkey! Like the guard at the warehouse!

Each wore a silver amulet about their neck, a snarling monkey face visible in the dim lamplight.

They had found them!

Chapter 29

Callisto recognized the screaming monkey emblem. The same as the one worn by the warehouse guard. The same as emblazoned on the chest she had snatched the gaudy jewelry from!

Her heart raced, her mind scrambling through the possibilities. She only had a small knife on her – not even a dagger. The hall was narrow, limiting her movement. They were trapped!

Callisto barely had time to shift into a ready stance, when a broad hand reached from behind the rearmost of the two men, gripping his throat. The tip of a long dagger pierced through his chest, as he wheezed in surprise.

She didn't wait to see how or what had happened. She had to take advantage of the lead swordsman's momentary surprise. She brought her foot across his face in a round kick. Blood was streaming from his nose. Her left hand gripped the wrist of his sword hand, keeping his weapon at bay.

Before he could recover, she had twisted his wrist, delivering a blow to the side of his elbow. She put her shoulder behind it. There was a sharp crack and a gasp as he dropped his weapon.

The rearmost swordsman had dropped to the floor. He had been stabbed through – twice! Taras stepped over the body, dagger in hand.

He gripped his second opponent by the throat – the one Callisto had disarmed. Taras' dagger plunged through his opponent's back, the tip of his long blade protruding through the chest each time he stabbed. Once, twice, three times. Any one of the thrusts could have been fatal. No one could accuse Taras of not being thorough – if unnecessarily so. The wounds had missed the heart, Callisto recognized. He evidently preferred to leave his victims choking on their own blood.

Taras released the swordsman. Blood covered his shirt and pooled at his feet. The stricken swordsman continued to wheeze, eyes wide, his dark tunic soaking in his own blood.

There was a grim look of satisfaction in Taras' eyes. Probably the most emotion Callisto had ever seen him display. He leaned over his victim to wipe his dagger on the dying swordsman's cloak. The swordsman was shivering, his jaw moving but unable to speak. Taras seemed to take a perverse pleasure in observing his victim's final moments.

Cetus' head appeared in the open doorway. "Are the two of you alright? The gods of fortune be praised. I'm relieved we arrived in time."

"Cetus?" Pontus was shaken, his back wedged against the far wall of the hallway. "What's this all about?"

"I'll explain as we go. We need to get the two of you out of here. Grab whatever belongings you can and come quickly. It's not safe for you here anymore. Taras will clean up the mess."

Callisto entered her room, gathering her pitiful few belongings onto her bedroll. Her new, scholar's wardrobe was kept in the servants' quarters at Cetus' suite. There wasn't much to gather from here. Just a change of clothes, and her blanket – her stash of notes to her grandmother tucked safely away inside.

By the time she had exited her small room, Taras had already dragged one of the two bodies out the door. He was bending over the remaining swordsman, searching for valuables. He removed the screaming monkey clasp from the cloak, examining both sides of it before slipping it into a pouch at his waist.

Callisto edged past Taras, stepping over the body. Pontus was still collecting his belongings as she descended the stairs to where Cetus was waiting. He glanced anxiously up the stairwell. After a few moments, Taras appeared, dragging the body. He gripped it by its feet, its head banging from step-to-step as he dragged it down.

"What's taking Pontus so long?" Cetus muttered.

Taras dragged the body to the end of the alley, tossing it unceremoniously into a small cart he had commandeered. It rocked as the body was hefted into place. The cart had been meant to have a donkey pulling it, but could be dragged by hand if the load was light – or if the person dragging it was strong enough.

The other bodies had already been loaded, their bloodied limbs hanging out over the edge. Three sets of hands. There were two others? The other swordsman and . . . Andros! His body was limp, and blood soaked, just like the others – vacant eyes staring into space.

The boy must have been their lookout, directing the two swordsmen to where they could find her and Pontus. A wave of sympathy swept through her for his mother. The response surprised her. His mother would probably never know if her worthless son had run off to find his fortune or had met an ill end in the alleys of Polonia.

As for Andros . . . the boy would have wound up on the wrong side of a blade sooner or later. If it had been up to him, she would have been the one lying dead in the wagon.

Taras pulled a tarp over the cart, hiding its contents before hefting the yoke across his broad shoulders, dragging it away. He headed down the street – towards the river.

"Callisto!" Pontus hissed. She pulled her attention away from the cart. He was standing at the top of the stairs, dragging a chest behind him. "Why are you standing there?! Get my chest!"

He left the chest, proceeding down the stairs. Callisto hurriedly sprang up after him. She slung her own belongings across her back, reaching around to lift Pontus' trunk.

The chest was awkward, and heavy. She had to brace it against her chest as she maneuvered down the steps.

"I thought I told you to be quick about it," Cetus said.

"You can't expect me to leave everything."

Callisto made it down the stairs, the muscles in her arms and shoulders already protesting. It was heavier than when they had arrived. She nearly dropped the chest a couple of times.

"Hurry along," Cetus said in an exasperated tone. "It's not safe here. There's no telling when someone might come."

Cetus started to lead the way in the direction Taras had disappeared to.

"We came as soon as we had word," Cetus said. "The cult members had been searching for whomever was responsible for stealing their gift to the emperor. A couple of days ago, they discovered one of the larger gems on the black market. All they had to do was track down who had sold it."

"I assure you, I took every precaution," Pontus said. "I would never sell to a snitch."

"They'll be looking. They'll have a general description by now," Cetus said. "The two of you will need to separate. I've arranged alternate lodging for the both of you. Pontus will stay in the accountants' district where foreign brokers usually reside – on the east side of the river."

"In the imperial city?! The papers to gain lodging there –"

"Were expensive, yes. A professional always has multiple aliases and safe rooms lined up. You will need to exchange your wardrobe accordingly. I'll set up an appointment with the seamstress in the morning. You should expect to depart every morning, heading in the direction of the shipyards. Ostensibly, you'll be going to verify and inventory cargo. You will not," and Cetus held that word, "be visiting your former haunts and fences. We can't afford to have anyone tracking you down again. Next time you might not be so lucky."

"Yes. I understand." It was one of the few times Callisto had ever seen Pontus genuinely contrite. Even when caught in a swindle with another thief, he would always attempt to talk his way out of it.

"Room and board at your lodgings will be due at the first of each week, Twelve drachmae per night. You'll be paying for the first week, in advance, in the morning."

"Twelve?! Why would I pay such an outlandish sum?!"

"Because," Cetus hissed, "you were the one who has a foreign cult on your tail! The last place they'll think of looking for you is the imperial city. Common thieves avoid the place. Being caught as a pickpocket in the imperial district is an almost certain death sentence."

"I can't pay for a room like that for weeks without end."

Cetus halted in the street, staring coldly at Pontus. They were one street away from the river and the docks.

"We're in this together, Pontus. We can afford no more distractions. When your lockpick finds what we're looking for –"

"If she finds it," Pontus countered.

"When she finds it, you can choose where and how you want to spend your share. Until then, you need to avoid drawing attention to yourself. I also have a lot invested in this scheme. If Taras hadn't arrived in time, I'd be looking for a new lockpick, wouldn't I? Starting all over, trying to smuggle someone in."

Pontus stood, absorbing the night's events. Without saying a word, he nodded his assent.

Taras appeared on the road ahead. He had stripped off his blood-stained shirt and donned a light jacket.

"Are they disposed of?" Cetus asked.

"Weighted and ready to dump," Taras replied.

"Good. Let's be on our way."

"Where will I stay?" Callisto asked, still straining to carry Pontus' trunk.

There was a look of surprise in Cetus' eyes, as if suddenly remembering her. "I forgot to mention. I found a loft in the upper floor, in one of the dormitories where academy students stay. It will cost Pontus three drachmae a night."

"Three!? For a lockpick?!"

Chapter 30

Dear grandma,

They've moved me into a small room above where paying students stay. It's small, but it's mine – my own space. I will have to report back at Cetus' suite daily, but I won't have Pontus watching my every move. I also won't have Cetus waiting in the next room while I change every day.

Is this how it will feel like when I'm on my own? When I can decide my own fate? Scary and exciting at the same time?

* * *

Callisto rolled from her bed to the floor. The first rays of dawn were streaming through gaps in the shuttered window.

She pulled off the loose gown she donned at night, shimmying into the dress she wore in her guise as an archivist's assistant. Even after all these weeks, the feeling of the soft fabric against her skin was new and exciting. So alien to the world of cast-offs and coarse linens she had grown to expect.

The small room which Cetus had arranged for her was only two streets away from the library, cutting down her travel time and affording her more time to peruse the library's stacks – during her excursions at night. It was small, located on the fourth floor of a stonework building. It was an attic room, where the ceiling sloped from the edge to its peak. Callisto had to bend down to avoid hitting her head, and a wooden cross-brace was located halfway across its span. Pontus had negotiated the price down from three to two drachmae per night. She was, after all, staying in what had been intended as a storage room, not a scholar's quarters.

It was nonetheless clean and dry – without the noise of porters shouting in the morning from a warehouse below.

Callisto fastened the hooks which secured her dress. She filled it out more than when she had first arrived. The curve of her hips had become more feminine, and her muscular frame –honed by constant activity – had become better defined.

She glanced at her wardrobe, hanging from hooks on the cross-brace. She still had another clean dress to wear, as well as the wine-red dress which the master seamstress, Danae had so generously gifted to her.

She shook out her shoulders and placed the scarf on her head. Her hair was growing out. She had always kept it cropped short, for almost as long as she had been on her own. She found herself having to brush strands from her face for the first time she could recall.

She cracked the window open, pushing the shutters wide. Outside, the morning air was cool, the sky blue. The scent of the sea and salt, intermingled with the aroma of fresh bread from bakeries below. She could get used to this.

* * *

Callisto turned the page, jotting down notes into her journal. Her writing had become neat and methodical over the past several weeks. She could probably pass as a scribe, should she have chosen to do so.

Her ears picked up Phaeton's familiar footsteps, walking between the bookshelves. He was heading towards her. She looked up from her notes. She had come to expect him. It was around mid-day, after all.

"Hi Mira. Making progress?"

"I've finished my survey and have been circling back to fill out my notes from the earlier volumes."

"Does this mean you'll be leaving soon?" There was a quiet pleading in his voice, as if he knew what the answer was – but didn't want to hear.

"I might be." Her voice was quiet. She didn't want to say the words. But she didn't want him to be surprised when the time came. "I've informed my patron of my progress and am awaiting his reply."

There was a pause. What was he thinking, she wondered? There was a mournful, hurt look in his eyes. He glanced at her notebook, at the list of numbers compiled in neat columns.

"What did you find?" he finally asked. She could tell when someone was struggling to change the topic.

"I've been compiling village names, crop reports, taxes, and census numbers."

"What do they tell you?"

"Each year, each decade, the number of settlements in the empire's census rolls stretches further north, pressing against the wilderness."

"Of course. The march of civilization. Bringing order to chaos. They teach children about it in school."

"Since the founding of the empire, the population of Bateria has increased eight-fold, and the area occupied has increased eighteen-fold."

"That's good, isn't it?"

"The empire has grown, but the rolls of the tax collectors show production has not kept pace with population. The further north they settled, the more rugged the land became. And the less productive."

"Is it a problem?"

"Maybe . . . It's like in the visions of Pythia. The wilderness can only be pushed so far before it begins to push back."

The quiet of the library was abruptly broken by a woman's shriek.

Callisto leapt to her feet, ready to flee or fight. They had come for her! But no, it made no sense.

At the end of the hall, two guards were dragging a woman towards the entrance of the library.

"Let me go! I didn't do anything!"

Her voice was shrill, her arms pinned behind her back. She was wearing a white blouse and navy-blue skirt. A student's uniform! Her scarf was missing, her sandy blonde hair trailing in a loose braid which had come partly undone.

It took Callisto a moment to register who it was. "Cassandra?"

Phaeton gripped Callisto's shoulder, easing her back into her chair. "Try not to notice. We wouldn't want to get involved."

"Stop! I was working for Master Zenodotus! There's been a mistake!" Cassandra was pulling against her captors, trying unsuccessfully to break free.

"What happened?" Callisto whispered, unable to tear her eyes away.

"There were rumors someone had been selling volumes from the archives to foreign buyers."

"But . . . No!"

"Someone suggested Cassandra as being the likely culprit." Someone? Had Phaeton known about this? "Some of the same documents which Cassandra had been requesting turned up missing."

Callisto turned to observe his expression. It was so unlike him. To be so calm, so unperturbed by the raucous cries echoing through the halls. He had known?!

"Phaeton . . . did you?"

"Shhhh! Me? No! I heard of it from the other journeymen. Cassandra had been asking for those volumes on behalf of Neilos. When he was questioned, he turned on her."

"But, but . . . what if she didn't do it?"

"Do you think they'll take her word over a senior journeyman?"

"I thought she was from a noble family."

"A lesser noble family. It won't help her here." There was a somber, pained look in Phaeton's eyes, confirming the hopelessness which seeped into his voice. "I tired to warn her. She wouldn't believe."

"What will happen to her?"

"She'll be taken for interrogation. The sooner she confesses, the easier it will likely be." Phaeton had taken a seat next to her at the table, trying to appear unobtrusive.

"Interrogation?" Callisto's voice came out in a squeak.

"Her family might be able to bribe the right official. Get her out – after the commotion has died down."

"I thought she was collecting works for the Imperial Historian, Master Zenodotus. Surely he'll intervene."

Phaeton frowned, shaking his head. "Zenodotus isn't known for streaks of kindness. He used to take pleasure in punishing apprentices who took too much time in their chores or took too much to eat at the dining hall. Thieves, if that's what she's accused of, receive much worse under his hand. She'd be better off if he didn't intervene."

Chapter 31

Dear grandma,

The empire is a dark, corrupt, evil beast. As quick to devour its own people in its unfeeling machinery as it is to trod-under a neighboring kingdom that's undefended. You already knew this, I'm sure. Each day, I am reminded of it again.

I don't know where I will go when I'm free, but it will be somewhere far away from here.

* * *

Callisto brought her two daggers up, snagging her opponents' sword between them. They were only practice weapons – blunt, heavy and wooden. The shock on the boy's face was nonetheless real. It was all she could do to suppress a smile as she twisted, prying the weapon out of the apprentice's hands.

She leveled a dagger at his throat.

"Thank you, Euthymius." Erebus' deep baritone filled the room. "That will be enough."

Callisto lowered her weapons. Each bowed, ending the match.

"Get cleaned up Euthymius. You know what you'll need to work on this week."

Euthymius bowed again towards their weapons master, then exited the room – leaving Callisto alone with Erebus.

A WOLF BEFORE THE STORM

"You're a natural, young lady. Any weapon I choose is lethal in your hands."

"Thank you, master Erebus."

"You need to be thinking about your future, beyond being a cutpurse for Pontus." Erebus leaned against his cane, his gaze intent. "With a more regular training regimen, you'd be unstoppable."

"Pontus will only let me practice once per week, when the . . . when the imperial offices are closed." It wasn't her place to reveal what robbery Pontus had in mind.

"You could be so much more than a common thief. More than a lockpick or burglar."

"Yes, master."

His voice dropped dangerously low. "You could be someone to make the empire afraid. Make even the emperor take notice."

Callisto let his words settle. "I don't know if I could be a killer," she whispered.

"A member of the Assassins' Guild is more than just a killer. They are not merely a sword-for-hire. There are plenty of those to be had, and they come cheap. A guild member need only take those contracts they want. True, there are plenty enough who select their jobs on the weight of payment alone. But there are also those, like me, who had our own reasons for which contracts to accept. Aristocrats who needed to be cut down. High officials to be eliminated."

"I don't know if I could do it, master. I don't see myself as having the instinct."

"You do, young lady. I've seen it in you. You nearly killed those boys when I found you only three weeks ago."

"They had it coming."

"They aren't the only ones. I'm just telling you." He inhaled, gathering his thoughts, judging her response. "You have the talent, Callisto. The ability to buy the freedom you deserve. You're not the stupid girl Pontus tells you. You're . . ." He stopped himself, waiting as she replaced the practice weapons. "Did I ever tell you about my younger sister, Hemera?"

"No, sir."

"She was a few years younger than me, back when I was a weapons master in the Imperial Army. You probably didn't know that about me, did you? I was a chief weapons master once. I trained noblemen's sons, as well as the elite of the Imperial Guard. That's where I received those silver *kopis* you've seen before. The ones with the wolf-head hilts. It was during an earlier werewolf war. You didn't know, did you?"

"No, sir." Callisto didn't raise her eyes, didn't turn to answer. Had her trainer, her mentor, been one of them? One of those who hunted down and killed her kind? She wasn't sure she could bear knowing.

"They call them werewolf wars, but they weren't really. At least, not like in the early days of the empire. They were an excuse for the emperor to extend and firm his grip over outlying settlements. A chance to settle old scores, eliminate rivals. Did you know that?"

"No, sir."

"I was recruited during one such werewolf war, more than a decade before Emperor Bessarion ascended the throne. I was naïve. I believed in the emperor's call for order. Like so many others. I looked the other way at the excesses, the brutality of the empire's soldiers. The inhuman methods of the inquisitors. It was not my place to question them. I accepted their excuses. How those identified for interrogation must have been guilty. Who knew? Maybe they were. Guilty of trying to eke out a living from this hard and rocky soil. Do you understand what I'm saying?"

"Yes, Master Erebus." The practice weapons had been replaced in their storage cabinets. But Callisto still could not bring herself to face her tutor of so many years. Couldn't let him see her eyes. Had he been one of them?

"I let myself believe their tales, ignored my own ears and eyes. Until, that is, I came home on leave. Came home to discover my sister had been named to the inquisition. Some jealous neighbor, maybe. Some official whose advances she'd refused. It doesn't really matter. She was about your age when it happened."

"I'm sorry," Callisto said, turning at last to look at him. Moisture had found its way to the corners of her eyes, obscuring her view.

"She never stood a chance. Confessed to whatever they demanded of her. By the time I came home, she had been executed according to the law of the land. It was the last day I served as a weapons master in the Imperial Army. I joined the Assassin's Guild, and with my already honed skills, became a first-blade. I vowed I would break the empire's grip at every turn and opportunity. There wasn't an official in the empire I would hesitate to kill. And there were always contracts, always scores to be settled. One nobleman's family or another. I was only sorry I couldn't do more."

There was a painful pause, as her teacher shifted his weight, settling himself slowly onto a bare wooden bench at the edge of the room.

"How much longer before this job of yours with Pontus is done?"

"Not long now." Why were her cheeks wet? What had come over her?

"Remember what I told you. You have the ability to make yourself into something more. When your business with Pontus is done, let me know and we can talk."

* * *

The shadows of the city's walls and buildings had grown long as Callisto made her way from the library. There were so many things running through her mind.

Erebus' words from the previous day. Her disturbing lack of progress towards finding the documents she had been sent to steal. A future which seemed cloudier than ever before.

What if she never found what she had been sent to retrieve? What if it wasn't there? Cetus seemed convinced it would be. Pontus less so. And what happened after? Was Erebus right? Was there a future for her in the Assassins Guild? Was it even the future she wanted?

Each step she took, it seemed her future was farther away than it had been before.

Her step missed a beat, shifting over an uneven stone in the walkway. Her ears perked up. Footsteps. A steady pattern. Nearly matching her pace, step-for-step. Behind her.

Who could it be? Had the cult found her again?

She turned down an adjacent street, careful not to look back, not to let on. She heard the pattern of the footsteps, still following, turning where she turned.

Her heart's pace quickened. She couldn't lead them back to her room. She had no weapons on her. Not even her knife. The streets of the imperial city were already emptying. Only a few shop keeps remained, still sweeping their entrances or closing their stores. Whomever it was would probably make their move soon.

Another street. She turned – and immediately flattened herself against a wall, hiding in the shadows. She feared whoever was following would surely hear her heart race. It was so loud in her ears.

The side street was vacant. If she was going to face them, whomever it was, now was the time. She listened as the footsteps drew nearer. Her muscles tensed, ready to spring. She imagined where her feet should be placed, readied her hands for the blows which would fall.

A figure rounded the corner, their face half-hidden in shadow. Callisto stepped forward, ready to pounce. She could already see it in her mind. A strike to the head, then to the groin. She inhaled, scenting the wind, muscles ready – then froze. Her stance wide, ready to strike. But the scent. She knew this scent.

"Phaeton?!"

He jumped back, startled by her sudden emergence. "Mira?"

"You were following me?"

"I didn't see you at lunch today."

"I was cross-referencing records from the second floor."

"I, well . . . I wanted to ask," he inhaled, gathering himself. "Would you join me for dinner? This Thursday? At . . . at my father's house?"

"You're inviting me to your family's estate?"

"No . . . I mean yes. Sort of. Just my father's home in the city. There won't be any other family members present. Just my father and I."

Callisto felt the blood rush to her cheeks. She was only grateful he couldn't see her blush in the dim light.

"Would you? Come that is?"

Chapter 32

Dear grandma,
A boy invited me to meet his family. A human boy. It's not something I'd ever thought I'd be telling you. If he knew who I was, what I was, I'm certain he'd shrink away in fear. But he doesn't know. And he likes me. I know it's an impossible arrangement. Just a dream I've been living, really. But it's been such a sweet dream.

* * *

"It all sounds very suspicious," Pontus said. "Why would the boy invite her to his father's home? What's his ploy?"

"Obviously, he has taken an interest in the girl," Cetus said, stroking his beard thoughtfully. "You never know when a contact, or informant, might prove useful."

"Why would he be interested in her? Maybe he suspects something. Could be looking to blackmail us."

"Don't be ridiculous, Pontus. If he had suspicions, he could report them to the imperial officials."

"It's very unusual. She's just a common street rat, after all. As far as the boy is aware, she's a peasant from the north. She wouldn't even have anything to wear to a formal dinner."

"Yes I do." Callisto was surprised to hear the sound of her own voice. She had been standing at the edge of the room, opposite where Cetus sat, and Pontus paced.

Pontus halted, turning to face her. "How would a common rag of a thief have a formal dress? Have you been holding out on me?"

"Danae sent me the dress, when she sent the others."

"Did I pay for this?!" Pontus took a step closer, raising his voice.

"You paid for what you agreed to pay," Cetus replied. "If Danae delivered something more, it's her business. Sometimes she takes a liking to people."

"I can assure you, she took no liking to me," Pontus said.

"Obviously," Cetus replied.

* * *

Callisto stood nervously on the steps. She felt very much out of place, the wine-red fabric hugging her hips and accentuating the curves she didn't know she had. She felt exposed without the scarf over her head. She ran her fingers across her hair. No, it was still tucked tightly into its clip.

Steps led up to the front entrance. Marble columns on either side supported an awning. It looked more like a temple to some lesser god than the entrance to a home.

She reached up to the knocker, its polished brass surface sculpted into the shape of a bull, with a ring piercing its nose. Its tone as she brought the knocker down was deep. It echoed from within, as if the space beyond was wide and vaulted.

The door opened and a young woman stood before her. A servant, judging by her simple, dark attire. She was a few years older than Callisto.

"Can I help you?" the young woman asked in an officious manner.

"I'm Mira. . . I was invited by Phaeton?"

Phaeton all but shoved the poor servant girl off the stairs as he came rushing to the door. His eyes were fixed on Callisto.

"Mira, you look . . . amazing."

A smile crossed her lips as Phaeton led her inside. A hot flash rushed across her cheeks. She knew she must have been as red as her dress.

The ceiling of the entryway was vaulted above them, lined with columns of white marble and painted with scenes from legend. Phaeton led her to a side chamber with a long dining table. It seemed very much out of place and empty, with a chair at one end and two smaller chairs on either side. Phaeton drew a chair back, offering her a seat.

Her breath caught. No one had ever offered her this courtesy before. Her, a common street rag, being treated like a lady. Her face tingled as she sat down. He slid her seat in and took the opposite chair.

Phaeton was wearing a black vest over his white shirt, its buttons freshly polished. He still had a youthful charm about him, although his shoulders were beginning to fill out.

"Sorry if my father is late. He's always busy with something or another. Did you have any problem finding the place?"

"No. No problem." Callisto suppressed a smile. She had noted the row of large homes along this same street during her first tour of the imperial city – a detail she thought better not to share. She had taken mental notes at the time, observing likely entry and exit points, assessing how easily an expert burglar might enter or leave. She decided it was wise not to share that information either. "Have you always lived here?"

"No. I grew up on our family's estate. It's about a day's journey from here. My oldest brother manages the manor in my father's absence. My father bought this house for his business in the imperial city."

The door opened and Phaeton rose. There was an obvious family resemblance, although his father was slightly taller, with a trimmed grey mustache. He wore a dark vest in a rich velvet fabric with silver needlework along its edges. Callisto followed Phaeton's example, attempting to play the suitably demur researcher's aide.

She could feel the tension rise as Phaeton's father entered. The waitstaff at the edges of the room came to stiff attention. Even Phaeton drew himself up, trying to appear taller. His father's eyes scanned the room, pausing for only a moment on her, before sliding off and to the side – as if she were hardly worthy of his regard.

The patriarch seated himself, and the two servants who had been standing behind him sprang into motion, bringing him a cloth napkin and setting a bowl of stew before him. Phaeton settled into his seat, and Callisto did likewise. The servants hastened to bring bowls to the two of them as Phaeton's father blew on the steaming hot broth. Scents of lamb, herbs and barley ascended from the bowls.

"Father, this is Mira, the girl I told you about. Mira, this is Damianus, my father."

"Pleased to meet you," Callisto replied.

Phaeton's father finished his first taste of the broth, wiping his lips before speaking. "I remember. The one you said was here on behalf of a patron from Symru. What would a nobleman from Symru be seeking from the archives of the empire?"

"I work for the honorable Lord Larkin, of Southfold," Callisto replied. "He has assigned me to collect records from the empire's first century."

"Records? To what end?" Phaeton's father slurped another spoonful of soup, his eyes never rising to meet hers.

"He has a fascination with the era of the early empire, as well as with the legends and lore of the time."

"Mira is something of an expert on stories of the destroyer," Phaeton added.

"The fables of the destroyer, you mean." Phaeton's father looked up from his meal to regard Phaeton. "I'm surprised anyone would pay to hear such fanciful tales."

"The oracles of Pythia," Callisto replied, "foretold the expansion of the human realm into the wilderness centuries before it happened."

"The expansion of the empire was inevitable. Anyone could have predicted it." Damianus turned his gaze towards her for the first time since they'd sat down.

"More than a century before the empire arose?"

"Men have always striven towards the establishment of order. To expand their command over the natural elements."

"Not all of nature can be tamed."

"In time, all of the wilderness will fall under the empire's dominion."

"Even the werewolves?" Phaeton cut in.

"Even the werewolves," Damianus answered. He finished his soup, pushing the plate away. "I'm always surprised by the fanciful interests of the landed gentry from overseas."

A servant stepped forward to take his bowl, while another brought a covered tray with the next course. The scents of vegetables, meats and herbs arose from it. Was that beef? The stew had been thick with lamb as it was. In Callisto's experience, even among the merchant class, it was rare to have more than one meat dish served in a single meal.

"That will be all," Damianus replied to the servant, wiping his hands on his napkin. "If you'll excuse me, I have business to attend to."

He pushed his chair back from the table, leaving his napkin in his chair, and exited the room.

"I'm sorry," Phaeton said to her, rising from his seat. "I'll be back in a moment."

A WOLF BEFORE THE STORM

Phaeton followed his father out of the room, leaving Callisto alone with the servants. She sipped at her soup, wondering if she had somehow erred. Should she not have spoken when Phaeton's father had asked the question? The demur researcher's aide was not a role which came easily to her.

The voices from the next room were muffled, carrying Phaeton's plaintive tones and his father's stern reply. It was doubtful any of the servants could have made out what was said. But then, they weren't werewolves.

"Father? I thought you'd be eating with us."

She was careful to maintain her composure, stirring and sipping quietly, listening in on their conversation.

"I have work to attend to, son. You . . . and your friend can finish without me."

She kept her eyes down, on her meal, absently stirring the stew, resisting the urge to glance at the servers.

"Dad, I thought you'd –"

"Phaeton, you're the youngest. You don't have the responsibilities of your brothers. Which is why I've indulged you for so long. You can do whatever you want with her. Find whatever uses she might have. Just don't expect me to approve. She's beneath your station."

"Father –"

"Don't embarrass me, Phaeton. Not again. You association with that crank of a tutor nearly cost me my license as an exporter."

"He was a scholar, father. Not a crank. A master at the academy."

"He was a heretic! A purveyor of subversive blasphemy."

"The empire is not above question. Just because we conquer something –"

"That!" Phaeton's father held the angry tone. Callisto could feel the strain in the server staff, their bodies stiffening in reaction. "That is precisely why he found himself beneath an executioner's axe." Damianus had lowered his voice again. There was a dangerous note in his speech. "Do whatever you want with this tart. I promise you; I won't let your missteps threaten your brother's inheritance."

The footsteps of Phaeton's father receded deeper into the house. Callisto blinked, trying to beat back the moisture which pressed against her eyes.

It was true. All of it. She and Phaeton came from different worlds. She had known this all along. Had never expected anything different. It was only, when he was kind to her, she had let herself imagine . . .

Beneath his station? If he only knew.

The faces of the servants remained stoic, giving no hint if they had understood what had transpired in the adjoining room. They wouldn't have had Callisto's hearing. But they would have heard the tone. The rocky relationship between Phaeton and his father was no doubt well known.

Phaeton returned; his face flushed. "I'm sorry, my father always seems to have some urgent business he needs to attend." He sat across from her, his eyes dropping to his lap.

"I understand," Callisto replied. "He must be a very busy man."

Chapter 33

Dear grandma,

Sometimes we acknowledge things only reluctantly. Even when we know something was just a dream. Even when the impossibility of it was obvious. It can still hurt to admit what could never be.

* * *

"A curious development," Cetus remarked. "It seems the boy Phaeton is at odds with his father. I wonder who else he might associate with."

Callisto had faithfully described her experience at Phaeton's family home. She left out only the conversation in the next room which she hadn't been meant to overhear.

"I fail to understand how this helps our task at the Imperial Library." Pontus was pacing the room, uneasy as always.

"Maybe not," Cetus was stroking his beard. "I've done some investigating. The boy's father has become something of a market speculator in Polonia, leveraging his family's land holdings to invest in merchant ships bound for the spice trade. It's something he knows little about, other than the promise of riches. He appears to be quite the risk taker. He gambled his family's fortune on a long-distance trade enterprise not too long ago. It could have resulted in utter ruin. He's only been fortunate none of his investments have been lost at sea. At least not yet."

"Sounds impulsive," Pontus replied. "Like the boy."

"I would agree. Once he hears there is a potential fortune to be made, he's apparently willing to gamble everything – betting there's an even bigger fortune ahead. Perhaps the boy's rebellion could be used as leverage."

Pontus halted his pacing to consider. "You really think the boy is that rebellious?"

"He did bring a peasant girl to see his father."

"Yes, I can see how it might work. After we recover the materials from the library, we could use the boy's impulsiveness to extort a price. Lure him into a compromising situation."

Callisto stood at the edge of the room, horrified. She had allowed others to make her decisions throughout most of her life. Where to go. What to steal.

She had no intention of staying around a single day after her task at the library was complete and her debt paid off. She certainly would not be helping them to extort money from Phaeton's family.

* * *

Callisto slid the tome back into place, aligning its textured cover with the neighboring volumes. The scent of the pages, the feeling of the leather against her skin was a welcome relief from the day.

The magical archives were dark and quiet. The solitude suited her. Time to herself. Time to think – or not think, as the case might be.

She drew out the next volume. It was a thin book, but with a large, oversized cover. Book of Visions? The title on the face of it didn't sound promising. There was no author listed.

She opened it up. At first, it seemed she was looking at a blank page. Then movement. Were the shadows playing tricks on her eyes? But no, there were lines on the page, drawn in dark ink. An illustration? Depicting a young girl in a cloak, with a hood drawn over her head. The illustration moved! The girl was walking down a lane carrying a satchel over her shoulder. Did she know this girl? Wait! Was there something following her? Yes! A person. A woodsman – with an axe, stalking her.

The ink drawings emerged out of the blank page before her eyes, moving across as if some unseen hand were drawing them as she watched.

The image of the girl turned, revealing a face beneath the hood for the first time. But not a girl's face. A wolf's face! Snarling up at her from the page!

Callisto slammed the book shut and replaced it on the shelf. She hated it when wizards had a sense of humor. She had found a couple of similar volumes before, all enchanted, all equally useless.

She sulked back to her notebook; the room illuminated by a single lamp. Another row of shelves completed, and no closer to tracking down her quarry. There were only a few more shelves left. What had she missed? Why hadn't she found what she had been sent to recover?

The night-time solitude of the library's magical annex suited her mood. She had seen Phaeton over lunch the previous day, but there had been a distance between them. A silence surrounding the subject of his father which neither of them had dared to broach. They had both tried to ignore it. But his embarrassment was still fresh, and her injury still raw.

It wasn't Phaeton's fault, she knew. There was no denying, however, the gulf between them. The chasm which had been reemphasized. Soon, she would either succeed in finding the documents she had been sent to recover or fail and be sent back to Centrola. In either instance, she would be unlikely to see him again. The two of them came from different worlds and lived in different realities. She could not expect to be accepted in his. It would not be safe for him in hers.

She flipped absently through the pages of her journal; the individual rows of the magical annex described in painstaking detail. Most of the volumes had proven elusive to her. Some were in languages she could only guess. She had been able to identify the flowing script of the fae easily enough, but there were others completely alien. Even those which had been penned in Baterian or in the common tongue were often beyond her reach, written in an esoteric fashion filled with symbolism. None of them had featured the names of either Gnotrix, or his apprentice Herrick.

What had she missed? Should she explore the adjoining room? The one Phaeton had said was used to store discarded, esoteric magical items? There was something about the other door which made her uneasy. She could hear sounds from it. Scratching, as if from rats – but more persistent. And murmurs. Too faint for human ears. Maybe she should open the door, just to see . . .

But no, here was where any writings should be kept. A journal was not a magical item.

So many volumes. So many ramblings or secret languages and codes. Still, there were a few volumes she had been able to appreciate. A few . . . like pages from a faded dream.

She strode to a familiar section of the library shelves. Even without bringing the lantern, she could easily find the volume she was seeking. The sixth shelf on the right, a large tome. She did not need the lantern to know its leather cover had been dyed a rich burgundy hue.

She drew it from the shelf, thumbing through the pages. The Prophesies of Pythia. Remembering again the passage, remembering how proud Phaeton had been to show it to her. Some wild things could not be tamed.

The texture of the binding, the scent of the ink on the page. Memories she would take with her. Memories – the only things she had ever been able to keep. She traced her fingers fondly across the pages. She could feel emotions welling up. It was a sweet dream. But she needed to stop indulging herself.

As she went to slide the tome back onto the shelf, something fell. Something – a scrap of parchment from between the pages. She bent to pick it up. At the top was written, "Collected writings of Herrick and correspondence from Gnotrix, two volumes." Beneath it was written, "Reserved for Master Zenodotus, delivered to Burcsteli." It was dated from six months earlier.

Chapter 34

Dear grandma,

Now it comes to an end. I've found what I was sent for, or at least where to find it. I was working for this day, longing for it. Now that it's here, why does it seem so melancholy? If I've won, why does my heart still dwell on what I've lost?

* * *

"It was there this whole time, locked away on the empire's island fortress." Pontus was pacing the room, a scowl across his lips. "Here we were wasting our time, while my lockpick dawdled away her hours."

"It was information unknown outside of these walls," Cetus said, leaning back in his chair. He was stroking the beard at his chin. "I doubt even Zenodotus is fully aware of the significance."

"Not that it matters," Pontus bemoaned. "It's beyond our reach. The island is an impenetrable fortress."

"It's not so impenetrable," Callisto blurted out. As their eyes turned to her, she realized her mistake. "I mean, I've seen the floor plan, from when they built the island. It was in the archive's records."

"You're sure you could slip through their defenses?" Cetus said, a thoughtful look on his face. "Would you even know where they might store something rare and valuable like this?"

"The administrative offices were in the tower. They'd be the only rooms fit for a nobleman like Zenodotus."

Cetus was deep in thought, considering the possibilities. Pontus, however, had fixed her in his icy stare. He had to have guessed. She had been there before. It was no accident she knew the arrangement of the island.

"Do you really think you could penetrate a well-guarded fortress like that?" Cetus said, an eager glint in his eyes. "They would be on alert, after the werewolf escape a few weeks ago. . . . Then again, their escape has already proven there are holes in their defenses."

Pontus was glancing between Callisto and Cetus. Was he nervous Cetus would also guess her secret? But no, Cetus was too consumed with visions of payment and riches to weigh such a remote possibility. Why would a common thief be involved with the escape of two werewolves?

"I'm willing to do it," Callisto said. "The payoff, being free of my debts, would be worth it."

"Then it's settled," Cetus said. "What tools will you need? Hooks? Rope? You can let your . . . acquaintances at the library know you've been recalled by your master in Southfold."

"She's still going to the library?" Pontus said in surprise.

"If she were to just disappear, it would arouse suspicion. Better to have them think she's been recalled with her notes."

* * *

"You're leaving? So soon?" The deflated look in Phaeton's eyes reminded her of a puppy which had a bone snatched away.

"Lord Larkin has recalled me."

She had waited until they were seated outside to tell him. Somewhere they could talk more freely, and unobserved. Sitting next to him now, in the outside air, she tried to frame a picture in her mind. The wavy locks of his hair. His dark, gentle eyes. One last image, to last her a lifetime.

"Why can't you stay? You could find a job in the city. Another patron would be sure to value your skills. A lot of girls can't even read."

"I'm an indentured servant, Phaeton. I'm under bond until my debt is paid off. If I tried to escape, I could be dragged into prison, or worse."

A silence settled between them. There was really nothing else to say. The two of them came from such different worlds. His would never accept her. Hers was not safe for him.

She knew she had to go through with this, had to tell him. It was the right thing to do. Why did it hurt so bad?

"You were the first girl I'd ever met, who could speak so freely," he said. "Who cared about lore and history and didn't back away from what she thought. I just . . . I just didn't think it would end."

She placed her hand on his. "I enjoyed our time here, for however brief it was. You were a good friend, Phaeton."

Chapter 35

Dear grandma,

In a few hours, it will all be over. I will be successful and free of my debts, or I will be caught, and my life will be ended. So many thoughts and emotions running through me now. So many might have beens.

I must set them aside. I only have time for the here and now. The focus I need to do the job and keep myself alive.

* * *

Callisto drew the lightweight dress over her darker thief's garments. It would be easier to reach the dockyard dressed as a peasant girl than to wait for the sun to set and take to the alleyways then.

She had already rolled her belongings into her bedroll and folded her fitted dresses for storage or transport. Where would she go when this was all over? She didn't know. But it would be a shame to leave the dresses behind. They were the first, and only tailored clothes she'd ever worn. She'd have to find a way to bring them with her.

She glanced around the bare room she had stayed in for the past couple of weeks. There was nothing here which could be mistaken for a home. No furniture. Only a worn, spare mattress and bed. Her folded-up clothing lay on top of it. Rented space. A rented existence.

Nonetheless, she felt like she would miss this place. Miss her time here. No sounds of laborers coming through the floorboards below. No shouts in the city street of people being robbed or stabbed in the night. And the library, only a few streets away.

She tucked her hair beneath a scarf, then locked the door behind her. She followed the stairwell down to the street below. Her steps were swift, purposeful. After tonight, it would all be over. Pontus would have his journal and letters, and whatever fortune it sold for. She would have her freedom. Either that, or . . . no, she couldn't think of it. Failure was not something she could afford to contemplate.

As she came down to the foot of the stairs and out, into the street, she saw him.

"Phaeton?" Had he followed her from the library? How long had he been standing there?

He was still dressed in his Imperial Library uniform, with its white shirt and grey vest. It was cool this evening, with clouds gathering on the western horizon. He really should have been wearing a jacket this time of day. His eyes were red, tired. His shirt, usually tucked neatly beneath his vest and belt, was wrinkled and unkept. His collar was unbuttoned and ajar.

"Mira, I was . . . You're not leaving now, are you?"

"I have errands to run."

"I wanted to talk. I know my father can be difficult, but I can persuade him. He could intervene, find a local nobleman who might buy your contract from Lord Larkin. I left him a letter –"

"Phaeton, I have to go." She stood, facing him at the edge of the street. A carriage rolled by. Students from the academy paused, glancing their way. They were too much in the open, too exposed. She couldn't afford to be having this discussion. Not here, not now.

"If you'll let me talk with him, give me another day –"

She gripped his hands in hers. "Phaeton, I have to go. I don't leave until tomorrow. We can talk then. I have to run errands tonight. Please understand."

She turned, adjusting the satchel over her shoulders. It was heavy with her tools and a long coil of rope. She headed down, towards the docks. There was a painful pressure behind her eyes, a pressure she attempted to wipe away as she turned the corner. It was all she could do to keep herself from looking back.

If she had, she might have seen a young man in a tussled white shirt and grey vest. He had a forlorn look on his face, as if searching for something he had lost. Something he had needed to say. He waited, despondent, until she had disappeared around the corner. Pulling himself from his reverie, he finally mustered his courage – and followed her.

* * *

"We'll be waiting for you here," Cetus said, as Callisto adjusted her dark hood. "Do you know where to find the rowboat you'll need?"

"The imperial fleet has several skiffs available at any time." Callisto replied. "They're usually moored at the lower docks or tethered to the larger ships."

"Do you have everything you need? Hooks? More rope?"

"The rope I have is fine." She wouldn't be using the hooks or rope – but she couldn't very well tell him that.

She adjusted the dagger at her hip, drawing her satchel of tools over her head. Cetus had arranged for a warehouse in the imperial city to be made available to them. It was in the tax assessor's district, where high-end luxury goods were usually impounded until they had paid their full import duties.

The air was filled with the scents of exotic spices, imported liquor, and seasoned wood. Crates were neatly arranged, bearing the names of distant ports of origin. Callisto had no idea whom Cetus knew or had bribed to have a whole warehouse this close to the imperial dockyards vacated for their use.

"Just make sure you come straight here with those journals," Pontus said. "No detours to look them over or deposit sections for safe keeping. I'll be keeping an eye on you. Make sure you don't forget."

He was wearing a new coat. One which better fit his alibi as a foreign trade broker. It was still too long for this time of year. He had likely sewn extra pockets to hide his assortment of knives and daggers. She knew from experience. His knives were always close at hand.

"Of course not," Callisto replied. She turned towards the door. She couldn't wait for the night to be over, to be rid of Pontus' paranoia and accusations.

She glanced outside. The sun had set. Long shadows were cast from the light of the moon, still low in the sky. Taras was standing watch near the entrance, his head barely shifting as she made her way past him, outside, and down the alleyway. When she glanced over her shoulder, she saw Pontus stepping out through the same narrow, side entrance. He would probably be pacing until her return, fretting about getting his full share.

The lower dockyards were deserted this time of night. It was the imperial city, after all, and the outer walls were well guarded. No one imagined a thief might make it this deep into the empire's inner sanctum. Only a few docks down, the great warships of the imperial navy were moored, a visible deterrent to any would-be intruder. Sailors hung about their decks, talking noisily. She could hear the murmur of their voices, even from this distance.

Callisto made her way down a sturdy dock with rowboats moored to either side. The dock was tall, built high above the water, providing space for larger ships to be moored. She'd have to climb down a ladder to reach the smaller boats below.

She paused, listening. Only the gentle ripple of the waves and current answered her. She lowered herself down to the skiff, loosened the moorings and was off, her strong strokes pulling her away from shore.

Her eyes scanned the decks of the big naval warships, where lanterns hung and watchmen paced. Ahead was the dark outline of the island fortress of Burcsteli.

Her eyes were intent upon the warships and their sailors. She had not noticed the young man who had followed her from the warehouse. Did not see as he came to the edge of the dock. His white shirt and grey vest were bright in the moonlight, as he peered into the darkness, perplexed. She had not noticed him, nor the second, taller, lean figure who followed him.

Chapter 36

Callisto clung to the outer wall, waiting. She was hanging on the shadowed side of the tower, listening as the guards on the wall below made their rounds.

The guard detail had become more businesslike, more frequent than the last time she had been there. The patrols were more closely spaced, and they made their rounds in pairs instead of alone. Below her, the courtyard was brightly illuminated. It had been dark during her prior visit. If she had meant to reach the prison cells at the far end of the courtyard, unnoticed, she would have been hard pressed to do so. Fortunately, this was not her aim on this night.

Her toes and fingers ached. Her claws had found grips in the stone, but she was unused to the steady strain. She forced her mind to relax, to focus on the task ahead, blocking out any momentary discomfort.

The guards on the wall below moved past. If she remained in the shadow of the tower, they were unlikely to spy her. To get to the window she needed to enter, however, she would have to climb across the inner face of the tower, where it was illuminated from below.

She had been counting her breaths, gaging the space between the regular patrols. A large part of a thief's success was patience. Once the guards moved past, there shouldn't be another patrol near this part of the wall for at least half a dozen minutes. She waited for them to pass out of earshot. Only when they had crossed to the stairway leading down, towards the inner courtyard, did she scramble across the face of the wall.

From what she had memorized of the tower floor plans, the wall facing outwards, towards the sea, largely hosted guard posts. They were arranged at neat intervals along a winding stairwell, with slots cut for archers or ballistae. They provided a clear view of any ships approaching from the sea.

The inner side of the tower, however, housed administrative quarters and had larger windows. It was one such window which she intended to slide through. It was open and lit from within, but she had heard nothing stir in the time she had been waiting. At least not from this window. Still, there was a risk the room was not fully vacant. She had no other choice but to find out.

The guards patrolling the wall reached the staircase, and she sprang into motion. She scrambled across the tower's face like some dark spider, swinging herself through the window. She landed in a crouch on the wooden floor. The boards were smooth and warm against her toes and fingertips. She paused to listen and take in her surroundings. Slowly, painfully, her fingers and toes reverted to their human form. Her claws retracted. Her bare feet shrank. Her heels settling onto the floor.

From the floor plans she had memorized, this would be the largest room in the tower. It was lit by two lanterns housed in recesses in the walls. A fire burned low on the far side of the room.

On one side was a large table with six chairs. A flask of wine and two cups sat at the edge, but any food had long since been cleared. At the opposite side was a desk and chair, piled with documents, books and writing materials.

There were two doors, one each on opposite sides of the room. The one to the right, she knew, would lead to the kitchen and servants' quarters below.

The walls of the room were covered by an alternating sequence of maps and bookshelves. Small tables and display stands were decorated with rarities gathered from across the empire and distant lands. Statues of heroes in poses drawn from legend. Paintings of the first rulers who had founded the empire. Stuffed birds embalmed and frozen in a death stare. Skulls, both human and goblin. Snakes and reptiles of all sizes and colors, their stiff bodies mounted on branches for display.

For a human, the display was no doubt intended to impress with its wealth and extravagant breadth. A chronicle of an empire which had grown to encompass territory three or four times the breadth of any neighboring kingdom. Jewels adorned ornaments and headdresses stolen from far-away lands. Gold and silver writing utensils were displayed prominently on the desk.

To Callisto, however, the room was rank from the skulls, hides and entombed bodies which adorned its displays. It was a revolting menagerie of death.

The bookshelves, however, were what she was there for. There were four of them, stretching more than twice her height, and anchored to the walls. It could take hours to comb through them all.

It was only as she stepped further into the room, however, that she saw it: sitting beneath a clear glass dome. A hand, covered in dark fur. It was attached to a display stand by the base of its severed forearm. It was embalmed, frozen like a clawed menace. A werewolf's hand. Irus' hand.

She couldn't have said how long she stood there; her breath caught in her throat. If she had not been so stunned, so distracted, so revolted, she might have heard the footsteps sooner. As it was, the door on the near side of the room was already unlatched and groaning open before she realized someone else was there.

Chapter 37

The door to the study opened, and an old man with grey hair stared in – as surprised to see her standing there as Callisto was to see him. He held a lantern in one hand, a sheaf of papers in the other. He had a long grey beard and wore a rich dark vest with baggy trousers. A golden chain hung around his neck.

Any hesitation Callisto might have had about killing an old man had evaporated when she had seen her kin's embalmed foreclaw. She sprang, a snarl on her lips as she drew her dagger.

The old man cried out only once, before her dagger drove up and into his chest, piercing his heart in a single stroke. He fell backwards beneath her rush. Across the floor, the metal lantern clattered.

Callisto was poised over him, her breathing still heavy, listening to see if the noise had drawn any attention. Her strike had been swift and precise. He had died instantly. No armor or weapons to shield him. From within, part of her raged – it had been too swift. It should have been longer, taken more. The rage. To feel her jaws crushing his bones. Her claws tearing his skin. He deserved to suffer.

There was no sound from the floors below. It was late and the servants who managed the kitchen or cleaned the rooms would have been fast asleep.

He stared blankly up, hi shirt and tunic stained with his own blood. A pendant hung from the golden chain on his neck. It was set with a red jewel in the center of a sunburst pattern. The imperial seal of Bateria. The inscription around the edges read, "Empire of Bateria," and beneath it, "History is Written." History . . . so this would be Zenodotus, the imperial historian. This was the man whom she had seen from the closet of the guard house. The one who had been carrying Irus' severed hand.

History is written . . . a twisted, corrupt retelling stained with the blood of its many victims.

She set the lantern upright. No sense in starting a fire from which she couldn't escape. She was here for a reason. The sooner she finished her task the sooner she could be out of this cursed place.

She stalked about the room; the wood of the floor smooth beneath her bare feet. She had to be long gone before daybreak. Before his body was found. Was there any rhyme or organization to the bookshelves? Reviewing all their contents would take hours, maybe days. She didn't have hours to spare.

The bookshelf immediately behind the desk appeared to contain writing supplies and newly penned volumes. The acrid scent of fresh ink was strongest here. She glanced over the volume laid out on the table, the letters still drying. "For the glorious advancement of the empire – " So began the line of text on the page. These were the histories Zenodotus was tasked with creating. Reimagined histories which would become official dogma. The tale of how the wilderness had been subjugated under to the emperor's hand.

She gripped the volume, hurling it across the room – into the fireplace. Flames licked its pages, its edges curling black as it was consumed. Glorious indeed.

The next bookcase appeared to be devoted to maps and travelogues from naval officers, merchants and explorers. Perhaps what she was seeking could be found there . . . but it seemed unlikely. These bindings were too recent, too fresh.

She continued to the next two bookcases. As near as she could tell, they were an eclectic collection of reference materials from across the history of the empire. Scanning across the spines, she could spot tomes from the earliest days of the empire as well as recent reports from expeditions to the east. It might take hours to make sense of it all, but this was the most likely place to look. The journals she was seeking would be over two centuries old. They could be anywhere in this convoluted collection.

A muffled sound caught her attention. Was there someone else there? No, it was too faint to be in the same room. From the floor plans she had memorized, she knew the inner wall of the room should adjoin and separate the administrative residence from the outer defenses of the tower. Was the noise coming from the other side? Had she alerted guards when she had killed the old man? He had cried out – just that once.

She swiveled her head around, trying to locate any hint of movement. No. She was hearing it through the open doorway. The one where Zenodotus still lay in his own blood.

She crossed over the body, drawing her dagger once more. There was a narrow hallway with a door on one side, and another at the far end. From the floorplans, the door on the right should lead to a bed chamber or study. Behind the door at the far end, there should be a stairwell, leading down to what had once been a private storeroom or wine cellar. She listened. The muffled sound came from the door at the end of the hall. Someone breathing? No. Sobbing.

Callisto pulled the door open. A fume of noxious chemicals ascended, burning her sinuses. The scents reminded her of a tannery, where animal hides were stripped and preserved. She drew her hood up, drawing its corner across her face, trying to filter the noxious odor. She made her way cautiously down. The stonework of the steps was cold against her bare feet.

It was a long, winding descent. The malodorous fume of the bark astringents almost drowned out the other scents reaching her nose: dried blood and urine.

When she had been listening from the watch-room closet weeks before, Zenodotus had bragged about how he had an expert embalmer on staff. Was this what she had found? Was this where he preserved his trophies for display?

At the bottom of the stairwell was another door, lantern light visible from beneath. She braced herself. There was no way of knowing what was on the other side. One, or many. Armed, or unawares.

She pulled the door open, knife in hand, ready to spring or flee.

Dark stains on the floor marked where wine racks had once stood. Bottles and vats filled with brackish liquids lined the wall. A spotted cat, partially mounted, was perched on a tree branch. It was missing only its glass eyes to make it complete – its empty sockets gaping blankly. Knives and tools had been arranged across a table.

In the center of the room was a stool, with chains and bindings for restraining subjects. It took a moment for Callisto to realize the figure lashed, face-down across the stool, was still alive. A slight figure – with long blonde hair. Her dirty dress was a mass of rent rags which hung about her shoulders. She drew back, whimpering as the door opened, straining against the chains which bound her wrists. Welts and red marks striped her back and shoulders. Her wrists were scored from the manacles which bound them.

The whimpering turned to a wail as the girl's eyes locked on the drawn dagger in Callisto's hand.

Callisto froze. The face! Despite the tangled hair and welt-scarred skin, she knew the face! Cassandra.

Chapter 38

Callisto lowered herself into a crouch, feet spread, ready to strike. It was not Cassandra's wail which had captured her attention, but the figure standing several feet behind her.

He was a young man, his dark hair and beard contrasting with his pale grey vest. His eyebrows were raised in surprise at Callisto's presence. There was a long, wicked looking blade in his hand.

She had seen his face once before. A journeyman at the imperial archives, calling for Cassandra. Neilos!

Callisto sprang, racing across the room. She leaped past where Cassandra was chained against the bench. The young journeyman had just enough time to bring his blade up before she reached him.

"Zenodotus?!" he shouted.

Callisto's dagger swatted across his weapon. It was a heavy blade, better suited as a meat cleaver than a weapon for combat.

Neilos swung at her, bringing his blade down as she sprang out of the way.

"Zenodotus!"

He had an advantage in reach over her. It wasn't just his arms which were longer. Is was his blade as well.

But he was inexperienced, at least when facing an armed foe. She let him bring his blade down, opening himself up. She drew her dagger across his arm. He yelped as her blade sliced through his skin.

He raised his hand, lashing out at her again. He was lunging towards the table, where more knives and implements lay.

Callisto brought her leg across, sweeping his leg out from under him. He stumbled, and she drove her dagger home – its blade plunging into his chest.

She yanked it free and stepped back as Neilos slumped lifeless, face-down before her.

Cassandra was still whimpering. The girl's back was towards them, her bindings preventing her from seeing over her shoulder. To her, it was just a terrifying cascade of sound. She was ignorant of everything which had happened.

As she wiped her dagger clean, Callisto took in her surroundings. A range of whips and knives had been laid out on the table. On the wall, long tresses of hair hung – most of them blonde or red in color.

Long blonde hair. The woman whose body had washed ashore. The one Phaeton had told her about. Zenodotus had been the killer? He must have been. Everyone had blamed it on werewolves.

Callisto sheathed her dagger. Cassandra was still wailing. The wine cellar had been converted into Zenodotus' personal torture chamber and trophy room. It was deep enough in the natural rock of the island to insulate most sounds and screams. Those few guards or servants who did hear anything would have known not to ask further. It was no wonder Zenodotus had chosen to reside on this desolate rock. Here he was free to pursue his perverse desires without interruptions.

What was she to do with Cassandra? Carry her out the window, slung over her shoulder? That wasn't practical. She couldn't leave her either. Callisto's eyes searched among the implements on the table. Knives. Pliers. There! A key!

Callisto adjusted her hood, keeping her face in the shadows. The less Cassandra knew, the better it would be for both. She leaned across, gripping Cassandra's wrist. Cassandra pulled away, her wails intensifying.

"Quiet, child." Callisto had partially transformed her lips and throat – extending her larynx, giving her voice a lower pitch. It came out as all but a growl.

Cassandra stopped her wailing. Callisto unlocked the manacle binding her wrist.

"Stay quiet, and you'll live." Callisto unlocked the second manacle. "Is there anyone else here?"

"Zenodotus. Is he –"

"He won't be coming back." Callisto spat out the words, the anger still fresh in her voice.

Callisto rose from her crouch. Cassandra was shivering, drawing the rags of her dress across her shoulders to cover herself.

"Stay here," Callisto growled.

She scaled the stairs again, drawing her dagger as she approached the top. She had to be sure there weren't any others. She passed through the door, into the hallway. Zenodotus' body was lying at the other end, where she had left it.

She pushed the side door open, prepared to pounce on whomever might be lurking within. It was a bedchamber, the posts of the bed supporting a dark canopy. A table sat to one side, with a platter of half-eaten meats and exotic fruit. Two wine cups and a pitcher sat beside them. There was another, smaller table on the other side of the room, beneath a wall-mounted lantern. Writing materials and leather-bound books were scattered across the table.

Callisto made a slow circuit, surveying the room. The tapestry on the far wall with its vibrant colors. A painting with an ornate frame. There was nothing here she wanted. Silver platters and wardrobes filled with rings were of no interest. She couldn't be weighted down.

As she turned to go, her eyes fell upon the table beneath the lantern. There was a scrap of parchment with notes jotted down, alongside a leather pouch, partially open. She picked up the pouch, examining its contents.

Letters! Letters addressed to the wizard Herrick, signed by the Arche-Mage Gnotrix. And a map! It depicted the lands of the far north. She examined the bound notebook. It was a journal, bearing the imprint of Herrick. She had found them!

She replaced the contents into the pouch, then stuffed the letters, map and journal into her satchel. She had what she had come for. But what to do with Cassandra?

She retraced her steps, descending again down the narrow stairwell and into the noxious fumes. When she arrived at the bottom, she paused. Neilos lay where he had fallen, face-down. Cassandra was tugging at arm. She jumped back as he rolled onto his back. His vacant eyes stared upwards. She kicked him, then jumped back as his body rocked – as if she couldn't believe her tormentor was really dead.

"I have to go," Callisto said, her voice a growl, her face shrouded beneath her hood in shadow.

Cassandra backed away, as if startled by the voice. She clutched the rags of her dress against her chest. The wild fear in her eyes unmistakable.

"I can't take you with me."

"I can escape when the servants come." Cassandra had edged closer to one of the tables, where knives had been laid out. Cassandra? With a knife? Callisto couldn't blame her for her fear, but the thought was laughable.

"Do you know where you'll go?"

"They come with breakfast. The servers. I recognized one of them. Her sister works for my father. She'll hide me."

Resourceful. Cassandra had more wits about her than Callisto had thought.

Cassandra's hand fell upon the table, groping for the handle of a knife.

"Please. Leave." Cassandra's words were little more than a whisper. "Leave!" she shouted more loudly. She brandished a knife in front of her, both hands gripping it, shaking. Callisto could have disarmed and overpowered her easily. There was something about this desperate girl's pleas which made her ache inside.

Callisto stepped backwards, into the shadows. She turned, leaving Cassandra to her fate, climbing the stairs. Would she ever see the girl again? It shouldn't have mattered. But she hoped the young noblewoman made it out without any more scars.

At the top of the stairwell, she stepped over the body of the slain imperial historian. She tore a strip of fabric from his shirt, using it to wrap the embalmed, severed hand of Irus. She couldn't imagine leaving it, as if it were some garish ornament for a nobleman's estate.

She made sure to douse the lanterns, before returning to the window. She listened, waiting for the patrol to pass beneath on the battlements, waiting for her opportunity to escape the sick, twisted world she had ascended into. Her fingertips and feet stretched, painfully transforming. Claws extended from her fingers and toes. It would all be over soon, she told herself. It would all be a memory, and she could move on with her life.

* * *

Callisto rowed hard towards the dockyards. The wind had picked up, and the waters had become choppy. The moon cast strange shadows as it peaked from behind the ragged clouds. She needed to get ashore and deliver her finds before dawn.

Coming to the dock from which she had borrowed the skiff, she slowed. The wooden braces loomed over her. The outer docks were unlit, just as she had left them. No sound of footsteps on the planks. She leapt out to moor the tiny boat.

She had tossed Irus' severed hand into the sea along the way, weighted down by a rock and wrapped in the knotted remains of Zenodotus' shirt. She tried not to think of the horrid hole she had retrieved it from. If the entire empire came crumbling down in a bath of flame, it would have suited her just fine. The emperor, his ministers, the bureaucrats, the noblemen – she hated the lot of them.

Would anyone ever suspect how she had stolen into the tower of Burcsteli and back again? No ordinary thief could have climbed the outside of the tower wall. More likely, they'd assume some rival had paid a guard to eliminate the historian.

What would happen to Cassandra? The girl had recovered remarkably well from the ordeal – although the nightmares would likely haunt her for the rest of her life. She was still a nobleman's daughter, however. Once free, her family would have the resources to help her find a new life, a new identity. They might never be friends, but she bore the girl no ill will. They both had their own reasons to hate the empire.

Gripping her satchel, Callisto scaled the ladder to the top of the dock – and halted.

There was a figure at the other end. He was thin, the moon casting long shadows across his gaunt cheeks. Pontus? He was crouched over something else – someone else. A body, laying prone across the dock.

Chapter 39

Pontus hovered over the body; the blade of his knife stained dark. Moonlight drew his features in sharp relief.

For a moment, Callisto held out a hope the figure lying beneath him might be someone else. Someone else wearing a white shirt and grey, blood-stained vest. Someone else, fallen and bent into a pose no living human would willingly accept – their head tipped, neck askew. Someone else. Someone other than Phaeton.

But her eyes were too sharp to spare her the details, and her scent was too keen. She could see the body, his chin, the vacant eyes. The way the curls of his hair framed his face. The way his chest lay motionless, no longer drawing breath. The scent of blood staining the knife in Pontus' hand.

"What have you done?!" She made no attempt to disguise the anguish in her voice.

"I've eliminated a witness." Pontus' voice was impassive, betraying neither anger nor malice. A simple statement of fact. "Did you find the papers?"

Callisto dropped the satchel to the ground. "You beast!"

"Don't get emotional on me. Hand the bag over. We need to get out of here before the morning watch comes."

"Everything that's innocent, everything that's pure – you destroy." Callisto drew the dagger from her belt. She cared nothing for the value of the papers. Nothing for the weeks of labor she had put into finding them. The only thing which mattered was the dead body, and the vengeance she would exact on Pontus' flesh.

"Don't do anything foolish, girl." Pontus was reaching for his coat pocket, the place where he kept his silver knives. They were shorter than the dagger he had used on Phaeton – the dagger he had dropped. Callisto knew them well. Knew how silver burned when it cut her flesh. Knew how it could leave a scar on her arms which would itch and never properly heal. She knew. Right now, she just didn't care.

She sprang. The dagger in her hand was swift and light, her movements practiced from years of training. Pontus never had the chance to draw the knife from its pocket.

It was quick, anticlimactic. After all the years, all the mistreatment, she had expected it to feel different to watch him die. When it happened, it barely registered in his eyes as she sank the dagger into his chest. His stare went blank, eyes still open. He collapsed, and she flung his body to the side. Away from her. Away from Phaeton.

The boy lay where he had fallen, his empty eyes still staring into the night sky. Callisto's hand brushed his cheek, and a whimper escaped her lips. Why? Why had he followed her? Why on this night? Why had he fallen into her world?

Sobs wracked her shoulders. Tears clouded her eyes, raining down in hot streams across her cheeks. Why? It was all so senseless.

Heavy drops of rain had begun to descend, pelting the ground, pelting her back and shoulders. The wind had picked up as the clouds began to open, the raindrops masking the sound of her sobs. Cold water mixed with hot tears. The storm above a mirror for the storm within. Why? A question for which there could be no answer.

"I have to thank you, of course, for finishing off a loose end."

She jerked her head up, spinning herself around. It was Cetus!

He had edged his way around her, keeping his distance as he made his way along the dock – towards the satchel which Callisto had discarded at the other end. He bent down, retrieving the sack, testing its weight in his hand. "You were successful?"

"Yes," Callisto nodded, wiping the salty tears from her cheeks. She was still kneeling. Still hovering where Phaeton had fallen. Why was Cetus here? Wasn't he supposed to wait for her at the warehouse?

Cetus smiled – a mirthless grin. "Excellent work, master lockpick. I'm sorry we have to part under such circumstances. I still have one loose end to extinguish."

Over her tears, the beating of her own heart against her eardrums, the pelting of the rain against the ground, Callisto hadn't heard. Not until it was too late.

The sound of a dagger, being drawn from its sheath. Movement in the shadows behind her.

She tried to spin around. A gasp and a wheeze escaped her as Taras' blade plunged through her back.

The pain was excruciating. Her lungs filling with blood, as if drowning. The cold steel cutting through her flesh. Taras' hand gripping her shoulder. The blade plunged in, then slid out, then plunged in again. Tearing a hole from her back, through her chest, its tip piercing the front of her tunic. He was preparing for another thrust.

She had one chance! One chance only.

With every reserve of strength she could summon, she lunged. Twisting, wrenching herself free. Shoving off with both legs.

Taras' fingers and nails dug into her skin. Her cloak tore, ripping as she pried herself free. She dove across the dock. Taras lurching after her – grunting as he stretched. She had to escape!

She plunged headfirst over the edge of the dock. Cold, salty waters enveloped her.

A splash, a moments' thrashing. Taras leaned over the edge, searching the darkness for signs of his victim. The rain was building.

"You let her get away?!" Cetus peered over Taras' shoulder.

"I can't see anything in the dark," Taras said. His features, his voice, remained impassive. Another kill. Another victim. Neither more nor less.

"You never miss."

"She twisted away."

"Could she have survived?"

There was a pause before he answered. "Not from my knife."

Cetus surveyed the trail of blood from the fallen bodies to the water's edge. "Come on. Search the boy. We'll want the ring as proof. We need to be long gone before the morning watch arrives. We have a meeting, and a payoff to arrange."

Chapter 40

Callisto pulled herself from the water – slowly, as quietly as possible. She clenched her jaw shut to avoid crying out. Her body was wracked with pain. Salt water flowed into her wound, into her lungs. She had to clamp down hard on her jaw. It hurt so bad. All of it hurt so bad.

She could hear Cetus and Taras speaking from the dock above. They were peering over the edge on the other side, where she had plunged in. They muttered. She might have been able to hear them, if she could focus. It was all she could do to keep from screaming from the pain.

Footsteps. Were they walking away? Had they left her for dead?

By all rights, she should be dead. No human could have survived having their lungs torn and punctured like that. No human would have the stamina to swim underwater after having been stabbed. She should be dead. She should have joined Phaeton, should have left this miserable world. But she wasn't human. And she wasn't dead.

Callisto remained where she was, shivering. One arm was hooked around the wooden brace. The saltwater burned where it seeped in. She was in no condition to fight. Not now. She needed to wait until they were gone.

What had gone wrong? How had everything gone so bad? Phaeton dead. Herself, shivering in the waters. In a couple more hours, the night watchman would make his circuit of the docks. He would find the bodies. Find her. She needed to be long gone if she wanted to live.

Callisto climbed up the trusses of the dock slowly, pulling herself up – every movement a searing stab of pain. She blotted it out. The way she had been taught to. The way she had always done before. Tears streamed down her cheeks. Was it the physical pain, or the emotional? Phaeton! Just a boy. Just a stupid boy who hadn't deserved to be in the middle of this.

By the time she had reached the dock, she could feel the wounds in her lungs beginning to close. The pain, while still throbbing, had begun to dull. It might be hours, even days before she was fully healed.

She didn't have days. She had to get out. Disappear before she was found.

She crawled on all fours to where Phaeton's body lay. The rain had become steady, cold, and raw. They had stripped whatever valuables they could from his body. His coin purse. His family ring. He was still lying there, just as before. But his skin was cold when she brushed the back of her hand against his cheek. Whatever warmth there was in this world had vanished from her heart. Why? Why had he followed her? Why tonight, of all nights?

* * *

She knocked on the door, her eyes scanning for any watchmen who might be out at this hour. Her hair was cold and wet, but she had changed out of her soaked and bloodstained clothing. The smock she wore was a couple sizes too large, but it hid the knotted bandages beneath.

She was clenching her right side, keeping pressure on the rags she had wrapped around her chest. Each movement, each time she coughed, threatened to tear open the wounds.

The door opened, and there was a moment of silence. "Callisto?"

She stepped inside. "I need a place to stay. Cetus double-crossed us."

Erebus shut the door behind her, then unshuttered his lantern. The training room was deserted – the weapons on its walls the only spectators.

"Pontus?" he asked.

"Dead," Callisto replied, leaving out the detail of how she been the one who had killed him. "Taras got the jump on me. They think I'm dead too." She was angry and embarrassed with herself for having been so careless. So distracted by her grief.

"You're injured? Let me have a look." Erebus gripped her elbow, helping her to steady herself.

"No!" Callisto drew back, leaning against the wall. "I'm fine. I'll be fine. I just need somewhere to rest. I couldn't take a chance on Cetus coming to clean out my room."

"Your clothes are fresh." Erebus led her across the training floor. Instead of leading her to one of the side rooms she knew, however, he pulled aside a wall hanging to reveal a hidden door. She had to duck her head to enter. There was a room, just beyond. There were no windows and few furnishings: a stool, a small table, and a mattress on the floor.

"I borrowed some clothes on my way. My others were too –"

"Bloody? Sounds like you've had quite the night. You can stay here until tomorrow. No one will bother you." Erebus placed the lantern on the floor and left.

It hurt when she lay down, but she knew she needed sleep. She wondered why she had never detected this hidden room on her own. Between the pain and weariness, sleep overtook her.

Even in slumber, however, her fevered mind would not let her rest. Her dreams were a tangle of painful memories. She saw Phaeton, over and over – in the library, on the street, at his father's home. Each time she went to call his name. Each time he turned away, as if he couldn't hear her. She'd run after, only to find herself in a strange room, facing a knife or sword-wielding opponent.

She'd dodge his thrusts, only to feel her attacker's kicks. Her body painful and feverish. No weapon in her hand.

She'd fight back, trying to disarm her foe. But she never could see who she was fighting. She'd be stabbed. Then the dream would rewind. She'd be calling after Phaeton again.

Chapter 41

I've lost, yah-yah. Lost everything which mattered to me. First you. Then myself. Now the only boy who saw me as something other than a street rag. I have lost, and I don't know where I can go, who I can turn to, what I should do.

* * *

Callisto awoke with a start. The vision of the nightmare was still fresh in her mind. Phaeton! Come back! Her heart racing. Her lungs laboring.

Erebus had drawn the tapestry which hid the entrance aside and was carrying a lantern and a bowl of hot stew. She could smell the savory aroma as it drifted through the air, becoming conscious of how hungry she was.

"I thought you might need to eat," Erebus said, setting the stew down on a low table.

She moved to a sitting position. It hurt when she stretched. She was stiff, and her side ached.

Her side! Someone had stripped off the rags she had been wearing, cleaning her wound and replacing them with fresh bandages.

Erebus had seen! Even with her wounds partially healed, he would have known. A stab wound like that should have been fatal. An entry wound in her back. An exit wound in her chest. Not once, but twice. She should have bled out from her torn and tattered lungs. How could he not suspect? She shouldn't be alive!

"You'll have to recover your strength, if you want to fight again."

Fight? Yes, she needed to fight. Needed to tear hole in Taras' chest. Needed to watch him and Cetus bleed. The way they had made her bleed. She crawled to the small table. She had to eat. Regather her strength.

"We can speak after you eat." Erebus exited the small chamber, leaving her with her food, and her thoughts.

Callisto devoured the meal ravenously. Her powers of recuperation were beyond anything a human might imagine, but they took a toll of their own – sapping her energy as her body healed.

The stew was hot, and although only mildly spiced, was a welcome warmth against her parched throat. She glanced about the room as she ate. There was a panel which could swing into place behind the tapestry, covering the entrance. From the outside, it would have completely sealed the opening, rendering it undetectable to an outside observer. There was another panel with a latch on the opposing ceiling of the room. An escape route, in the event the building was searched.

She finished her meal and crawled towards the entry. She waited, listening, before drawing the tapestry aside. The studio was empty. It was unusual for this time of day. Erebus typically had students throughout the day – learning the skills of a lockpick, cutpurse, or weapons training.

She inhaled. The heavy aroma of coffee, thick and dark with mud, wafted from the kitchen. She followed the scent.

Erebus was seated at a table, a small cup of rich, dark coffee on the table before him.

"Feeling better?"

Callisto nodded. "Thank you for letting me stay." She took a seat across from him at the table. She had been in Erebus' kitchen a couple of times before. Pale light drifted in from the window – daylight but overcast. Raindrops pelted the panes of glass. How long had she been asleep?

"I've been asking around. Cetus has arranged for a meeting with someone offering a small fortune for some rare documents. I assume this was your last job with Pontus? Retrieving those documents?"

She nodded.

"There were several customers who have been offering large rewards for these items. Most have been foreign buyers, although a new contender recently came forward. Cetus has set up a meeting with one of them tonight. He will likely depart shortly after." He paused, studying her. "What do you intend to do?"

"I'm going to kill them. Both of them." There was a certainty in her voice. Taras' size did not intimidate her, nor did Cetus' wealth or connections. She was going to make them pay.

"You're certain? You believe you've recovered strength enough to face Cetus and his hired sword?"

He had seen her wounds. He would know. No human should be able to fight after having been stabbed like that. How could he not suspect?

"I'm certain." Callisto's voice was low, almost a growl. "Thank you again for letting me stay. You've been most kind." She rose to leave.

"There's more to this story, if you'll stay to hear it." He waited until she had seated herself again. "It seems Cetus' had a little run-in with a foreign cult. Oddly enough, they were one of the buyers interested in the documents. He seems to have made himself some enemies in the process."

"The cult with the monkey pendants?"

"The same. Despite his attempts to cover his tracks, his henchman couldn't resist a chance to collect an early share in the profit. He sold two broaches he reportedly collected from the cultists. A pair of rather unique pieces of jewelry." Erebus drew a folded parchment from his pocket, holding it up. "There's a contract out on Cetus, and his bodyguard. They've assumed he was also in on the earlier, warehouse robbery from a few weeks ago. The reward is considerable. Are you interested?"

Callisto's hand reached out before she had thought through her response. Erebus drew the parchment back.

"Make sure you're ready for this. If you accept the contract, you must execute."

"I don't need a contract to want to kill them."

"Accept the contract, and you'll be bound by the rules of the guild. Complete it, and you'll be a third-blade, a ranking member under the guild's rules. Once you accept, there's no turning back."

Callisto snatched the parchment. "I have no reason not to."

She had meant to glance only briefly at the document but stopped when she saw the reward being offered. "Four hundred?"

"Paid in gold, not silver. Not all of it would be yours to keep, mind you. The guild takes a commission. I asked you once before, what it was you wanted – when all of this was over. When your debt to Pontus was paid. Do you know now?"

"I want vengeance."

"On Cetus?"

"On all of them. On every corrupt official in the empire. Everyone who has made life a misery. Every one of them, everywhere."

Erebus lifted a wooden box from the floor and sat it on the table. It was the chest, with the two snarling wolves inlaid into its surface.

"I have trained many students over the years. You are faster, and stronger, than any of them have ever been. You could hear the motion of the pins and plates inside of locks. Could see targets in the light too dim for humans to distinguish."

How long, Callisto wondered, had he suspected?

"I couldn't be sure at first. But your cuts and bruises from the sparing matches would heal before the training match was even over. You are something special, Callisto. You could achieve what I could not. Make the empire take notice. Make them pay for everything they've done."

He slid the box towards her.

"A lot of things happened in decades past. Things I cannot undo. I am not proud of all of them. I can think of no better use for these, if you should want them."

"I am . . . honored, master."

"Carry these, and everyone will know your name, Callisto. The assassin who carries silver blades from a werewolf war fought decades ago. Carry them, and no one will suspect who you really are."

Chapter 42

Dear grandma,

I understand now. I was not meant for a life at peace, any more than you were. I cannot change what happened to you, or to me. But I can find those who did this to us. Not just one of them – all of them. I can make them regret every home and every family they tore apart.

Erebus was right, yah-yah. Freedom would never have been enough for me. I need something more in my life. Somewhere I can plant my blade or sink my claws for every wound which ever scarred my soul.

* * *

"You can leave my bags here," Cetus said. The porter all but dropped the heavy trunk at his feet. A light but steady drizzle poured down. The waiting carriage was poorly lit by the lantern which hung outside the rear entrance to the inn.

Cetus paid the porter an obol for his trouble, waiting until he had left before turning to Taras. "Load my bags onto the carriage. We'll be leaving as soon as I return with payment."

"Should I go with you?"

"The buyer specified I was to come alone. I'll be back soon enough."

Cetus made his way down the alleyway, leaving Taras to heft the heavy trunks into the back of the carriage. The chassis rocked as they were jolted into place.

"Take it easy with those!" The carriage driver was a skinny man who seemed to have a case of the sniffles. He had raised the collar of his coat to stave off the rain and had a rag in hand for his nose. He watched as Taras lashed the trunks into place.

"Mind to your own, carriage boy." Taras turned a disparaging eye towards him. The hilt of his dagger was visible at his waist. His short sword, which he carried when they traveled, was on his other hip.

The carriage driver withdrew, blowing his nose into his rag. He walked towards the front of the carriage to inspect the harness.

Abruptly, the coach jerked, as the horses heaved against the carriage brake.

"Hey! Carriage boy! Steady those animals!" Taras shouted.

"I'm on it!" The carriage driver responded. "Something's unsettling them!" He wiped his nose again, muttering a curse under his breath as the rain soaked into his scalp. He gripped the horse's noseband, steadying the animal.

Satisfied the horse had calmed down, he turned – just as the kick caught him square across the jaw. His head rocked back, just once – and he collapsed to the ground.

In the back of her mind, Callisto knew she could easily have slit the carriage driver's throat. It would have made less noise. It might also have avoided alerting Taras to her presence.

Then again, she didn't much care if he knew she was coming.

She stalked, like a leopard on the hunt, rounding the corner of the carriage. She had drawn her cloak and hood up, over her shoulders. Her twin blades already drawn.

Taras was waiting, a sword in hand.

There was a momentary flicker of recognition and surprise in his eyes. Then they returned to the same, passionless expression he always wore. "You should not have come back."

Callisto leapt, bringing both blades down in rapid succession. Taras parried. He was faster than she had expected. And strong. She felt the jolt of the blow as his sword struck her own. It shook her arms. She felt it in her shoulders and joints.

Yes, he was fast. Yes, he was strong. But she was faster. She brought each blade down in a rapid rhythm, driving him back.

Taras parried, then tried for a thrust. Callisto brought her left blade down against his, the axe-like forward curve of the *kopis* deflecting his short sword out of the way.

Blow by blow, step by step, he was losing ground. She had been preparing since she was old enough to hold a knife. She was not about to lose now.

Taras thrust, his blade grazing her arm as she pivoted to avoid him.

Another stroke, another parry. He wasn't tiring. At least not yet. She and Taras could be going on like this for many minutes more. Time enough for someone to raise the alarm. Time enough for the imperial city's sentries to arrive. She needed to bring this to a close.

She drew back in a feint, appearing to allow an opening. The trap was set.

Taras lunged – and she leapt. The trap was sprung.

Using her left-hand blade, she drew his sword back and out of the way. Her right blade followed through, its edge raking along his exposed arm.

Taras cried out – an angry shout as his sword clattered to the ground. Instead of drawing away, however, he sprang forward. His good hand reached out, trying to grip her.

Callisto leapt up, driving the tip of her left blade down and into his shoulder, just above the collarbone. There was a momentary flash of pain in his eyes. Her lips were drawn back into an angry snarl. She plunged her blade downwards, deeper – into his chest. He collapsed, his blood pooling at her feet.

Callisto stood, recovering her breath. She had expected to feel something. Triumph? Satisfaction? But it was rage which still burned inside her. It had been far too swift.

She bent down to unfasten the dagger from his belt. The same dagger which had killed the two cult members. It had been specified in the contract – proof the job had been complete. She only had one more task to fulfill, and she had to move quickly, or his scent could become lost in the rain.

Chapter 43

Dear grandma,

There's a price to be paid. A debt for all the years, all the misery. A price I am going to exact.

I can't bring you back, yah-yah. But I'm not running anymore. I claim my own path, my own destiny. They will never take that from me again.

* * *

Callisto crept along the balcony, careful to test each floorboard before committing her weight. The lower floor of the spice market exchange would have been crowded during daylight hours. Porters, assessors, traders, and profiteers. At night, however, it should have been vacant. Should have been but wasn't.

Tonight, the usual watchmen were absent – relieved of their responsibilities. It took connections to vacate a building like this. In the imperial city, no less. Connections which implied a well-placed buyer.

The upper level of the exchange, where the balcony was located, held offices. Each door held a trader or guild seal. Each door was locked shut for the night. Below was the floor of the exchange, where imported spices were brought, weighed, and sold.

The scent of exotic herbs, roots and salts mingled in the air, as Callisto crept cautiously towards the edge. She could have waited for Cetus to conclude his bargain for the documents. He was the one she had been contracted to kill. He was the one who would feel her vengeance.

She was also curious, however, about whom his buyer might be. She wanted a perch, from which she could observe the transaction. She would wait for Cetus to conclude his business. There was no way she was going to let him escape alive. But she wanted to know, needed to know, over whom and what all this misery had been inflicted.

There was a dim light from the trading room floor. Someone had lit a lantern. One lantern, and no more. From the balcony's edge, she could see Cetus, waiting for his buyer to arrive. A leather pouch was tucked under his arm, his trimmed beard and head nervously turning, peering into the surrounding darkness as he waited.

Callisto waited patiently in the shadows. Patience. Patience was what separated a successful thief from an amateur. Waiting for the right time to strike. Stealing a sheaf of papers. Stealing someone's life. He was not going to escape her.

From somewhere in the back of the building, a door opened and closed. Footsteps. Two of them – their patterns distinct. She could see someone emerging from the shadows. A lean figure who moved with a fluid grace.

"Is your master coming?" Cetus asked, his eyes on the darkly clad swordsman.

"He's coming," the swordsman replied. "And I have no master, only clients." His stance was wide, his hands resting above his weapons. A saber on one hip, a dagger on the other. Callisto leaned forward, straining to see the figure at the edge of the lamplight. Could it be?

A dark, tightly trimmed beard. A scar across his eyebrow. Xystos! Someone had hired an assassin? As a bodyguard? It was unusual, although not entirely unheard of for the very wealthy. What had he been hired to do? Was he there as a bodyguard, or something more? His presence could complicate her task. She would need to wait for him to depart. There was no need to confront Cetus while Xystos was present – if she could avoid it.

There was more motion from the back of the building. The second set of footsteps she had heard enter. It was still too dark to see. The glare of the lamplight was more a hindrance than help.

"Do you have the documents?" The voice was familiar, but she couldn't quite place it.

"I have them. Are you prepared to pay the advertised sum? It's not the kind of change someone can just carry around." Cetus rested his hand on the leather pouch beneath his arm, unfastening the clasp.

"I'm prepared." A smartly dressed figure emerged into the light, a paper held in his hand. "A banknote with the promised sum, written against my estate as collateral. If, that is, you have the promised wares – letters from the Arche-Mage Gnotrix."

It was all she could do to contain herself. Grey hair. Trimmed mustache. Damianus! Phaeton's father!

"I must admit," Cetus continued, "your boldness surprised even me. Offering double the sum promised by the Order of Marcus Maximus?"

"With so many seeking these papers, it was obviously worth something much more to someone else. I only need determine who their buyer is. Xystos will ensure their safe delivery – assuming you have the documents."

"I have them, but first things first." Cetus was reaching into the leather pouch, drawing something out. Xystos tensed, his hand hovering over his saber, prepared – as if Cetus might be foolish enough to draw a weapon. "Not many noblemen would put a contract out, for the life of their own son."

Chapter 44

Callisto stiffened. The words echoing in her mind like the ringing of a bell sounding inside a narrow tower. Contract? Son? Could it be? Had Phaeton's own father . . . contracted for Phaeton's death?

"The boy was foolish and impudent. Willing to sell his family name for some churl of a peasant. Threatening to expose me. Threatening his brother's inheritance. The boy almost ruined me last time. It was a risk I couldn't take."

Writing . . . the letter Phaeton had mentioned?

Cetus withdrew a small object from his coat pocket, holding it up for Damianus to see. It glittered silver in the lamplight. A ring, with a red stone. "I believe the price for the boy was a hundred coins? Gold, if I'm not mistaken? Bearing Trevio's mint?"

A momentary look of surprise flashed through Damianus' eyes. He quickly marshaled his control. "I had heard the boy went missing yesterday."

Cetus tossed the signet ring to Damianus, who caught it in his free hand. "His body was left lying on the imperial dockyards, should you wish to claim it. I suppose you won't be needing the services of an assassin after all."

Damianus was examining the ring. "Well . . . yes. There's still the matter of the girl." His voice took on a harder edge.

Cetus reached into the pouch again, drawing out a wine-red cloth. He tossed it on the ground at Damianus' feet. "I've taken care of that loose end for you too."

Her dress! The one Danae had gifted to her! The one she had worn to dinner at Phaeton's home!

"I'm impressed," Damianus replied. "I hadn't realized you engaged in such . . . unsavory matters."

"It was mutually beneficial, I assure you."

Callisto felt the wind escape her lungs, as if she couldn't breathe, as if her life had stopped. She had been targeted. Phaeton had been targeted. It had been no accident. Phaeton's own father had plotted their deaths, to protect whatever family secrets Phaeton had threatened to reveal.

"I regret having missed my chance," Xystos said. "I had hoped to even my score with her."

"You knew the girl?" Phaeton's father said in surprise.

Callisto slid her hand over her boot, gripping the handle of her knife.

"The wench fancied herself an assassin in training."

She drew her knife out slowly, quietly, watching Xystos for any response. His eyes were on the dress, lying on the floor of the exchange.

"An assassin?" Damianus scoffed. "The wench was barely a stick. A bone caught in the throat of progress, which might choke a less careful diner."

Her life. Phaeton's life. They were being counted out for a handful of coins. This sick, corrupt empire was rotten to its very core.

"The bounty for the girl, I believe, was set at thirty gold florins, if I'm not mistaken," Cetus said. "To be added, of course, to my payment for retrieving the documents."

Callisto launched herself over the edge of the balcony. She put the weight of her body behind the dagger, throwing it from across the room, pushing off against the railing.

She rolled into her landing as she struck the floor, not looking to where her dagger had struck. She had heard the dull thump as it found its mark. She knew. Her aim had been flawless. Damianus had gone down first. The man who had contracted for his own son's death. For Phaeton's death. She was not letting him leave this hall alive.

As she came to her feet, drawing her twin blades in unison, Xystos was already charging down on her. His saber drawn. His other hand gripped a dagger. "You!"

She had caught a glimpse of Cetus from the corner of her eye. The surprise, the terror in his expression, was unmistakable. Like someone who had seen a ghost risen from the dead.

She was only dimly aware of which direction Cetus fled to – the leather pouch tucked under his arm. Her focus was on Xystos. She barely had time to bring her blades up as his first stroke fell.

"So much the better!" Xystos' strokes fell hard, the full force of his anger behind each blow. "I get to finish you myself!"

Callisto was on the defensive, having only just rolled to her feet. Xystos might not have been as strong as Taras had been, but he was faster. She swung each of her blades, barely finding time to deflect his blows as she regained her footing.

He thrust, his blade barely missing her. He had a clear advantage in reach. He also had the skill which Taras had lacked. He was quite likely the most dangerous adversary she had ever faced. The pace of his blows was furious. Like a wildcat defending its territory.

She drew back in a feint, attempting to draw him in, but his dagger was ready. He was too experienced to be fooled in the same manner as Taras. Her sword rang against the guard of this dagger. Another strike parried! She needed to get ahead of him. She needed to think!

She brought her blades into a steady rhythm, the practiced movements of her training routines. Stroke, parry, thrust. She forced herself to clear her mind, allow her senses to reach out. The scent of the room. The stench of his sweat. The rhythm of his breathing.

That's right. He inhaled before each lunge. A sharp, measured instinct, reinforced by years of training.

She struck harder, drawing on her reserves. The force of her blows jolted her joints and muscles. They must have been jolting his too. More strength than a girl her size should possess.

She could see the uncertainty in his eyes. She only had to wait for it. Listen for the rhythm of his breath.

Stroke. Parry. He inhaled sharply. This was it!

He lunged, and she brought both blades to bare. Her right blade parried his saber. Her left raked across his arm and wrist. He cried in pain as the sword was wrenched from his grasp.

She followed through. One thrust. Quick. The point of her blade cutting through fabric, leather, and flesh. Sinking deep into his chest. There was only a moment's surprise in his eyes. Xystos collapsed at her feet.

She stood. Chest heaving. Teeth still clenched. They were dead. Xystos and Damianus both. Damianus – the father who couldn't value his own son above his own ambitions. The man who had put a bounty on the head of a peasant girl whom his son had . . .

No, she didn't have time for sentiment. Not yet. She sheathed her blades. Unfastening her weapons belt.

There was still one more score to settle. One more she had to hunt down.

* * *

Cetus had withdrawn to a safe room several buildings down. It was likely one of many escape routes he had prepared. What had he said? A professional would always have multiple aliases and safe rooms? He was in a small room in the corner of a garment shop – unoccupied at this late hour.

His breathing was raspy, and his body stank of fear. Callisto could smell it clearly. He was cowering in a corner, probably hoping Damianus' hired sword would finish her off. He had likely assumed he would be safe here. Had assumed no one could track him down to this hole. He had assumed wrong.

She could smell him, hear him breathing from behind the door. Her hackles were already raised. She stalked forward, careful to keep her claws from scraping against the floor. From the sound of his breathing, she judged he was on the far side of the room.

There was no light glimmering from beneath the door. He was probably hoping to go unnoticed. Armed or unarmed, she couldn't tell. Armed or unarmed, it wouldn't matter.

A floorboard groaned beneath her step.

"Taras? Is that you?" Cetus whispered.

She launched herself against the door, claws bared. It shattered into a cascade of scrap wood and splinters. She landed squarely in the center of the room.

It was a typical safe room. A bed, a table, and dried supplies were stacked to one side. A lone window, high on the wall, allowed light to filter in.

Cetus was leaning against the far wall, cowering like a cornered hare.

"What are you?! This can't be happening!"

She approached him slowly. He had a knife in one hand, his other hand gripping a satchel. In the light of the window, her shadow was long, but unmistakable. Her amber eyes glimmered bright. Her paws ended in long, curved claws. Hair stood stiffly across her back. She was a werewolf. A beast many believed to be extinct from these lands. A beast they had hunted to oblivion. This was who she was, what she was – no matter what she might have appeared only minutes before. And tonight, this cowering man would pay for everything which had been done to her and her kind.

Callisto leapt, her jaws clamping down on his neck and shoulder. If he moved to stab her with his dagger, she didn't notice.

There was a cracking sound as his chest and shoulder bones were crushed beneath her grip. A wheezing sound escaped from his lips. She shook her head, his neck snapping as she whipped his body from side to side.

In the morning, when the first tailors arrived, they would find the bloodied remains of what had once been a man. Who, or what they had once been would never be confirmed. Strips of flesh and cracked bones were all they found – crushed beyond recognition.

Chapter 45

Dear grandma,

Would you be proud of me, seeing me now? Would you be disappointed by what I've become?

I did not choose this life I've lived. It happened, and I cannot change it. The years separating us now. The shadows haunting my nightmares. The painful memories. I cannot change what happened. But I can change what happens from now on. I will be the shadow haunting their nightmares. The angry memory hunting them down. They will fear me, yah-yah.

You and I will be the only ones who will know. Know that somewhere deep inside, I'm still the little girl, just trying to be the brave little wolf you told me to be.

* * *

"This is all there was?" The priest looked dubiously at the paltry few pages in his hand. The journal pages all bore Herrick's signature. Still, he had expected something more. Something from his master, Gnotrix.

"The reward was twenty gold florins per page, two hundred per page if any were signed by Gnotrix. I don't believe a minimum number was specified. These pages were all there was." Callisto kept her tone even, her left hand resting on the pommel of her blade.

She wore a dark tunic, trousers, and boots, with a hood and cloak over her shoulders. While the outside of her cloak was dark, the inside was a rich, wine-red shade. The same shade as a dress she had once worn. Danae had tailored them to match her slim frame. Eliminating Cetus and his henchman had paid well.

The three priests, each wearing the symbol of the palm-forward hand, had gathered around to inspect the documents. Two armed guards stood at the rear of the room. They were bulky enough to impress most. Their movements, however, were sluggish and betrayed their lack of discipline or training. They were hired muscle, nothing more.

"You were the assassin who eliminated Cetus and his bodyguard?" the older of the three glanced up at her.

"I don't discuss contracts with another party."

"Why didn't you sell the pages to the monkey cult?"

"I sell to the highest bidder," Callisto replied. "Who they are is no concern of mine."

The older priest nodded to his associate, who retired to a corner to retrieve a heavy chest. Unlocking the cask, they counted out the coins – gold glittering in their hand. The coins were deposited into a sack and handed to her.

"Our thanks, assassin. It seems the trail ends here."

* * *

The magical archives were dark and empty, as they usually were at this hour. It felt strange being there again, after so much had happened. So much had changed.

Had Phaeton's brothers shed a tear when he passed, she wondered? She liked to believe so. From the vantage point where she had watched, she couldn't be sure. They had appeared, dressed primly as was proper to their station. They had appeared, but had avoided drawing attention to themselves, as the plain wooden boxes were lowered into the ground. A father and son buried on the same day – both dead under mysterious circumstances.

She had left a note for Phaeton's brothers, ensuring they knew where to claim his body. She left the signet ring as well. The death of two family members, under such inauspicious circumstances, was not something they would want discussed widely. The burial rites were suitably subdued.

Callisto drew her hood back, as the freshly lit lantern flooded the chamber with its glow. Long shadows stretched across the walls and ceiling. The musty scents of the leather-bound volumes, with their cured hides and dried inks, permeated the air. It was not merely a library. Not for her. It was a crypt. A place where memories came to be buried.

She counted down the rows. The sixth shelf on the right. A thick volume, dyed a deep red hue.

Reaching into her satchel, she drew out a leather pouch, clasped shut by a buckle. She unlatched it, glancing through the pages one more time. Letters. The signature of Gnotrix clearly visible.

She shut the pouch tight once more, clasping the buckle shut, sliding it onto the shelf. This would be its resting place, alongside the volume Phaeton had been so proud to share with her. The oracles of Pythia. The legend of the destroyer.

She could have sold the letters to the religious freaks, like she did the journals of Herrick. She didn't need the extra gold, however. And she couldn't bear to sell these pages to foreigners. Let those cultists believe the trail had run dry. Let the pages of Herrick's journal suffice to keep them at bay. The letters would remain here. Her own private burial for Phaeton and all he had meant to her.

Someday, maybe someday, Phaeton's vision of a place where everyone could come and learn, would come true. Maybe someday, the great destroyer would arise to pass judgement on this empire. On everyone who so richly deserved it.

Callisto turned, making her way with confident steps towards the entrance. She ran her fingers across the bookshelves, the tables, the chairs as she passed. Places which still reminded her of him. Full of foolish innocence.

This place. Its memories and stories. Tucked away in the prison of the empire. The locked doorway and gate separating the archives. The stairway leading up. The banners with their sunburst symbol lining the walls. The same imperial symbol, on the uniforms of the guards, or flying from the heights.

"Someday," she said softly to herself. "Judgement is coming for you. All of you. I swear it."

A WOLF BEFORE THE STORM

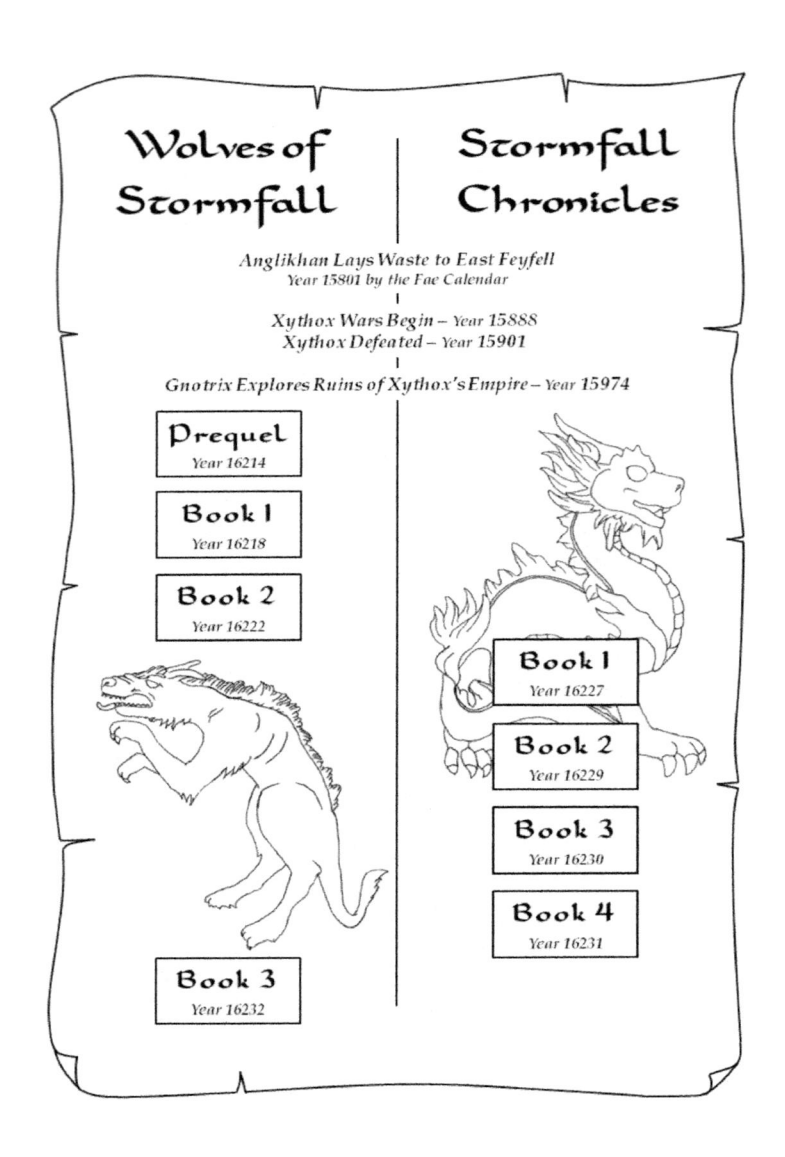

Wolves of Stormfall | Stormfall Chronicles

Anglikhan Lays Waste to East Feyfell
Year 15801 by the Fae Calendar

Xythox Wars Begin – Year 15888
Xythox Defeated – Year 15901

Gnotrix Explores Ruins of Xythox's Empire – Year 15974

Prequel
Year 16214

Book 1
Year 16218

Book 2
Year 16222

Book 1
Year 16227

Book 2
Year 16229

Book 3
Year 16230

Book 4
Year 16231

Book 3
Year 16232

A NOTE FROM THE AUTHOR

Welcome to the world of Stormfall. I hope you enjoyed reading this story as much as I enjoyed writing it.

If you did, please consider telling your friends or posting a short review online. Word of mouth is an author's best friend and is much appreciated.

The Stormfall Chronicles is an epic fantasy series set in the same world. Callisto appears in Books 3 and 4 of *The Stormfall Chronicles*. The second installment for *The Wolves of Stormfall* is expected to be released first on Kindle Vella before being issued as an eBook on Kindle and in paperback. I look forward to Callisto's continued tale.

For information on upcoming releases, please visit my author's blog:
https://jwgolan.blogspot.com

Character Guide

Name	Description
Andros AHN-drohs	Son of a warehouse steward who sublets a room to Pontus
Atreus ah-TRAY-us	A younger member of Pontus gang. Brother or cousin to Theia.
Bessarion beh-SAYR-ee-un	Emperor of Bateria
Callimachus kuh-LEE-mah-kuhs	Master Archivist at the Imperial Library of Bateria
Callisto kuh-LEES-toh	Assassin who is also sister to Makednos
Cassandra kuh-SAHN-druh	Lesser nobleman's daughter, and a student at the Imperial Academy
Cetus KEE-tuhs	Pontus' business partner
Crius KREE-us	A thief from the city of Centrola
Damianus DAY-mee-ah-nus	A minor nobleman in Bateria. Phaeton's father
Danae dah-NAH-ee	A master seamstress in Polonia
Darios DAR-ee-ohs	A general and former inquisitor in the army of Bateria

Name	Description
Erebus AYR-eh-vaws	Weapons master and retired member of the Assassins' Guild
Eratosthenes ayr-uh-TAWS-thuh-nees	Master Geographer in the Empire of Bateria
Euthymius eh-THEE-mee-us	A pupil of Erebus in Polonia
Hemera ee-MAIR-ah	Younger sister of Erebus
Irus EER-oos	A werewolf and personal bodyguard of Rog En-Rogeth
Larkin LAR-kin	A nobleman from Southfold in the Kingdom of Symru
Lethe LEE-thee	A former member of Pontus' gang of thieves
Marcus Maximus MAR-kus MAKS-ee-mus	Founder of a cult in Trevio
Memnon MEHM-nawn	A first-blade to the Assassins' Guild of Bateria
Mira MEE-rah	Callisto's assumed name, used to infiltrate the Imperial Library
Neilos NIE-lohs	Senior journeyman reporting to Master Historian Zenodotus

Name	Description
Phaeton FIE-thawn	Youngest son of a minor nobleman, and a journeyman archivist
Pontus PAWN-tus	A master thief, to whom Callisto owes a debt for her years of training
Pythia PITH-ee-ah	A fabled seer who foretold the coming of the destroyer
Rog-En-Airden ROHG-en-AYR-dehn	The Alpha-Were who negotiated a truce with the fae
Taras TAH-rahs	Hired sword and bodyguard to Cetus
Theia THAY-ah	A younger member of Pontus' gang. Sister or cousin to Atreus.
Xystos KSIS-tohs	A third-blade in Bateria's Assassins' Guild
Xythox KSIE-thoks	A wizard who waged war on the Fae Kingdom centuries ago
Zenodotus zay-NAW-doh-tus	Master Historian in the Empire of Bateria

Printed in Great Britain
by Amazon